Also By

Standalone

Called into Action

Love on the Winter Steppes

Three Keys Ranch Series

Hearts Unleashed

Wrangled by Love

Navy SEALs of Little Creek Series

Issued

Matched

Assigned

Hartford Minotaurs Hockey Series

Totally Pucked

The Perfect Snipe

Wrangled By Love

Three Keys Ranch Book 2

Paris Wynters

Copyright © 2021 by Paris Wynters

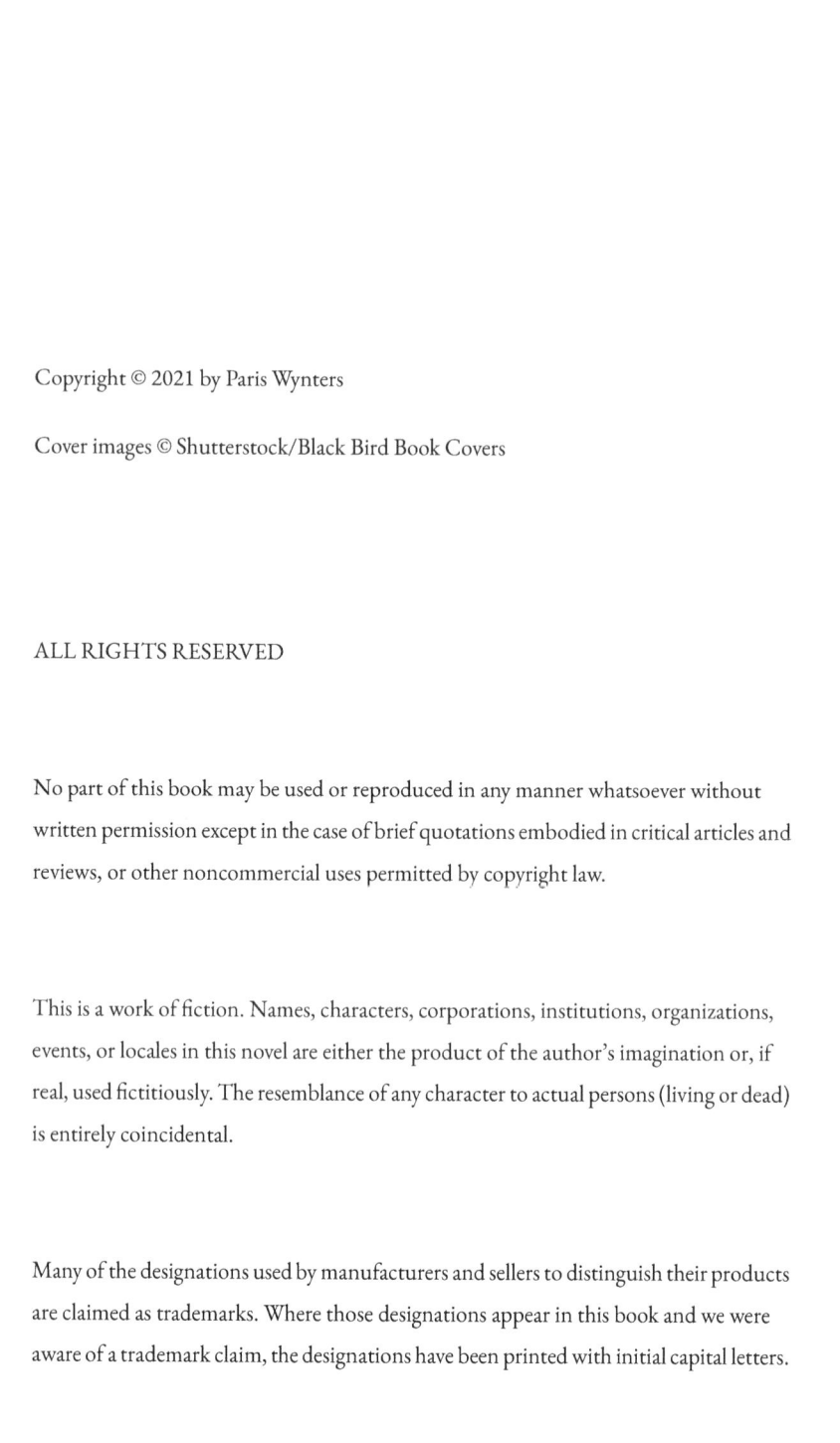

Cover images © Shutterstock/Black Bird Book Covers

ALL RIGHTS RESERVED

No part of this book may be used or reproduced in any manner whatsoever without written permission except in the case of brief quotations embodied in critical articles and reviews, or other noncommercial uses permitted by copyright law.

This is a work of fiction. Names, characters, corporations, institutions, organizations, events, or locales in this novel are either the product of the author's imagination or, if real, used fictitiously. The resemblance of any character to actual persons (living or dead) is entirely coincidental.

Many of the designations used by manufacturers and sellers to distinguish their products are claimed as trademarks. Where those designations appear in this book and we were aware of a trademark claim, the designations have been printed with initial capital letters.

Chapter 1

Emma

Emma Wallace lowers the windows of her white Ford Fiesta, her skin glistening and the nape of her neck damp as she lifts the cold cup of iced guava white tea and places the straw in her mouth. The sweltering heat of summer came to New York earlier than usual and Emma isn't sure if she will be able to last two more months if the temperature continues to rise.

A lone drop of sweat makes its way down her back, leaving a trail of temporary coolness in its wake. Emma places her venti-sized plastic cup back in the holder as she makes a left down her street. To her surprise, Emma finds a parking spot not far from her apartment, an unusual occurrence for Brooklyn. Then again, she'd normally be at work this time of day. Thanks to being laid off because of a merger last month, Emma currently works from home as a freelancer. Which explains why she is able to take a midday car trip to run some errands including stopping at her favorite coffee shop for her favorite iced tea.

After putting the car in park, she grabs her purse, the mini sunflowers she purchased at the store, and her drink before stepping out of the car. Once the vehicle is locked, she strolls toward her building. Her sandals clop against the cement sidewalk, the June sun's rays beating down on her skin. At least her apartment will offer a respite from the heat. But the moment her building comes into view, Emma stops in her tracks.

Ray, the private investigator she hired a couple of months ago, sits on the stoop in the shade under the canopy of green leaves. He stands the moment he spots her and she takes a tentative step forward. Her fingers tighten around the cup in her hands and her heart begins to pound in her chest.

"Ms. Wallace." Ray nods a greeting.

"Hi." It's the only word she's able to conjure up, her eyes focusing on the manila envelope in his large hand.

Ray lifts his head simultaneously shielding his eyes with his free hand. "Gonna be a hot summer. Hope your air condition's workin'."

When he looks back to her, she offers a weak smile, her throat constricting with each passing second. "Uh, did you find something out?"

"Yes, ma'am." Ray holds the envelope out to her. "Everything I could find is in here, including some pictures. And the bill for my services."

"Thank you." She takes the envelope. "I'll get a check in the mail tomorrow."

When Ray leaves, Emma pulls out her keys and unlocks the main door to the building, then walks through the second door. Sweat drips down the side of her face and she wipes it with the back of a shaky hand. Today isn't the day to wait for the slow elevator.

But walking up three flights of stairs is no fun either in this humidity.

Though walking might quell the bubble of anxiety about to burst in her chest by offering it an outlet. So, Emma grabs the black banister and races up the carpeted steps. Once on the third floor she speed walks to her door, her keys jingling as she fights to steady her fingers so she can open the lock.

Once inside, she heads into the kitchen and places the flowers, along with her purse and the envelope, on the kitchen counter near the window of her Brooklyn apartment. The once beautiful yellow petals already begin to curl at the edges from the summer heat.

When she picks them up their heads fall with gravity toward the linoleum-tiled floor.

Emma shakes herself as if to rid her body of lingering mosquitoes. She reaches over, grabs the white ceramic vase, and fills it with water before placing the miniature sunflowers into it, hoping they will recover. After grabbing the manila envelope, she heads into the living room, then places the vase on the coffee table and flops down onto the polyester alloy-grey couch. Her finger skates over the sealed flap of manila envelope. After a few months of searching for her birth father, Ray has found him and now she will finally get some answers.

Hopefully.

The last time she attempted to speak to one of her birth parents, the universe smacked her upside the head. Well, crushed her heart actually. What mother can look their daughter straight in the face and reject them?

Her birth mother, that's who. The woman refused to give her more than five minutes' worth of time, and refused to answer half of Emma's questions. But she caught the way the woman's face hardened when Emma inquired about her father. Her birth mother eventually wrote down what little information she had on the man after Emma stuck her foot in the doorway and refused to leave.

"What am I waiting for?" she asks the empty air of her apartment.

Sucking in a sharp breath, she tears the seal open and pulls out a packet containing some photos. She stares at the man in the handful of pictures.

Mitch Locke.

She chuckles. Huh, her biological father kinda looks like Sam Elliott and Tom Selleck had a love child. A little craggy. A little leathery. A beautiful full head of gray hair and quite the '70s mustache.

Emma puts the photos down onto the table and reads the report the private investigator also included. Her biological father owns a cattle ranch in Absarokee, Montana—wherever the hell that is. So fitting, though. He looks like a movie cowboy. She sifts through the photos and, sure enough, there's one of him in a cowboy hat, one that looks like it's been trampled a few times.

There's also a photo of him with his arm around a young woman who is a little shorter and a little thinner than Emma. She turns to the second page of the report and sits back on the couch. A sister. She has a sister. An actual biological sister who even looks like her.

She always wanted a sister. Emma met plenty of girls her age bouncing between one foster home and another, but none of them ever got close enough to call any of them a sibling. Hell, they barely got close enough to call each other friend before one would move on to a new place.

Emma always wanted a father, too. Most of the foster parents were decent enough folks. Nobody ever laid a hand on her and there were always clothes on her back and food on her plate. They just weren't... dads. They were barely interested in her, much less invested in her. They definitely hadn't loved her.

Montana. A ranch. A father. A sister. What would that all be like? She indulges in a brief fantasy. The hard arm of a man who smells like soap and leather around her shoulder telling her he's proud of her. Someone who looks like her borrowing her clothes and staying up late whispering about... well, whatever it is that sisters whisper about.

Easy there. She's also always dreamed about having a mother and look how that had turned out.

She reads a bit more. Her sister, Katie, is a year older than her. What the actual hell? Her stomach sours. Why didn't they give up her sister, too? Why did her father keep one daughter and not the other? What was wrong with her that nobody wanted her?

She lets out a harsh breath.

After a particularly lonely Valentine's day—the first where she was the only one of her friends single—Emma decided to search for her father. Thanks to her birth mother, she had a name and state to focus her search on. So, she hired Ray, hoping that this time maybe her other parent would offer her the closure she needs, to put her childhood behind her and go happily into her future.

But now she isn't so sure. What if there is no closure? What if there's no way to tick that box of a task accomplished? Her stomach churns a little as she wonders if she'll ever be able to fill that little empty spot in her heart and what it will mean if she can't.

Emma places the packet and pictures down on the coffee table and gets up from the couch, the cheap polyester material sticking to the back of her thighs. Her sandals clomp against the hardwood floor as she paces around the small room. She reminds herself that a biological father and sister doesn't mean she has a family and that she doesn't really need one. She's a grown ass woman and she is her own family and has made a home for herself. It's always been just her and her alone and if that's the way it stays, well, it's fine. She'll be happy. She just needs some answers to a few basic questions.

She looks down at the photo of Mitch and Katie and wonders what it would be like to be part of that photo. She snorts. She could totally Photoshop herself in. Make them one big happy family. No mess. No stress.

Also no reality.

The phone in the pocket of her khaki shorts rings, pulling Emma from her thoughts, and she pulls it out then taps the green button on the screen. "Hello?"

"Good Afternoon, Ms. Wallace. This is Mr. Sanchez. I was wondering if you had a moment to go over the logo you sent us."

Not exactly. But Emma can't say that. Not to a customer, especially one she needs. Which is all of them at the moment. At least, until she gets another full-time gig. "Of course. Just let me grab my laptop."

Emma walks over to her work desk and opens the top of her Asus, then hits the power button. The second the startup screen loads, she enters her password and clicks on the folder containing the images for Mr. Sanchez's project.

After being laid off, Emma had to turn to freelance opportunities to support herself and to further build her portfolio. Graphic design is a competitive field and New York is one of the most competitive places to find a job. She has resumes and work samples out, including one to Tik Talk Media, the most prestigious marketing firm in New York City. No nibbles yet, though she has all of her fingers and toes crossed.

Once the images load onto the screen, Emma sits in the chair and turns her attention back to the client on the line. "Okay, Mr. Sanchez. What can I do for you?"

"I am really impressed with the design, but it's a bit too bold." Mr. Sanchez goes quiet for a minute. "I wanted to bring in more elegance, something more modern and sleek."

Emma bites her inner cheek as she taps a Pinktini colored nail against the top of her wooden desk. "What colors do you want to keep?"

"The royal blue is nice."

"How about something using the blue along with different shades of silver?" Emma flips through some of the designs she sent over. "Maybe doing the dragon in an alloy with blue eyes. Making the lines sleek."

"I'd be interested in seeing that. Send over some mock-ups at your earliest convenience."

Emma bids her client goodbye and starts to redesign his logo. She ties her dark brown hair up into a messy bun, the humidity licking at the back of her neck. She wipes her forehead and continues to modify Mr. Sanchez's project.

A couple of hours later she sends the updated file to her client and leans back in the chair. She sips at the cold iced tea in her hand as drops of condensation coat her fingers, her mind circling back to the image of her father and sister in one of the pictures and her gut twinges with a pang of hurt. Abandonment. Maybe even jealousy.

Emma aged out of the foster care system, never having found a family of her own. Instead of hoping to be adopted, Emma concentrated on her schoolwork, earning one of the highest GPAs in her school and qualifying for numerous merit scholarships for college. But no matter how hard she worked, how much she only relied on herself, she always wanted to know if her family regretted giving her up. If they thought about her. If they wondered where she was and who she'd become.

She certainly has spent some time wondering about them.

With the sun beginning its descent over the Brooklyn skyline, Emma stands and walks over to the coffee table. She grabs the report with her biological father's information, then goes to the kitchen to grab her wallet from her purse, stopping momentarily to stare out the window to the street below her apartment. Nothing like summer city chaos. Cars and taxis honking. Motorcycles revving their engines. People talking and shouting as they make their way down the block.

The pulse of the city makes its way into her bloodstream. Emma worked hard to get here. She just needs to get this one issue settled, to get some closure, then she can relax and enjoy the life she's built.

She's going to meet her biological father and sister. Cross that off her bucket list and move on.

After retrieving her wallet, Emma heads back to the laptop and taps the touchpad to open the internet browser. She types in one of the popular travel websites and researches the cost of a hotel room and flight to Montana. Financially this might not be the best time for a trip, but she's saved money over the years, and since she's working freelance she has no set schedule to adhere to. She can work anywhere in the world as long as she has access to Wi-Fi.

Surely, there's Wi-Fi in Montana. Even in Absarokee.

There isn't much on her social calendar either. A brunch with some college friends. Drinks with some former colleagues, which is as much about networking as it is about catching up and chitchatting.

And if I end up getting hired by Tik Talk Media, who knows when I'll be able to take this trip? It could be months before I have vacation time.

Blowing out a breath, she flips the report to the page with her father's address and enters the information into the required fields. After pressing the button to continue, Emma pulls a credit card from her wallet and finishes up with the payment section. Once the confirmation page pops up, she exits the website and powers down the electronic device.

The last item to take care of is a bill from Ray. She sighs. She paid for the privilege of having her heart broken when she went to see her mother. Is she about to make the same mistake again?

Chapter 2

Otto

Otto Prescott taps the steering wheel of his red Ford F-150 to the beat of SAINt JHN's Roses. Nothing calms his nerves like a drive with the windows down as he blasts upbeat music. Well, other than riding the range on a horse without a single human soul in sight. Or snuggling up with his daughter.

At least that used to be the case.

Three years ago, while he was deployed, his then-wife filed for divorce. Veronica was tired of moving because of his job. She was tired of having no family around, especially with such a young child. And being off in another country he really didn't have the opportunity to stop her, to try to convince her to stay.

Truth is, he understood. Addison changed their lives and he wasn't there enough. The only thing his now ex-wife failed to see was that he hurt too from missing out on his daughter's life. Then two years ago, Veronica moved to Montana with Addie, leaving him behind in North Carolina, making it even harder for him to have a real relationship with his child.

So, when the opportunity came, Otto retired from the military—before he truly wanted to—and moved out west a couple of months ago to follow them. But Veronica continued to give him a hard time, not making it easy for him to have a consistent visitation schedule. She even nitpicked about the temporary apartment he was renting.

At the time, Otto was just trying to keep his head above emotional water. He struggled with trying to reintegrate into civilian life, struggled with having to fight to see his daughter, and struggled because he was the one without a job or family close by.

Fortunately, an Army buddy of his had a friend who lived in Absarokee. The man even had a job opening on his father-in-law's ranch that he now managed with his wife. John Rathborne was a lifesaver for him. Not only did Otto now have a steady income but the ranch also had a residence building that was more upscale then the apartment he'd been living in.

Upscale. Ha.

More like he didn't have neighbors fighting every day, the electric worked, and there weren't drug deals going on in the hallways. The residence building was new, something his boss had built to help living on the ranch be more accommodating than just a cabin for everyone to sleep in. Though, that existed too, but either brand new hands or seasonal workers slept there.

Besides the accommodations, living at the ranch is a safe place and full of space and adventure for Addison. She loves coming to visit. She loves the ranch dogs, Koda and Nickel, along with some goats and...the *chickens*.

He shudders at the thought of them.

But Veronica continues to interfere with his visitation rights, which is why he's on his way to see a lawyer.

He squints out the windshield to his right. What in the world? He slows his truck down, taking in the sight of the brunette waving her arms like she's trying to signal a 747 where to land, her sunflower-covered sundress fluttering in the breeze like some kind of floral surrender flag.

He looks past her to the silver Jetta tilted into the ditch on the side of the road with a rental company name embossed onto the license plate holder. He hadn't needed to see that to know she's from out of town. No one from around here would be traipsing around this area in that outfit.

He could keep going. There's no law saying he has to stop. If he does, he'll be late to the lawyer and the whole meeting is about how he can get more time to spend with Addie. A smile curls at his lips at the thought of his daughter. Forty pounds of piss and vinegar. There's nothing more important to him than that little girl.

Nothing.

Except now little Miss Sunflower is standing there on the side of the road—one many don't come down—looking as out of place as socks on a rooster. He can't leave her here, all hair and legs and sunflower sundress. Besides, she's someone's little girl, too. How would he want someone to treat Addie if she were in a similar predicament? Although he hopes to raise her to be smart enough not to end up with her car in a ditch while wearing ridiculous clothing.

Story of his life, needing to be two places at once. He'd wanted to be in Afghanistan, shoulder to shoulder with his fellow soldiers and back East with Veronica and Addie. Now he wants to be at his lawyer's office getting joint custody of Addie and helping this woman out of the predicament she has solidly gotten her own self into. He grinds his teeth and pulls to the side of the road, just past the Jetta. He gets out and tips his Stetson at Little Miss Sunflower. "Ma'am. What seems to be the trouble?"

The woman bites her lower lip and stares at the ground before turning and pointing to her car. "I spun out and lodged my rental in the ditch."

It's a nice set of lips. Plump and pretty and stained a pretty shade of pink. He can imagine biting that lower one, too. Otto ignores the uptick in his pulse and focuses on the Jetta to his left. "Did a nice job wedging the car in there."

"Thanks. Although I would have preferred not to have overachieved on this one." She places a hand on her hip and sighs and looks at him full on for the first time. Damn, she's pretty. All big brown eyes with a spray of freckles across her nose. She looks familiar in some way although he'd damn sure remember meeting her if he had. "There was a bunny—"

He quirks a brow. "A bunny?"

"You know, a rabbit." She puts her index fingers up behind her head like long ears and wiggles them. "It ran across the road. I swerved to keep from hitting it and then the car was spinning and, well, I ended up here. Not used to the dirty roads. But things could be worse. At least the weather's nice."

Her cheeks turn pink and she glances away when he looks at her. She's right. The weather could've been worse. The rain could've made everything muddy and much more complicated. Going to a lawyer's in muddy dress pants and shoes wouldn't have been ideal, so guess it works out for both of them that the sun is out today. "Let me grab a rope from my truck and see if I can pull you out." He walks back to his truck.

She follows after him. "Oh, no. I couldn't...that would be asking too much. I can't seem to get any service on my phone here. Maybe I could borrow yours and call Triple A? Or the rental company?" She stays with him, but her foot hits some gravel in those platform sandals and she stumbles.

On reflex, Otto reaches out and catches her and now she's right up against him, her soft curves pressed into him, big brown eyes wide and staring at him, pink blush rising up on her cheeks. A faint peach scent floats in the air from either her perfume or lotion that makes her smell good enough to eat. He shakes his head to dislodge that thought. Once he's sure she's stable, he releases her. "Easy there. Don't want to turn an ankle in those things." He gestures to her feet.

Her teeth sink further into her lower lip and her brown hair floats in front of her face when a gentle breeze swirls by and he finds himself wanting to tuck it behind her ear for her. "They seemed like a good idea at the time. Who knew I'd end up in a ditch?"

He snorts, but doesn't comment further on expecting the unexpected when driving around rural Montana, pulling the rope out of the toolbox in the back of the pickup. "I don't get much more service than you do and even if you reach a tow company, it could be hours before they make it out here." He secures one end of the rope around the trailer hitch of his truck. "Best to get to it ourselves."

"If you toss the other end down here, I'll tie it here."

Otto spins around to find the woman standing in front of the Jetta. He shakes his head. She plans on tying the rope directly to the bumper and Lord only knows what kind of knots she might tie. "Only if you want to do some serious damage to your rental. Look, I'll take care of it. Pop the trunk for me."

The woman clicks on the key fob and a moment later Otto grabs the front hook from the spare tire Styrofoam pack then heads to the front of the car, wincing a bit when his dress shoes slip and his knee twinges. Once everything is secured and in place, Otto double checks the knot one last time. "Let's get you outta this ditch and on your way."

She places her hand on his shoulder to stop him. "I really appreciate this."

Her touch is electric, burning its way through his dress shirt and making him way too aware of how long it's been since he was touched by a woman. He pulls away, not wanting to admit how nice it feels. He clears his throat and shrugs away the tingle left behind. "No problem. Now put the car in drive and aim for the road and I'll pull you out."

"Just like that?"

"Just like that," he says.

She stands, looking at him, her brow furrowed and her teeth biting into that lower lip again. Otto reaches up and scratches the back of his head. "Helps if you get in the car."

The woman's eyes go wide as she straightens her back. The pink tinge on her cheeks from earlier returns. "Yes, of course."

She turns and scurries away and Otto can't help but smile now that she can't see. The woman is definitely out of her element, but she's doing her best in a bad situation. No whining or wailing. Gotta give her credit for that. He turns and makes his way back to his truck. Once in the driver's seat he starts the engine and opens the window. He sticks his head out and looks back at her. "On three, okay?"

She gives him a double thumbs up. He nods and turns forward, his lips hitching into a smile. She's got plenty of spirit, that's for sure. Turning his attention back to the steering wheel, he holds a hand out the window and lifts a finger. "One."

He shifts into drive and holds up another finger. "Two."

With his foot on the gas pedal, he holds up a final finger and floors it. "Three!"

The truck surges forward and stops, straining, trying to gain traction on the dirt road. Then, slowly, inch by inch, the Jetta rolls up and out of the ditch. He continues a few feet to make sure they clear the edge of the road and puts the truck into park before climbing out.

The woman meets him in front of the hood of the Jetta. "That was amazing! I really can't thank you enough." She reaches into the purse now on her shoulder. "Can I pay you something for your time?"

Otto backs away, a little offended, hands held up in front of him to stop her. "People around here help each other out because it's the right thing to do. We don't expect to get paid for it."

Her smile fades. "I'm sorry. It's a little different in New York."

Otto leans down to untie the rope. So, that's where she's from. Explains a lot. "Gonna leave the tow hook in case you need to use it again."

She crosses her arms in front of her chest and purses her lips. "Thanks for the vote of confidence, Mr, um?"

"Otto."

"I'm Emma." She sticks her hand out and he takes it. Her palms are soft, but her grip is firm. She releases his hand and backs up toward the driver side door. "Anyway, thank you again. You're my hero."

Now his own cheeks begin to heat. "No heroics. Just a tow. Take care."

He walks back to his vehicle and undoes the rope from the hitch before tossing it into the bed. She isn't the only one who needs to get going. He pinches the bridge of his nose as if it could ward off the anxiety forming in his chest over this lawyer meeting.

He makes his way back into the truck and straps on his seatbelt. If he's going to make it on time he'll have to drive faster than he cares to. The reflection in the rearview mirror shows Emma sitting in her car, her fingers punching at the rental's GPS. She's so out of place and something in his chest squeezes at the thought of leaving her there, but there's another girl in his life that's more important. One he needs to fight for.

His daughter. And she will always be his first priority.

Chapter 3

EMMA

Emma drives up the winding gravel driveway, sweaty palms gripping the steering wheel. So far the day hasn't been going according to plan. Whether that's due to the universe forewarning her this meeting is a bad idea or a bad case of nerves one thing is for sure, Emma wants nothing more than to turn the car around and head back to the hotel. She could be back in Brooklyn tomorrow if she wants to with no one the wiser.

She sucks in a deep breath and concentrates on the positive aspects of the day. The sun is shining, the ranch is fairly simple to find, and a handsome man came to her rescue and held her for a moment. She hadn't minded the way those arms had felt around her one bit and there'd been a look in his eye for a second or two that made her think that he hadn't hated it either. Then his face had slammed shut and he was back to being all business and he'd shied away from her touch like she'd burned him. He'd even gotten his nice suit all dusty to do it.

Her gut clenches. If she hadn't been so nervous, she wouldn't have overcorrected when she swerved to avoid hitting the rabbit that ran across the road. Now the poor guy is probably heading to work in a ruined suit thanks to her.

She hadn't totally been joking when she'd called him a hero. He had that kind of air about him. He's capable. A guy who would keep people around him safe.

Emma swallows hard when the huge white house with its wraparound porch comes into view. Large prairie grid windows dot the outside of the house and a gigantic oak tree spreads its thick limbs over much of the roof. It's beautiful. Grand, yet somehow unassuming at the same time. The big blue Montana sky opens up behind it like a movie backdrop. What would it have been like to grow up here? To have all this space? She'll never know, that's for sure. Even the nicest of the foster homes she grew up in didn't hold a candle to this place. She'd been lucky if there'd been a yard.

Emma turns into a spot next to a red Prius. After turning off the engine, she takes a few seconds for herself. This is it. Inside will be her father and sister. God only knows how they are going to react when she fills them in on who she is. She pulls down the visor and checks her hair, pushing back the strands that are stuck to her clammy skin. Then after taking a few more deep breaths, she grabs her purse and exits the car.

To her left is a big red barn, and beyond that, in open fields, is a huge herd of cattle. What kind she doesn't know. Hell, the only cows she knows about are those black and white ones that people like to put in commercials and ads. She'd done a layout of a brochure for an ice cream place a few weeks back that had used stock photos of them. That's pretty much as close as she's ever gotten to a cow. She wrinkles her nose at the smell when a breeze blows in her direction. How do the people here stand it?

Emma grabs hold of the rails as she climbs the steps of the house up to the main entrance. The front door is open, although the screen is shut, allowing her to peer down the hallway. She stands there, frozen in place, staring at the white button on the right. After running a hand over her floral sundress to smooth out the material, she straightens to her full height while clutching her keys tight in her left hand. If her biological father kicks her off his property, she'll be ready to get in the car and drive off faster than she had when she met her biological mother. She's ready this time.

With a slight nod, she reaches out and pushes the button setting off a wave of deep chimes. A moment later a chorus of high and low pitched barks cut through the air along with the scraping sound of nails on wood.

"Nickel. Two Bits. Go place." While the deep voice is a bit scratchy, the tone is full of authority, and Emma shrinks in on herself a tiny bit.

But when she looks down, two large dogs are staring at her. One gray with semi-floppy ears who is thin and has a white streak down its muzzle. The other tan with a black muzzle and black accents around its eyes as if the dog is wearing thick eyeliner. Not to mention the darker fur that also gives the appearance of eyebrows.

Emma chews the inside of her cheek and takes a step back. While the dogs appear friendly, this is their home and she's a stranger. Plus, they haven't listened to whatever command they'd been given. She's not going any further without an invitation.

Heavy footsteps catch her attention and Emma looks up from the dogs to the tall man, his tan weathered skin and thick gray mustache coming into view the closer he gets to the screen door. His eyes are deep set, his bushy brows scrunch together. "Can I help you?"

God, it's like looking at the photo all over again. She's practically memorized the image. But seeing her biological father in person makes Emma's stomach summersault. All she can do is stare at him and fidget with the strap of her purse.

Her father reaches out and pulls on the handle to the screen door as he nudges the two canines away with his lanky leg. "Ma'am?"

"Oh, sorry. Hi. Hello. I'm Emma." The words tumble out on their own. Not the ones she rehearsed of course. Those seem to have deserted her.

"Hello, Emma. Is there something I can help you with?" She reaches up and scratches the side of her head behind her ear.

"I was wondering if I could speak with you?"

"Me?"

"Yes, sir."

He curtly nods and squeezes through the screen door, careful not to let out the two dogs. She takes a minute to study the man who is her father, biting back a smile when she notices how he fastens the very top button of his shirt. Very few people she knows do that. As a matter of fact, the only people she knows who do that wore suits and ties, not denim and cowboy boots.

He extends an arm toward the wicker chairs on the porch to her right. "Why don't we take a seat. Based on your expression, this looks like it must be important."

"It is." She follows behind and sits down, the blue cushion firmer than she expected, yet comfortable. She places her purse in her lap and clutches in tight against her as if it were a shield. "It's important enough to me that I flew here from New York to see you."

Her father leans back into the chair, placing the ankle of one leg on top of the knee of his other. "Must've been a long flight. So what is it that I can do for you that's worth a trip like that?"

What can he do? Maybe hear her out. Be empathetic. Not berate her and kick her out the way her birth mother had. Gripping the leather material of her purse, she sucks in a deep breath. "Isobel gave me your information. Well, some of it. Just your name and the town, really. I hired a private investigator to find out the rest."

At the mention of her biological mother's name, the man tenses, but he remains silent. So, she continues on. "I'm your daughter. My moth—, Isobel was pregnant when she left you. After I was born she gave me up for adoption."

Except she wasn't adopted. Instead she'd bounced around the foster care system until she'd turned eighteen. Emma stares at her father, who hasn't moved or spoken. She even glances down to his chest so she can catch any movement to ensure he's still breathing. The last thing she wants to do is kill the man by dropping this info bomb on him. But the longer he doesn't move or speak, the more uncomfortable she becomes. Hell, has he even blinked?

"Hey, Dad. Think you can help for a second with Snowbird?"

Emma swings her head sideways toward the red barn where a woman wearing indigo jeans, cowboy boots, and a jade t-shirt stands. Her dark brown hair is pulled back into a braid and a cowboy hat sits atop her head.

Katie.

Her sister.

Emma has spent plenty of time staring at her picture, too, imagining what she might be like. Now here she is in the flesh, looking like she belongs in this place in a way that Emma will never be able to emulate.

Her heart beats so hard as if trying to break free of its bony cage. Would they be ganging up on her? Would her sister be angry their father seems so upset? Maybe she should leave. But she wants some answers. Needs some answers to questions that have been haunting her.

Her sister's gaze bounces from their father to Emma. When no one says a word, Katie crosses her arms. "Don't mean to interrupt, but I was hoping we could get Snowbird set up so I can help John with the herd out in the north pasture."

"I'm sorry. I should go. This doesn't appear to be the best time." Emma moves to stand but her father holds out a hand, palm facing her, and she stops.

"Katie, call John and tell him you'll be late. I think you should be part of this conversation," he says, his voice calm and even.

Her sister's eyes narrow when they land back on Emma, her animosity clear. Great. This might be worse than how Isobel handled her visit. At least her biological mother had waited to know who she was before she'd rejected her. Emma's leg starts to bounce as her nerves began to fire off.

She sucks in a deep breath and blows it out slowly. She doesn't need them. Doesn't need their acceptance. Doesn't need their support. She's been on her own for years, made her own way through college and into the work force. All she wants is the answers to a few simple questions.

Why didn't you want me? Why didn't you look for me?

Her father steeples his fingers and places them against his mouth, momentarily closing his eyes as Katie pulls out her cell phone and steps away. Then she returns and leans against the railing, arms and legs crossed, eyes narrow and suspicious.

Their father's gaze now turns to focus on the daughter he'd raised. "Katydid, this here is Emma. Your sister. And my daughter." He says it so simply, so straightforward, like he's announcing that the sky is blue.

Emma's leg bounces faster as she looks down at her purse to avoid meeting her sister's gaze. She closes her eyes for a moment, hoping for peace and courtesy. When she opens them she looks to Katie who's gone pale.

"My what?" Katie looks back to her father. "I don't understand. I have a sister?"

"Yup." The word flies from Emma's mouth before she can stop it as her hands flick into the air, palms facing upward. "It was news to me, too."

They both turn to look at her.

She sighs. "Look, I grew up in foster homes. When I aged out of the system, I was happy. No more bouncing around. I went to college, got a good job, rented my own apartment. Then one day the itch of finding my biological mother began. I hired a private detective who found her for me. I went to visit her, but Isobel turned me away." She stops for a second, looking out toward the barn until she regains her composure. The memory of the hurt and humiliation is still so deep it's hard to talk about out loud. "But she gave me your name. I asked the private investigator to look for you. He found out where you were. So, here I am."

Katie's eyes narrow further. "And of course, you wouldn't object to a DNA test, right?"

"Katie!" Their father's tone is stern and disapproving.

Katie stands and walks over to their father, placing a hand on his shoulder. "Mom walked out on us. And we both suspect she was probably cheating on you. Now, after everything that's happened, some stranger walks into our lives again. Someone claiming to have family ties. Just remember what Peter did."

The older man scrubs his face with his hands. "This is different."

"How? Let's say she really is my sister. But your daughter? Are you seriously telling me my mother would have walked out pregnant with your kid and not asked you for a dime?" Katie throws her hands up in the air and paces the length of the porch.

Emma's fingernails dig into the material of her purse, her heart thundering in her chest. Who the hell did they think she was? And who the hell was Peter? "I'm more than happy to take a DNA test. In fact, I think it might be a good idea. Just know that I'm here because I wanted to meet my biological father. I have questions I want to ask. Nothing more."

Katie whips around to face her. "Yeah right. You don't want a cut of the ranch? Please, I'm not some airhead pushover."

They think she's here for the ranch? What on earth would she do with a ranch? Or a piece of one? She shakes her head. "Um, no. I don't. Not the life I want. I've got a line on my dream job in New York City. I had some time free when the investigator got me the info on who and where you all were and I thought I'd come see for myself. Now I have. I'll be going back home shortly." Maybe even more shortly than she'd planned.

Her father, some of the color coming back into his face, rubs the back of his neck. "Look, Emma, this is a shock for all of us. For me. I hope you'll believe me when I tell you that I didn't know . . . had no idea that you even existed until now. It's a lot to come to terms with at a moment's notice."

When he quiets and rubs his chest, Katie sprints over to him. "Dad, why don't you go lay down. I'll take care of this."

Emma's eyes widen and she leans forward. "Are you feeling okay? I'm sorry I didn't mean to upset you."

Katie sneers. "He had a heart attack almost a year and we've all been through a lot. This wasn't the best time for you to stop by. Even if you are who you say you are."

"Oh God." Emma springs up from her chair, tears forming in her eyes. She grabs her bag from the chairs and runs for the stairs. What a fool she has been. It isn't nerves but the universe trying to keep her away all morning. She should have stayed in the stupid ditch. Or turned around and headed back to the hotel after her hero had pulled the car back onto the road. Instead, she pushed on and now she might actually have caused her biological father to have another heart attack. He could die before she even gets to know who he is. Tears run down her cheeks and she bounds down the steps, the soles of her sandals too smooth so that she slides and almost wipes out again, but this time there's no big strong man with arms like steel to catch her.

"Emma, wait," her father calls out. "Please."

She stops at the bottom of the steps and turns to face him using the back of her hand to wipe away the tears still flowing down her face.

He makes his way toward her. "There's no need for any DNA test. I believe you are who you say you are. You've come all this way. Why don't you stay at the ranch? We can talk some more. Maybe get to know one another. You said you had questions after all and I sure have a few myself now. There are plenty of empty rooms with Katie having moved out and all."

Katie tenses and turns red. Clearly, she's not a fan of the idea. And what does Emma know about this man anyway? Would it be safe? She shakes her head. She'd stayed in some pretty shady foster homes growing up. This place doesn't seem so bad in comparison, but better to be safe than sorry. She's already got the hotel room for the night anyway. "Let me think about it."

"At least come by for breakfast tomorrow." Her father stares at her, bushy eyebrows pulled up, the wrinkles in his forehead deepening.

Emma blinks a few times, then looks at her sister who turns away rather than make eye contact. "Sure. I can do breakfast. I'll be here around eight."

And with that, she turns and walks back to the car, wanting nothing more than the calm and quiet of her hotel room.

Chapter 4

Otto

Otto sits on the sofa in the common area of the employee housing, elbows on knees, and his face buried in his palms. The meeting with his lawyer yesterday didn't go so well. He probably should've just stayed with Little Miss Sunflower. At least she appreciated him. Imagine offering to pay him for pulling her out of that ditch. He could think of a few other ways she might be able to show her appreciation, though. She'd felt damn good pressed up against him.

He shook his head. No. He had no time or place in his life for those kinds of fantasies now. He needed a plan that would help him get joint custody of Addie. He hadn't been able to sleep, tossing and turning all night long trying to figure one out. Veronica and her lawyer fought tooth and nail against him the entire meeting. The biggest argument now...his job is still new therefore the housing is temporary. If he gets fired, he'll be homeless.

Like he'd get fired. Who do they think he is? Some kid who is wet behind the ears? After three tours in Afghanistan, he knows plenty about responsibility and what it means to have people rely on him. He knows what it's like to have to make decisions that can mean life or death for himself or the soldier next to him. He can do his damn job just fine.

But, once again his service seems to count for nothing and joint custody is out of the question. He's stuck with a measly every other weekend visitation schedule. He's glad to have that, but he wants more. A lot more.

"Hey, hermano. You ready to get some breakfast?"

Otto lifts his head. Mario Perez is standing by the door, waiting. With a groan, Otto hoists himself off the chair. "Yeah."

"Meeting didn't go well, huh." Mario presses his lips into a thin line. The former hockey player started out as his co-worker and is rapidly becoming his best friend out here. He's as pissed as Otto is about the custody situation. Mario believes no matter what, family shouldn't be kept from one another. Then again, he comes from a big family, who may argue but they stick together. No divorced parents. No divorced siblings.

Otto grunts, but says nothing and falls into step next to Mario as they walk the fifty yards or so to the main house. The two men are about the same size, a little over six feet, and broad-shouldered. They're a good match for chores around the ranch, even in strength and stature. Otto's stomach growls loud enough for his friend to hear.

Mario's grin shows off his white teeth against his deep brown skin. He pulls a quarter out of his pocket. "Wanna wager on who cooked this morning?"

"Not sure there's a winning choice." While the boss's daughter is a great cook, Katie is also absentminded. They're as likely to be called to the table by the smoke alarm going off as they are a dinner bell. John, who's also become Otto's friend, loves mentioning how when the two first met, Katie forgot about the banana bread in the oven and nearly burned the place down. Though lately the ranch owner, Mitch Locke, has been making breakfast since he was on light duty due to a mild heart attack he'd had. All the man cooks is eggs and bacon. And while the bacon comes out both crispy and juicy, having the same meal every day only reminds Otto of being back on deployment with limited options of what to eat and when he can eat it.

"Ah, shit. Ready to run?" Mario's voice has both a hint of fear and laughter.

Otto follows his friend's line of sight over to the oak tree, where a flock of five hens has started toward them. "I don't understand what the hell is wrong with them."

Mario claps a hand on his shoulder. "Those gallinas are in love with you."

"More like obsessed." As the last word leaves his mouth the hens come bolting toward him as if summoned. Mario increases his pace until the man has climbed the stairs of the main porch and entered into the house. Otto on the other hand continues strolling. While his fowl groupies are an annoyance, he isn't particularly interested in sitting with a bunch of people right now. Hopefully, he'll be able to saddle up Bayberry and head out for most of the day. He's found more peace in solitude out here than he thought possible when he first arrived. There's something in the land here that speaks to his soul. The vastness gives him a sense of perspective and the beauty soothes something inside him.

The hens surround Otto. The dark brown one he's named Matilda pecks at the heads and necks of the others to keep them away from Otto. She's the boss and she doesn't like to share. He reaches down and scratches her head with his forefinger and sighs. If only she could peck his ex-wife a few times. An unworthy thought, he knows, but he's only human.

He chuckles to himself, then makes his way up the steps only to stop at the screen door. Parked alongside Katie's car is a silver Jetta, just like the one he helped pull from the ditch yesterday. Weird. Why would it be here? He shakes his head. It can't be the same one.

He pulls on the screen door and enters the house. To his right Nickel, one of the ranch dogs, is fast asleep under the large bay windows facing the east so the warmth of the morning sun fills the living room. The dog's leg twitches in her sleep, then she settles down with a snore.

Otto snorts. Some watch dog. Nothing like Koda, John's Malinois. Then again, Koda is a former military working dog and has the training and dedication to prove it.

Speaking of John, Otto needs to speak to him to make sure it will be okay for Addison to stay over on nights he has visitation. Employee housing doesn't always cover families—or incurs some form of rent if they do—Otto wants to make sure it will be okay. He doesn't want to do anything to do endanger this job. It's the lifeline that connects him with Addie and without that ...well, without that he's not sure who he is or what he's doing. The military told him all that for years, but he is without its discipline and demands now. He has to forge this new path on his own and the one thing he's sure of is that he loves being Addie's dad.

He cuts through the living room and heads into the high-ceilinged dining room. A massive table made from a giant slab of reclaimed wood dominates the room, morning light from east-facing windows spills across it. Mario and John are seated at one end of it while Katie and Linda, the ranch veterinarian, sit at the other. Linda Taylor has been the ranch veterinarian for almost thirteen years and spends enough time here she often takes meals with the family and staff. Hell, she's actually the mother figure to Katie. The two women's heads are close together and whatever Katie's hearing, she doesn't much like, based on the scowl on her face.

Otto slips into the spot between John and Mario as quietly as he can and looks at Mario with a lifted eyebrow.

"You shoulda stayed outside with the *gallinas*." Mario grabs his glass of water and takes a swig, his attention still focused on the two women deep in conversation.

John reaches down to scratch Koda, who sits attentively next to her owner, between the ears. "Can we talk about something else?"

Otto looks around, trying to pick up a clue as to what's going on. Mitch isn't at the table yet. Eggs and bacon again, it is, although he swears he can smell something else cooking. Though Sawyer Beckett, Mitch's nephew who'd come to help out after the attack on the ranch a couple of months ago, is also missing. Was Sawyer the source of Katie's scowl? "Something happen to Sawyer?"

John shakes his head. "Nah, he's in Billings handling some paperwork. Will be back later this afternoon."

That's a relief. "So, what's all the tension about?"

Before either of his friends can answer Mitch enters the room carrying a plate of bacon, followed by....

Holy shit.

Little Miss Sunflower.

The woman from yesterday who'd put her rented Jetta in a ditch to keep from hitting . . . what had she said? A bunny? She's got on cut-offs and a tank top today rather than a sundress, but it's definitely her.

There's an uptick in his pulse, and over the aroma of the food, he catches a whiff of the peach scent he'd smelled on her yesterday. He blinks once. Twice. Then swallows hard. What is she doing here? Without thinking, he half stands.

When her gaze lands on him she freezes, the bowl of fruit in her hands wobbling and those big brown eyes getting even bigger. "You?"

"Sunflower?" he says, sure that his own eyes have widened as well.

"You two know each other?" Katie's voice cuts through the air like a knife, accusatory and threatening.

Otto snaps to attention. "We've met. Pulled her car out of a ditch on my way into Billings yesterday." He looks down at his empty plate, not wanting his face to betray the confused emotions running through his brain.

Mario turns to face him. "On the way to your lawyer appointment? In your Sunday best?"

Otto gives him a look and his friend raises his hands in front of himself. Otto sits back down and takes a sip of the orange juice sitting in front of his plate.

The woman sighs. "There was a bunny. I swerved to keep from hitting it and ended up in the ditch. Otto came along. I wanted to use his cell phone to call for help, but he pulled me out of the ditch himself instead."

Katie doesn't look like she's done asking questions, but before she can, Mitch steps closer to the table, eyes locked with Otto's. "Well, thank you for helping my daughter."

Otto sputters and coughs when the orange juice goes down the wrong pipe. What did his boss just say? Daughter? That can't be right. Since he started working here Katie was the only Locke child he knew of. Mitch never spoke of another. The only other family member around is Sawyer. "Sorry, sir. Did you say your daughter?"

"Yes, he did." Emma places the bowl of fruit onto the table with a loud thunk, her straight brown hair falling over her shoulder. "My name's Emma, remember?"

Right. Emma. She's only Sunflower in his mind and maybe a little bit in a dream he had last night. Otto swallows hard. Best to shut all that down and fast, even in his fantasies. Talk about off limits. She's the boss's daughter. Getting fired for messing around with a family member is the last thing he needs. Not to mention, Addie is the only lady he has time for in his life. Building a relationship with his daughter after being gone for so long is his first and only priority outside of work.

John claps his hands and grabs the serving spoon by the bowl. "Fruit looks mighty delicious. Heard you helped Mitch cook and that there were some pancakes. Beats another day of eggs."

Otto's gaze bounces from his friend to Katie who stares daggers at her husband. John may be trying to ease the tension, but if he isn't careful Otto won't be the only one with a lawyer on retainer. John seems blissfully ignorant of his wife's look and helps himself to a healthy portion of strawberries, blueberries, and melon. Otto keeps his own face carefully neutral.

"In fact I did. There's plain and banana pancakes. I'll be right back with them." Sunflower—Emma—gives him a long look before turning and heading back into the kitchen.

Mario chuckles. "Looks like the gallinas might have some competition."

"Those hens still giving you a problem." Linda eyes him, obviously having caught Mario's comment.

"Yes, ma'am. Matilda's even gotten prickly with the rest when they come near me. Pecks at them something fierce." Otto takes the bowl of fruit from John and ladles some onto his plate.

The entire table erupts into laughter so loud, Koda springs up to her feet eyeing everyone. Otto's not quite sure what's so funny. John gives Koda a quiet command and she settles next to him again.

Mario nudges Otto with an elbow. "You *named* the chicken?"

Ah. That was the joke he didn't get. "Gotta call her something." He sinks down in his chair a bit.

"I'm sure Emma wouldn't mind being pecked a few times. If she can't deal, she can head back to New York." Katie smirks while looking down at her empty plate.

"Enough." Mitch's thunderous tone catches his daughter's attention and she slinks down into her seat, too, her face turning pink.

A little noise of distress makes Otto look to the doorway where Emma stands with a plateful of pancakes. Her chest rises and falls rapidly and there's a bit of a tremble in her lower lip. He pushes back his chair. "Here, let me take those for you."

"No, I've got it." She shakes her head, blinking back the shine in her eyes, and straightens to her full height planting the plate full of pancakes down on the table, then sits down next to her sister and looks right at her. There's a definite resemblance there. Emma is a bit softer and rounder, her skin lighter, but it's there. "If *Matilda* isn't careful, we might be eating chicken parmigiana for dinner."

Otto can't help but smile. And neither can Mitch. While the mustache covers most of his lips, Otto doesn't miss the way the corners of the older man's eyes wrinkle as his cheeks pull up the slightest bit. Mario, on the other hand, is biting his fist, gaze bouncing between the two sisters like they might leap up from the table and throw down. Linda, seemingly unconcerned with whatever kind of hen fight is brewing, grabs some bacon.

Otto adds banana pancakes to the fruit on his plate. "No one is cooking Matilda."

Mitch quirks a bushy eyebrow at him. "Interesting. Thought you'd be happy to get rid of her."

John snorts. "Don't let him fool you. He acts all grumpy, but he has a soft spot for her. Wouldn't be surprised if sooner or later she ends up sleeping in his bed instead of the coop."

The whole table laughs again. Otto glances up at Emma. Her cheeks turn a bright shade of pink and her eyes sparkle with laughter instead of unshed tears. Otto can't look away. "How long will you be staying?"

Emma looks quickly between Mitch and Katie and then back down to her plate where she seems to mainly be pushing the fruit around without eating much.

"Emma's agreed to stick around for a bit so we can get a chance to know each other." Mitch smiles at his daughter encouragingly.

Everyone continues digging into the food as Mitch officially introduces Emma. Turns out his boss didn't know he had another daughter until she came knocking the other day. Can't imagine what that would've felt like. If Veronica had done something similar to him, he'd be livid. He'd missed enough of Addie's life when he was OCONUS. To have someone deliberately keep the precious seconds he did have away from him? Just the thought of it makes him sad and angry on Mitch's behalf.

Katie, who has been stabbing at her food like it might not be dead yet, rolls her eyes and reaches for more pancakes. "Whatever. Dad could use a break from cooking and relax more. Especially since the heart attack."

Emma angles her head to look around her sister at her father. "If you had a heart attack, why are you eating bacon? Isn't that kind of on the no-fly list for cardiac patients?"

Katie waves a triangle of pancake on the end of her fork in the air. "Because he refuses to listen to anyone. When we won't allow him to do too strenuous work, he cooks. And when we try to get him to cook healthy food, he does something else he shouldn't be doing. And round and round it goes." She points at everyone besides her sister. "They're all stubborn."

"Just like you," John says, then takes a swig from his glass of juice.

She sticks her tongue out at her husband, who smiles at his wife. Otto shakes his head, chuckling. Being around those two gives him hope that there could be someone out there for him. They'd both gone through so much, yet managed to find love. To find each other. And seeing how John readjusted back into civilian life helps Otto not give up on those days he struggles.

"Did you and John serve together?"

Emma's question catches him off guard. He hadn't realized he'd checked out of the conversation. "No." It comes out terser and harsher than he intends.

"John was a canine handler meanwhile this vato was a Beret." Mario shoves another piece of bacon into his mouth and swallows before continuing. "What do you do?"

"Graphic design. My company was bought out so I was let go, but I've got some resumes out I'm hopeful about. There's an opening at one of the top companies in New York, one I've wanted to work for since I graduated college. What about you? Did you serve?"

"A healthy dose of hip checks," Katie says.

Mario points his fork at Katie. "Finally caught on to the terminology." He then turns back to Emma who looks a little confused. "Played hockey. Was drafted, but played in the minors. Career ending injury. So here I am."

Otto watches as Emma takes in everyone around her, learning who they are and whatever they want to share about themselves. She appears to loosen up as time goes by as does her sister. Though, he catches Katie eye rolling a couple of times when Emma speaks.

"Well, if there's anything you want for dinner let me know. Since I agreed to stay here for a few weeks I'll be helping with some of the chores, including cooking," Emma says.

Otto stops chewing, unable to swallow for a second. When Mitch had said she might stay, Otto thought his boss meant a couple of days. Not a couple of weeks. Sure, the Lockes could use the help, but Otto would just as soon not have the distraction of a woman who shows up in his dreams and causes his heart to beat faster and makes him smile when she doesn't back down to Katie or anyone.

    Especially when that woman is the boss's daughter.

Chapter 5

Emma

Emma slips and falls on her ass. Again. She slaps the compacted dirt and groans. Less than a week of living on Three Keys Ranch and she's already rocking some serious bruises on her butt.

She's also ready to throw her sneakers into the fiery pits of hell. While she doesn't want to invest in a pair of boots she'll never wear again once she heads back home, her Chucks offer little support or traction when it comes to helping out her father on the ranch. The family ranch. She supposes it's part hers, too. That seems to be a big reason why Katie is so pissed Emma turned up.

She hoists herself back up and smacks the dirt off her blue designer jeans, also not really made for ranch work, growling at the sight of chicken shit on her back thigh. How far away is the nearest dry cleaner? A single cluck fills the air and she glances over her shoulder and her eyes narrow. "Matilda."

   The brown chicken stands there, head slightly cocked to one side, scratching at the dirt with one foot. Emma has no idea why but she gets the distinct feeling the bird doesn't like her. It seems entirely possible that particular pile of chicken shit was strategically placed. Well, the feeling is mutual. The idea of Matilda parmigiana becomes more likely with each passing moment.

   Emma blows a lock of hair out of her face and turns forward, determined to get the damn cow in front of her milked. "Can you please move your big ass and work with me?"

   The cow doesn't respond. Not so much as a moo.

   Emma grumbles and pushes the cow again. She's almost gotten her to the stall where the bench and pail are waiting. When her father asked if she'd help with the milking at breakfast, Emma jumped at the chance to be helpful. Katie had been sitting across from her, following the conversation with her lips pressed tightly together. Emma hadn't wanted to give her sister the satisfaction of admitting she didn't know the first thing about cows or how to milk them. Instead, she'd flipped open her laptop and watched a couple of video online tutorials when she went upstairs to get her shoes.

It hadn't looked that hard. She's pretty sure she's got the basic idea. But then, all the cows in the videos were already in a stall. No one mentioned how to move a cow, much less how stubborn the animals could be. She's been shoving at this cow for half an hour and has only moved a few feet.

She throws her hands in the air. "Seriously, you are the biggest diva I've ever met. Do you think this is fun for me?"

The red cow turns its neck to look at her and moos. Damned if Emma doesn't pick up a massive attitude coming from the sound. Who does this cow think she is?

Emma narrows her eyes and purses her lips. "Yeah well, mooo you, too."

"Those are pretty tough words coming from a woman who's easily a thousand pounds smaller than that old girl," a husky voice says from the barn doorway.

She looks over the cow, wiping yet another lock of hair out of her face with her forearm. Otto.

His Stetson is pushed back a bit so she can see his eyes and hell if her pulse doesn't quicken even if the grin plastered on his tanned face irritates the heck out of her. One more person happy to see her fail apparently. He'll have to get in line behind Katie.

Emma exhales sharply. "Glad to see my misfortune brings a smile to your face. Here I thought my presence only made you frown."

He winces and pulls his Stetson off, examining it as if trying to avoid her gaze. "Didn't mean to be quite so rude the day we met. I had an appointment I didn't want to be late for. Then you were kind of a surprise yesterday morning." He looks back up. "I don't take pleasure in seeing anyone struggle, though."

"Then why are you still smiling?" She grunts as she pushes the stubborn cow once more.

"Well, you're arguing with a cow like you're expecting her to answer you back." Otto places the Stetson back on his head and strides into the barn. Then he takes the cow by the neck and angles her snout to where he wants her to go.

And fucking hell, that bitch moves. Emma's mouth hangs open. "How'd you—"

"You don't want to fight her. You won't win. You want her to work with you." He walks the cow along slowly. "She's a good old girl. Show her where you want her to go and she'll likely oblige you."

A ruckus of buck-buck-buck fills the barn. By God, what the hell are they all doing here? Emma glares at the chickens who seem to glare right back at her. Matilda scratches at the dirt as if she's getting ready to charge Emma like an angry bull.

Otto groans. "I swear them chickens won't leave me alone."

She looks at him, then back to the flock. Matilda has her head up and her chest thrust out and now she's pacing back and forth like she's on a catwalk. A giggle erupts before Emma can stop it. Her hand flies over her mouth attempting to muffle the volume but it's too late. "It's like she's prancing for you."

He bows his head. "More like stalking me. Everywhere I turn, there they are. Damn Matilda even tries to get inside the residents' building."

The giggle grows to a full out laugh. "Poor you." Emma wipes the tears running down her cheek. She hasn't laughed so hard in…forever. "At least they aren't trying to make your life a living hell. I swear if she could Matilda would leave a bag of flaming poop on my doorstep then ring the bell and run away."

Otto smiles and leans an elbow on the back haunches of the cow. Damn if he doesn't look sexy as hell. The cowboy could rock a t-shirt, worn jeans, and day-old stubble like no one else. His biceps are tan, the muscles prominent. He's solid, built, and looks capable of a lot.

When he'd driven away after pulling her car from the ditch, she'd never expected to see him again, much less find him working for her newly-found family. Not that she minded. That moment when he'd caught her before she fell played over and over in her mind. The way the hard planes of his body pressed against her and the sensation of the rock-solid muscles of his arms wrapped around her had sent a jolt through her and that was on top of the way his smile played on those plump sexy lips. What the hell was a man with a jaw that square and hard doing with the kind of lips Hollywood starlets paid top dollar for anyway?

He'd looked every bit as gobsmacked as she'd felt when she walked into the room that first day at breakfast. Maybe more. And what had he called her? Sunflower? Where the hell had that come from?

Now that the cow is in place in the barn, Emma takes a seat on the footstool. "Okay. I got this."

She's not sure if she's speaking to Otto or herself. Although now that she's faced with the cow's actual udder, she's not so sure what she's got. Otto's gone back to the other side of the cow and she slips her phone out of her pocket and taps open the website containing the step-by-step procedure on how to milk a cow, complete with illustrations.

Okay. Step One: she needs to wash the udder. She looks around for something even close to soap and water, but before she can get up, Otto is placing a bucket next to her. "You're going to want to wash your hands good, too."

"Thanks." She places the phone on the ground and gets busy with water, jumping a little every time the cow shifts her weight.

"Are you . . . are you using the internet to figure out how to milk a cow?" Otto crouches down next to her and points to her phone. His face remains neutral, but the doubt in his voice comes through loud and clear.

Emma shoves a lock of hair off her face with the back of her hand. "How else am I supposed to learn?" It isn't like anybody is taking much time to explain anything to her.

"Not from Google. That's for sure." He scratches the back of his neck and takes a deep breath. "Okay. You've washed the udder and your hands. Now you're going to need some lubricant."

She sits straight up. "Lube? What is it exactly that you think I'm going to do to Bessie here?"

He shakes his head and pats the cow's haunch. "Her name is Clara and you don't want to damage anything when you milk her. It's best if your hand can slip freely." He walks over to a nearby bench and comes back with something called udder budder and two pairs of gloves.

He's actually going to help. Relief floods through Emma. He really is a hero. They both glove up and he puts some udder budder on her hand and then slips behind her on the footstool. With his arms on either side of her, he guides her hands as they lubricate the cow's udder. His breath is warm on her neck and his hard chest is against her back, the muscles shifting and moving as he guides her. "That's right. Just want to make it so there's not too much friction."

Once they're done, Emma straightens, resting her arms on his thighs that are on either side of her. "Okay. Now what?"

He chuckles and it vibrates her whole body. "Now's the fun part."

Otto grabs her hand and puts it on the udder. She recoils and scrunches her face. It's the oddest thing to touch. But he is patient and shows her how to grip the teat. "Start at the top, and squeeze while sliding down."

He guides her a few more times, milk spitting into the bucket below. Then he removes his hand and stands up. "Now try on your own."

She does it and more milk streams out. She gasps. She's doing it! She's milking a cow! Emma glances over her shoulder to thank Otto, but finds him full on staring down her top at her cleavage. Oh uh. No way is he getting away with that. She angles the udder and squeezes on the downward stroke, blasting him in the face with milk.

"What the fu—" He pulls a bandana out of his back pocket and mops his face.

She smiles and shrugs. "Clara may be sharing hers, but I'm not sharing mine."

He leans closer, his face next to hers. He smells like trees in sunlight. She leans toward him as if she's being pulled. It's hard to take her eyes off the strong clean lines of his jaw. His lips are inches away from hers. Then his hand shoots out and grabs a teat and sprays her right back. She nearly falls off the footstool, spluttering, with milk running down her face.

Otto chuckles and dabs at the milk on her face. He's close enough that his woodsy scent nearly overwhelms her as much as the tenderness of his touch. Then he stands and saunters toward the barn door. "Have yourself a good day, Sunflower."

Then, with a tip of his hat, he's gone with Matilda and company strutting along behind him as if they'd won some contest.

Chapter 6

Otto

All day Otto's haunted by the sensation of having Emma in his arms again, the faint peach scent of her hair and skin, and the glee on her face when she realized she was actually milking a cow. Which, of course, he then ruined by getting caught ogling her breasts. It's hardly his fault, though. They're beautiful, from what he's been able to see.

Something hits him square in the middle of the back. "Ow!"

He turns to find Sawyer grinning at him. "You done with whatever daydream took you a few miles away? We've still got some irrigation lines to check and I'd like to have it all done in time to shower before supper."

Good set of goals.

Otto gives himself a shake and sets his mind on what's before him. Not difficult to do since the work is hard and demanding and requires attention. One false move can lead to accidents with injuries every bit as bad as the ones he saw over in Afghanistan. He came through his multiple deployments unscathed, physically at least, and it would be a damn shame to have survived all that to get injured now.

"Well, then we best get moving." He gives Bayberry a little nudge with his heels and the three men are off into the open plain.

Time seems to fly even though the work is tedious. The work here is like that for Otto. It soothes. Along with the easy camaraderie that's formed between him and Mario and Sawyer, it's made being a ranch hand a better experience than he'd even hoped for. Before long they're back at the residents' building, showered, and ready to eat. Otto ambles toward the main house with Sawyer and Mario who lifts his head to the sky and sniffs. "Smells good. Tomatoes. Garlic. What do you think is cooking?"

"I don't know, but I'd like to find out." Sawyer picks up the pace.

When they get into the kitchen, Emma is bent over peering into the oven, her short skirt riding up in back to a tantalizing height. Otto's eyes travel up the smooth lines of her legs, imagining what's just out of reach and the many things he'd like to do with it.

Mario elbows him hard. "Catching some flies there?"

Otto shuts his mouth quickly and just in time as Emma straightens and smiles at them. "Go on in to the dining room. This needs about five more minutes. There's salad and bread to get you started."

Otto swallows hard. Salad and bread. Right. He's hungry for dinner.

They walk into the dining room as everyone laughs at something Mitch has said. His boss's eyes twinkle with mischief in a way Otto hasn't seen for a while. Katie is lifting her napkin to dab her eyes. Linda reaches over to give Mitch's hand a squeeze, making sure it's back in her own lap before Katie's put her napkin down. Otto looks over to Mario and Sawyer to see if they noticed it, too. Everyone has been curious if there is some sort of secret relationship between the two, but Katie always shoots the idea down. And no one ever has ever witnessed anything more to suggest the rumors might be true.

Otto takes a seat, maneuvering so he's between Mario and Sawyer and the only other empty place at the table is to Mario's left. If he sits next to Emma, he's not sure if he'll be able to eat. Already all he can think about is running his hands up her smooth legs and underneath her skirt. He drains the glass of ice water in front of him, hoping the cold water inside him will have more of an impact than the cold shower.

"Frena, amigo." Mario passes the salad bowl to him. "There's plenty where that came from."

Otto nods and takes the salad, filling his plate and then passing it onto Sawyer. By the time the bread has made it around, Emma is coming in with a big tray of something that smells damn good. The platter makes the rounds and when it reaches Otto he freezes. "Emma...what's this?"

"Chicken Parmigiana." Emma smooths her napkin onto her lap.

Otto nearly drops the platter, his stomach sinking.

Emma rolls her eyes. "Don't worry. It's not Matilda. I promise."

Mario bumps his shoulder and laughs hard enough that tears are coming to his eyes. "You should see your face!"

"I'm afraid like most of the animals here, Matilda is smarter and wilier than me." Emma takes a bite of salad. "Even Clara's got it over me."

Katie laughs. "Clara? The cow? The red one? The one who's practically like a dog?"

Emma nods. "She and I had a bit of a failure to communicate this morning."

Otto holds his breath. *Please don't say anything about me looking down your shirt. Not with your dad here.*

"I, uh, hadn't ever actually milked a cow before and was trying to use YouTube to figure out how." She keeps her head down looking at her plate.

Mitch lets out an audible breath and sets his fork down. "You should have said something, EmmaBear."

Emma's head shoots up and everyone's heads swivel to Mitch. Katie coughs and John gives her a pound on the back between her shoulder blades. Once she recovers, she asks Mitch, "EmmaBear? Where did that come from?"

Mitch shrugs. "Not sure. Just came out."

Otto scoops a serving of the chicken parm onto his plate then looks over to Emma who's toying with the napkin on her lap. "Anyway, Otto was passing by and stopped to help me get started. Of course Matilda came in at that very minute looking as if she wanted to tackle me and peck me to death. But Otto led her away before anything happened."

Otto slumps into his chair, letting out the breath he'd been holding. No mention of his ogling. Thank God. Well, one good deed deserves another. "You woulda had it figured out with or without me. I just sped up the process for you a little."

Katie snorts derisively.

Emma tears into a piece of bread, completely ignoring her sister. "I've never been around animals much before. One place I lived had a cat, but that's been pretty much it."

Linda places her fork down. "Do you know how to ride?"

"Like a horse?" Emma eyes go wide. "No."

"We'll have to see if we can do something about that." Mitch returns to eating.

Mario pats his belly then reaches for the platter for a second helping of the chicken parmigiana. "Where'd you learn to cook?"

Emma laughs. "Mainly YouTube there, too. It helped in the system. If you could do something like cook, you were useful. Useful kids didn't have to move so much and got treated a little better."

"You know, Katie actually used the internet to learn how to cook. Guess it might not be such a bad way to learn." Mitch grabs the glass of water in front of him and takes a swig.

Katie looks like she's about to choke, her face getting red.

Otto chews on some salad, lingering on the importance of the statement Emma made. It explains why someone would try to learn to milk a cow by watching videos on the internet. Being useful and self-sufficient was how Emma made it through her childhood. She's using the same techniques here, finding ways to learn what she needs to know to get along without ever asking anyone for help. Brave. Possibly misguided, but definitely brave.

The conversation turns to the irrigation repairs and what tasks need to be done tomorrow. With plates finally nearly licked clean, Mitch leans back and pats his stomach. "I'm full as a tick."

Emma stands and begins collecting plates. "I hope you left room for dessert. I made a cobbler with some jarred fruit I found in the root cellar. What is a chokecherry anyway?"

"Only about my favorite thing on the earth," Mitch says, a big smile on his face.

Otto doesn't miss Katie's eye roll. She opens her mouth like she's about to say something, but Linda lays a gentle hand on her arm. Otto's not sure what passes between the two women, but Katie slumps back in her chair and John puts his arm around her, pulling her against him.

Ah. Otto gets it. Can't be easy to have been the apple of her daddy's eye for twenty-six years, only to have some usurper come in and steal the spotlight. Given the year Katie had, it'd make sense she might be struggling to come up with some graciousness. Hell, he isn't sure how Addie would take it if she suddenly had to share his attention with a sibling.

Emma's arrival at Three Keys Ranch is unsettling for everyone it seems.

Chapter 7

Emma

A chorus of murmurs of assent rises from around the table as everyone digs into the chokecherry cobbler. Even Katie is eating with gusto. Emma relaxes a fraction. She'd been twelve the first time a foster parent told her to have dinner on the table by six and to figure out what to make based on what was in the kitchen. It had been a heck of a lot easier here at Three Keys Ranch where there's a freezer full of meat and vegetables in the refrigerator and the root cellar. And there's more of that sweet tea her father served her that first afternoon. She's not sure when she ever tasted something this good.

Hell, it's even beat out the iced guava white tea as being her favorite drink.

A few minutes go by with no one speaking, the best compliment any cook can get. It's a good silence, companionable. These people are silent a lot, though. Emma must've said ten sentences for every one of her father's when they'd talked that first morning. Although each of his had been important, including the one when he asked her to stay longer to give them a chance to get to know one another and not let Isobel steal one more minute from them.

The idea someone wants to be her dad pretty much undid Emma. Any thought of going back to New York flew out of her head as fast as that bunny had run across the road in front of the rented Jetta.

Katie finishes chewing, then looks over at her. "So, if our mother gave you up, how come nobody ever adopted you?"

Her father slams his fork down on the table, his face stormy. "Katie."

Emma lifts up a hand to stop any tirade that might be forthcoming. Her sister might be trying to bait her, but it's probably good to get all the information out on the table. "Isobel gave me up, but refused to give the name of my father. While I could've still been adopted, if my biological father had ever stepped forward wanting custody, it could've placed the established adoption in jeopardy. My only guess is most people didn't want to live like that, so passed me over. And once I hit a certain age, it became harder regardless. Teens have such a difficult time finding anyone who might even want to foster them let alone adopt them." She picks at the cobbler in front of her, appetite suddenly waning. The memory of those court hearings still hurts.

"Oh," Katie says, her voice small. "I, uh, didn't know that."

"It is what it is." She forces herself to take a big bite of food. If she's chewing and swallowing, they can't expect her to say more.

Conversation at the table turns to who's doing what in which pasture the following day. It's like listening to people speak in a foreign language. Tuning out what people are saying, she casts a furtive glance over at Otto who seems to be enjoying every bite of the cobbler. She's glad he's not angry at her for squirting him in the face with milk. Heat creeps up in her own face as she thinks about those moments when he sat behind her on the milking stool, his chest pressed against her back, his arms strong around hers.

He always seems to be right there when she needs some help. Between getting her car out of the ditch and the way he jumped up to help her with the pancakes that first morning and then again out in the yard with Clara the cow. He's like a guardian angel who is there one minute and gone the next.

So now, not only is she contending with a bratty older sister but she's also crushing on a worker on her father's ranch. Yeah, definitely not what she expected when she made the choice to come out here. Maybe she should rethink her plans to stay longer. It's so tempting, though. When she'd come back that first morning and Mitch had told her how much he wanted to get to know her and how she could actually be a help, it had been impossible to refuse, even with Katie glaring at her and stomping around like she was trying to squish cockroaches.

After dessert, Emma stacks some dishes and carries them to the double basin stainless steel sink in the kitchen. She braces her hands on the edge of the counter and takes a breath.

"Need some help?"

Emma looks over her shoulder to find Mario carrying the salad bowl to the sink. In all honesty, she isn't in the mood to talk to anyone. Would be nice to be left alone with her thoughts and let them settle. However, the earnest look on his face causes her to push that need for solitude away, for now. "Um, sure. I don't think all of this will fit in the dishwasher, so we'll have to do some stuff by hand. How about I wash and you dry?"

"Mitch and Katie must appreciate how much you're doing around here." Mario places the salad bowl down on the granite counter and grabs a dishtowel.

"It's not a problem." Emma looks down at the dishes in the sink and grabs one along with a sponge. There's a decent amount in there, waiting to be scrubbed clean, and having something mundane to do to keep her from thinking too hard and too much is a welcome distraction. She can do them on autopilot and let her mind go blank. After pumping a small amount of soap onto the sponge, she turns the faucet on. "Though I'm sure the only thing Katie would appreciate is me leaving."

Sounds petty but the words slip out of her before she can do anything about it, and she can't take them back any more than she can take back the hot tears forming in her eyes. Instead, she focuses on the dish in her hand, lathering it with soap and water.

"Not so sure about that. Watching over her dad, the ranch, and her husband is stressful. Used to have a housekeeper here to help. But she had some family stuff and had to quit. Truth be told, Mitch seemed happy. Not that he disliked the woman, he just hates being waited on. Wants to do things for himself, but the heart attack has slowed him down considerably. With you here, some of the pressure can be taken off Katie's shoulders. Give her some time to get used to it. You were kind of a big surprise."

Emma jerks her head sideways to face Mario. The dish nearly slips out of her hand and falls back into the sink. Luckily, she tightens her grip just in time. "Why does she need to look after her husband?"

Mario straightens, blinking his eyes rapidly. Learning her biological father had a heart attack had been quite a shock, but

Emma hadn't seen anything wrong with John. If anything, the man looks as solid and sturdy as a titanium hammer. She knows, of course, that there are things that happen, things she can't see going on beneath the surface, but it's hard for her to put John and weak in the same sentence.

Mario rubs the back of his neck, his eyes cast down, clearly unwilling to speak.

"Mario." Her eyes soften. "Please. Tell me."

For a moment, she doesn't think he will. But after sucking in a deep breath, he glances back up at her. "Last year, there was an incident."

Emma blinks. She thinks she knows what he's referring too. "My father's heart attack." She takes a steady breath and focuses on the new dish in her hand, waiting for him to respond.

"Not just that. There was a worker here who had ulterior motives." Mario sets his dish down, but doesn't grab a new one. His eyes are everywhere – the sink, the floor, the kitchen door – but not on her.

Emma tries not to read into that, and instead turns the sponge over to the rough side and tries to scrub off the dried foods. She grimaces, putting more pressure on the plate, hoping to calm her nerves.

Mario clears his throat, then continues. "He was the son of a man who used to be partners with your father. I'm not sure why that ended, but the man died early. The son blamed the Lockes and wanted revenge. He attacked the family and John."

Is that who Peter is, the person Katie referenced when Emma first arrived? Emma swallows hard. There's so much she doesn't know. Why hadn't she done more research on them before she came out here? She furrows her brows and turns her attention back to scrubbing the plate, needing to do something with her hands while her mind whirred. "He's in jail now, right?"

"Yes." From her peripheral, Emma sees him flex his fingers before dropping his arms to his sides. "But not before he caused enough damage. He'd been responsible for the attack Katie'd endured as well."

The plate almost slips from her hand at his words. She takes a moment. There's no sound in the kitchen save for the running water. She rests her hands on the edge of the sink, needing to hold onto something.

Mario comes to stand next to her and reaches to grab the dishes she's already cleaned and dries them. She grabs another avoiding eye contact. "Was it bad?"

She's not sure she wants to know, but she'd be foolish not to try to find out. Ignorance most definitely isn't bliss. What is she stepping into here?

Mario doesn't answer right away. Emma tries not to read into the silence, despite how overwhelming it is. Instead, she grabs a glass and quickly washes it, not even putting much effort into ensuring it's shining afterwards. When she hands it to him she makes the mistake of meeting his gaze. Sympathy fills his brown eyes and a lump forms in her throat. If that look doesn't say everything he's not, she's not sure what else would.

"She'd been a nurse, someone attacked her and beat her bad. No one had known who the assailant was then. It all came out after. Seems Peter—that's the former worker's name—hired some guy. When that didn't work he adjusted his plan. Even shot at both Katie and John. He wanted to kill your sister." He places the glass into the rack and takes the next one she hands him. "John is a veteran and had some injuries. Probably some similar to the ones I suffered when I played hockey. You know, the head trauma, numerous concussions. He got hit and it made him worse for a while. Screwed some of the healing up."

She winces, tilting her head so her hair falls into her face, shielding it from Mario's view. What more can she say? Should she say sorry? But she's not even sure what she should be sorry about.

It isn't like what happened is her fault. And more than that, Mario isn't related. He's just filling her in on what happened to her family. Or is he? Did any of this happen to him? "Did you get hurt?"

"Nah." His features soften, appreciating her concern, but he casually waves it away. "Didn't start working here until a couple of months ago. Otto and I are new."

Not as new as she is. And not nearly as out of place.

Chapter 8

OTTO

Otto kicks the dust off his boots in the doorway, then tosses his Stetson onto the coffee table along with the package of fudge cookies he's picked up from the market. Spending the past two days in the south pasture removing spotted knapweed has been hell on his back. And while he just wants to spend time with his daughter, he longs for a hot shower and a soft bed, maybe a game of Candyland, but that's not gonna happen tonight. Not when he has to take Addie to a Girl Scout meeting. Veronica signed their daughter up as a way to meet new friends, something he actually supports. It's a good choice. The right thing to do. But he would've appreciated learning about it sooner than an hour ago because his ex-wife's schedule had changed and she couldn't get Addie there herself.

"Daddy!" Addison's little voice echoes through the apartment, followed by the patter of little feet running from her bedroom to the kitchen.

He bends down and spreads his arms, feeling that familiar catch in his chest when they're filled with his six-year-old daughter. She squeezes him back hard. It never ceases to amaze him how she brings instant joy to his heart. He inhales the sweet scent of her strawberry-scented shampoo and then pulls away the slightest bit to give her a kiss on the top of her head. "Got the cookies for your meeting tonight. Did you have fun with Sawyer?"

Addie gives him the biggest toothy grin he's ever seen. "We played Wii. But Sawyer isn't very good, especially at tennis. He's kinda slow."

"I heard that." The timbre of the voice from the bedroom was deep with a hint of a Texan accent.

Otto laughs and stands as Sawyer appears in the doorway, his brown hair a sweaty mess. He looks more like Mitch than either Katie or Emma do, his face already craggy even though he's only in his twenties. Maybe the girls take more after their mother. It's not like there are any photos of her around. No one even seems to mention the woman's name either.

"Thanks again for watching Addie. Wasn't expecting to have to go to a meeting nor that I'd have to bring a snack."

"You know it's no problem." Sawyer looks over at Addie, that craggy face softening much like Mitch's does when he looks at Katie or Emma. When it comes to his co-workers, Otto can't imagine a better group of people. While he and John connect in a way only veterans who share those experiences can, Sawyer and Mario are like brothers to him. And like the good uncles they are, they'd instantly offered to help with Addie. They are, well, family.

Also helps Sawyer is a lawyer. Or was. Hell, Otto wasn't sure where the man stood on his former career now that he'd been working on the ranch. Either way, Veronica didn't seem to be giving him a lot of grief when he asked if his *lawyer* friend could pick Addie up.

Otto had had to run into town after work to grab something to bring to this meeting because Veronica didn't even bother to send that, but he suspects it's all part of the game she's playing. Well, he's not playing. He's deadly serious and he'll take whatever she throws at him if it means getting joint custody of Addie.

Sawyer claps a hand down on his shoulder. "Was my pleasure. And I'm not slow, I'm cautious. Do you know what it's like to play a videogame while trying to keep track of someone who barely comes up to your waist. Last thing I need is you beating me up for trampling your little girl."

"Uh-huh." One thing Otto learned quickly was how cautious Sawyer is. Too cautious sometimes it seemed, but the man is used to paying attention to the tiniest details. Though, Otto suspects his friend was like that way before he started his legal career. The man notices when a painting across the room is the slightest bit tilted. Hard to know what came first, the profession or the predilection.

Otto turns his attention to his daughter. "Are you ready for your troop meeting?"

Addie's brown curls sway and she nods. "My uniform is on the bed. Sawyer ironed it for me because it got wrinkles from being in the suitcase."

"Well, go get dressed while I get ready myself." He shoos her back toward her room.

She hustles past Sawyer and into her room. His friend walks into the kitchen as the bedroom door closes, grabs an apple from the bowl on the counter and bites into it, a smirk spreads across his lips. "Hope by *getting ready* you mean taking a shower. You smell like a barrel full of manure."

Otto grimaces. "I have no intention of embarrassing myself or my daughter going anywhere smelling like this."

Sawyer grabs the package of cookies from the table. "From what I gather, most of the moms bake cookies. Or buy cookies directly from the bakery. Not sure these are going to pass the test."

Otto pinches the bridge of his nose. So not knocking it out of the park. Maybe more of a bunt. "Just doing the best I can. Not used to being a single parent. Deployment kept me away most of the time. And when I was around, Veronica was always there to lead the way."

"I'm just poking at you. You're doing a great job." Sawyer swallows whatever chewed up bits of apple he has, then smiles, making the corners of his eyes crinkle. "Addison thinks the world of you. Don't let anyone else tell you otherwise."

Otto holds out his hand to Sawyer. "Anyway, I should go get ready. Thanks again for watching Addie."

His friend takes his hand and shakes it as he quirks an eyebrow. "Maybe later you can tell me what's up with you and my newfound cousin."

His good mood evaporates and his gaze jerks toward the bedroom door, which thankfully is still closed. This isn't a conversation, or even something to casually speak about in front of his daughter. Plus, nothing is going on with Emma. She's off limits. "Nothing to talk about. Just helped get her car out of a ditch and showed her how to milk a cow."

"If you say so." Sawyer walks over to the door and exits the apartment.

Once the door closes Otto heads to the bathroom. He strips out of his clothes and steps into the shower. Luckily, the hot water comes fast thanks to the tankless water heater Mitch has installed. Otto scrubs his scalp and skin trying to wash off all the dirt and stink he can. Sometimes the smell just won't leave, like the way fisherman always have the faint odor of fish coming off them.

As the droplets of water run over his brown hair to wash away the soap, his mind wanders over to Sawyer's comment. Is the chemistry between them that obvious? He knows he feels it and he thinks Emma does, too. Most likely Mario has put some insane idea into Sawyer's head. Though, maybe Sawyer actually spoke to his cousin. Did Emma say something about him? Crap. He hopes not. Sawyer's his friend, but he's also the boss's nephew. Best to step carefully around all of them.

His pulse begins to pick up speed. Just thinking about Emma makes his dick swell. She's gorgeous, but she's also strong. Maybe not Montana ranching strong, but a different kind of fortitude. It can't be easy to show up to meet your biological family out of the blue for the first time then remain calm as your biological sister acts like a brat toward you in front of staff. And Katie was definitely being a brat.

He clears his throat and looks down, his dick already at half-mast. What he wouldn't give to rub one out and relieve some stress, but he doesn't have the time and his little daughter is in the next room. Not exactly an aphrodisiac. So, he finishes up in the shower, then steps out and dries off, running a comb through his thick hair. He wishes he had time to shave, but the Girl Scouts are going to have to deal with his five o'clock shadow.

Thirty minutes later, he's standing by the refreshment table at the meeting while his daughter is off with the other girls. Sawyer was right. All the snacks look freshly baked and are prettily displayed on platters. Someone even brought a casserole. He's starving and takes a big helping. When he looks up, a redhead winks at him from her perch behind the table causing him to inwardly squirm.

A brief glance around the room tells him the redhead isn't the only woman assessing him. He gets it. He's pretty much the only father in the place and he's an unknown quantity, too. Someone new in a small town. Maybe staying for the meeting isn't the best idea. He came to the Girl Scout meeting to bring Addie, not to pick up women. He quickly cleans his plate and disposes of it. He finds Addie sitting with a circle of girls doing something that seems to involve winding yarn around popsicle sticks. He kisses the top of her head. "See you in an hour, baby girl."

She looks up at him, kisses his cheek, and then goes back to chatting with her friends, barely registering that he's leaving. He should be glad she doesn't worry about him coming back, but his heart sinks a little anyway. After all, he'll be missing her while he's gone.

He heads toward the door only to catch sight of the redhead coming at him from the side like a cowboy separating a cow from the herd. He should have moved faster. "Hi, I'm Gracie Johnson. You must be Addison's father."

He nods. "Yes, ma'am."

"Addison said you recently moved out here. Are you finding everything okay?" Gracie bats her lashes and steps closer into his space, her perfume scenting the air around him.

"Not much to find. I'm mainly working and taking care of Addie, ma'am." Hopefully, the woman will take the hint by his clipped tone and walk away.

He's not that lucky. "It's important to take a little time for yourself now and then. You don't want to burn out. All work and no play and all that." She crosses her arms over her chest, which he's pretty sure she knows plumps her breasts up. He certainly notices, despite himself. "If you don't have plans for tomorrow night, there's a new movie playing at the drive-in."

A drive-in. Really. He looks hard at Gracie. She's not bad looking. Quite the opposite, really. She's just not his type. "Sorry, ma'am. Ranch is very busy, so outside of work I only have time for Addison."

"Sounds like you work too hard." Gracie licks her lips. "You should really take a break."

Damn, she's persistent. Maybe he should have skipped the shower. "Wish I could, ma'am, but cows don't understand what a break is." He touches the tip of his hat with one hand and grabs the door handle with the other. "Have a good evening."

Otto steps out into the cool evening air and takes a relieved breath. He does the mental math of the last time he'd brought a woman into his bed and runs a hand over his scruffy jaw.

Too long.

He can't do anything about his personal life. Any way he goes, he's screwed, and not in the good way. Getting involved with a woman around here is trouble. With only a few thousand people, word spreads fast, everyone knows everyone. There's no way he could even have a one-night stand without Veronica finding out. If Otto hooked up with someone, there'd be rumors. Moms talk to other Moms. And worse yet, it would eventually get back to Addie and...just...nope. Bad idea all around, no matter how tempting.

It isn't only about him anymore. If keeping his daughter in a secure environment means he lives more celibate than a priest and works even harder on the ranch, it's worth it.

At least, that is what he's telling himself. Until he reaches his truck and his thoughts get interrupted by a familiar voice, spitting nasty curse words as if she'd been part of the military herself.

Chapter 9

EMMA

Emma blows a lock of brown hair out of her face and glances around. She's sandwiched between an old-looking bank made of all brick and an antiques shop with not a soul in sight. It's just her luck. Again.

She kicks the tire of her damn rental car. Hard. This Jetta is the worst, maybe it's even cursed. Smoke billows out from under the hood. "Piece of shit."

It's a sign. She should go back to New York. She doesn't belong here. Hell, she only went into town to pick up a few things at the drugstore like a new toothbrush since hers has gone missing. *Maybe Matilda found a way to break into the main house with the rest of the flock and took it out of spite.*

Then Emma had gotten distracted by the town's mix of old and new buildings, blending and contrasting so many materials and textures and styles. It had practically begged her to shoot some photos for her portfolio. When she was done, she'd headed back to the car, got in, turned the key and nothing happened except a bunch of smoke coming up from under the hood.

With a huff, she looks up and she shakes her fist at the sky and growls.

"Excuse me, ma'am?"

Her skin heats instantly at the sound of the husky baritone voice rumbling behind her. Emma looks over her shoulder and finds Otto who's fighting a smile. Again. He looks better than ever with a slight scruff of beard on his face and a tight white T-shirt showing his shoulders. She bites the inside of her cheek to reign in her thoughts and points to the car. "It's acting up again."

"Let me take a look." He rounds the rental and pops open the hood. He shakes his head and looks over the engine then bends over the engine, tan arms flexing and his shirt pulling tight over well-defined shoulders and Good Lord the way those jeans look on him. No wonder Matilda wants him for herself.

Still pumped up from her frustration over the stupid rental car, Emma lifts her hair off the back of her neck to let the breeze cool her down. She looks down at her yellow Chucks. "At least I have better shoes on this time."

Otto straightens and looks over at her, his gaze starting at her feet and sliding up her legs with an attention that she can practically feel. She lets her hair drop back around her shoulders.

"Looks like you're overheating."

Her eyes widen as she coughs. Once she regains her composure she looks him in the eye. "I'm perfectly fine."

Otto chuckles. "I mean the car. The coolant is low. I have some in my truck."

She deflates a little, feeling both embarrassed and a little defiant. "You just happen to drive around with coolant?"

"It's a good idea to have some basic vehicle maintenance items with you around here. You can wait a long time without someone coming around to help. I'll be right back." He walks back to the corner giving her an eyeful of his back and ass.

Her hero, once again.

About five minutes later he pulls his truck up next to the Jetta, cuts the engine, and hops out while carrying a blue jug before going back under the hood. "Maybe you should bring the car back and ask for a new one."

"Thought crossed my mind." Though she has to admit, the rental is bringing her some nice views. Her eyes trail over Otto once more as he leans over the car, big hands busy under the hood. It isn't difficult to imagine those hands on her, strong and rough. She fans her face to cool off her hot cheeks.

"Start her up and see if that helped," he says.

She slides into the driver's seat and turns the key. The engine comes to life and best of all there's no smoke coming from under the hood. She drops her head to the steering wheel. "You are a lifesaver."

Emma turns the engine off and gets out of the car only to find him smiling at her once again. He walks closer, leans against the car, and tips his Stetson. "Happy to assist."

Her body lights up. Apparently she has a thing for cowboys. Who knew? It's not like she gets much of a chance to hang around them in New York. The naked one in Times Square doesn't count. She leans closer to Otto as if some kind of magnetic force is drawing her to that broad chest. "Seriously, what do I owe this time? At least let me pay you for the coolant."

He frowns. "No. It's fine."

"Missed you at dinner tonight." Nobody mentioned where he was and Emma had been too embarrassed to ask. "We had pasta primavera."

He runs his hands over his face. "Sounds good. Sorry I missed it. I had . . . another engagement."

"Matilda was bereft." She smiles, but it's actually true. The chicken with her posse had come right up onto the porch and circled several times, clucking loudly. When she'd finally gone back to the coop, her head had hung down.

"Matilda will get over it. What are you doing back here anyway?"

She chews the inside of her cheek, fingers toying with the hem of her sundress. Is he being polite or might he actually be interested in discussing the aesthetics of the town and her photos and what she wants to do with them? Probably best to keep it simple. "Just exploring."

His eyes remain focused on her, almost penetrating through her. He leans a smidge closer, his jaw ticking. "And what do you think so far?"

Heat flows in waves through her body. Her breath hitches at how close she is to Otto, how close their lips are, at the way her heart races. She swallows hard and looks down at her feet, trying to break the spell. "It's nice."

It's nice.

She must sound like such an idiot. Why couldn't she mention how different the town is from the city she lives in, how the architecture of the buildings is different? Maybe because the scent of warm woods, amber, and coconut wafting off Otto short-circuits her brain.

Her gaze falls to his neck where a vein pulses visibly, like he's struggling for control, too. What would happen if either of them gave into what they both clearly want to do? What harm could it be? No one would need to know except the two of them. She stifles a low whimper, wanting to see what he tastes like. She looks back up and his blue eyes dilate. And when she bites her bottom lip, Otto slides his hand into her hair and pulls her the rest of the way to him. His warm soft lips crash down onto hers. She kisses him back with equal ferocity. He tastes so good, like sweet tea on a sunny day, a flavor she didn't even know she craved before she tasted it.

He pulls her close, solid arms wrapping around her as he consumes her in a way she's never been before, exploring her mouth, nipping at her lips, claiming her completely. Her entire body buzzes as she melds herself to him, wanting every inch of herself pressed against his body. It feels so right, like they're meant to be together this way, like she belongs in his arms. His kiss is insistent and commanding, but tender.

She wants more, though, wants to tempt his control so she scrapes her front teeth against his lip and murmurs his name. "Otto."

A low growl rumbles from his chest and vibrates against her breasts, her nipples rising and tightening. Emma grabs the back of his neck and pulls him even closer. She's lonely and tired and dispirited. She doesn't belong here in Montana and yet she doesn't want to leave. She's found her family, but still doesn't have a home. Every second feels like a struggle to prove herself. Her head spins. She wants to not think for a minute, to shut down all the strife. Otto can give her that. She wants his heat, his strength, his passion. She wants to be overwhelmed.

He meets her and then some. His hands slide down to her ass and yank her against him.

"I want you," she says against his mouth, then bites his bottom lip.

"I want you, too." He kisses down her neck, leaving a trail of gooseflesh on the way and making her body light up like the New Year's Eve ball in Times Square. There's not a square inch of her that doesn't need more of him.

"Otto, please." Her voice is raspy, needy. She claws at his shoulders and grinds her hips against him. Why not? Why not find some oblivion in his arms? What would it really hurt? He clearly wants her as much as she wants him. Maybe he has troubles he wants to escape, too. Maybe she'd be giving him some solace as well. They're consenting adults. As long as nobody else finds out, they'll be fine. Whose business is it anyway?

"You sure?" he says against her throat.

The ache between her legs gets more insistent. "Yes." She's never been more sure in her life.

Emma wraps her legs around Otto's waist when he lifts her up and walks the couple of feet over to his truck. They're alone in a dark empty lot, and fortunately for them, they aren't anywhere near a streetlamp. The way the spot is hidden that she was cursing a few minutes before is now more than welcome. It's become a haven, an island built just for two.

His hand stalls on the truck door handle and he looks at her, eyes level and serious. "You absolutely sure about this?"

She tries like hell to think clearly through the fog of lust that seems to envelop her whenever Otto comes near her. "Yes, but let's be clear. This is casual. One time. No strings and no need for anyone except you and me to know. Is that okay with you?"

"Yes, ma'am." He opens the door and lifts her into the front seat. His mouth meets hers once again as he takes off his Stetson and flings it into the passenger's side. He kisses his way down her neck to her breasts as he lifts her sundress, then slides off her undoubtedly soaked cotton panties. The cool breeze hits between her spread thighs and she tries to squeeze them shut, but Otto stops her.

"Sunflower, I'm about to warm you up."

Before she can utter a word, Otto buries his face between her thighs and licks her as he hoists one of her legs over his shoulder, unerringly finding that most sensitive spot. She arches against him, wanting more, needing more. Everything inside her clenches down as the sensations he creates with his tongue and his breath vibrate through her whole body. She gasps as he drives his tongue inside her, plunging in and out. Then he slides his hands beneath her to lift her, opening her wider. She's helpless before his onslaught, pleasure coursing through her like a wildfire run amok. There's nothing she can do, but hold on, her hands shoved deep into his hair. It's like he knows every inch of her already.

"Fucking hell, you're delicious, Sunflower," he groans between her legs, his sexy drawl vibrating her flesh.

She can't speak. She can't think. All she can do is ride the waves of sensation to the white hot heat just out of reach. She arches and twists, tightening and quivering at his touch, pleasure climbing higher and higher until she thinks she won't be able to stand another second of it. Then she's there. She comes apart as her orgasm rips through her, the world disappearing around her, aware only of Otto as he stays with her, leading her through every ounce of pleasure, drinking her in like a fine wine.

She comes back to herself, chest heaving and her whole body still trembling. That had been amazing, a climax to end all climaxes, but there's still something empty inside her. She still wants more. She wants him to fill her, to take her, to feel him inside her. She wants to move with him and feel his strength. She rises up on her elbows to look at him, standing between her legs in the open truck door. "Take me. Please. Now."

Otto rises, then leans over her and reaches for the glove compartment. Inside is a box of condoms. As he grabs one she practically rips his shirt open and runs her hands over his chest, gratified to feel him moan. Then she unfastens both his belt buckle and jeans. He backs out of the truck and stands there staring at her. Well, more like devouring her with his eyes, his hunger for her apparent, making her feel more desired than she's ever felt before.

A wave of anticipation washes over her. He looks into her eyes. "No strings?"

She shakes her head. "None. Just this once. Just us."

He grabs her thighs and yanks her lower body out of the truck until his body is wedged between her legs. Her body starts to heat again in anticipation.

He shoves his jeans low on his hips and rips open the condom, wrapping himself quickly. "Hold on tight."

Emma's eyes go wide and she instinctively grabs onto the headrest of the seat with one hand and the steering wheel with the other. What has she gotten herself into? Otto tightens his grip on her hips and plunges into her—hard—causing her breath to stall as her body struggles to adjust to his thickness. He's solid as stone and feels so amazing, it snaps her still-simmering orgasm from earlier into full gear. She contracts around him, spasming.

"Fuck, Emma. You keep milking my cock like that and I won't last much longer," he says through gritted teeth.

She chokes out a sob, another orgasm taking over her senses and leaving her a trembling mess. Yet she needs more. Wants to give him more, so she lifts each time he surges forward, taking him a little deeper.

He growls, and her sex flutters around him. His fingers dig into her ass and he fucks her harder, his chest beaded with sweat, despite the chill of the evening air. She squeezes her eyes shut and tries to slow her breathing. "You're…you're going to make me come again."

"Good," he says, and drives faster. Harder. "I want to feel you."

His hips slam into the backs of her thighs and the truck rocks with each wicked thrust. She cries out, so close to giving him what he wants. He reaches down and circles her clit with his thumb as he impales her on his cock over and over. Heat, blinding in its intensity, flashes through her body, and she screams. "Otto!"

"I'm there, too…I'm coming…," he rasps, taking her over and over, fucking her through her pleasure.

He thrusts deep one last time and shudders, flexing his hips, riding out his own orgasm buried to the hilt with his head thrown back and his mouth open on a groan.

She loves the idea, the feel, of this strong man coming apart for her as she dissolved for him, each taking the other to a place that's beyond rational thought, where the lines between them blur, and they're condensed down to their elemental selves. Man and woman. Yin and yang. Heat and desire. There's no ranch and no difficult sister, no crappy rental car and no recalcitrant cows. There's only Emma and Otto, finding pleasure and peace in the front seat of a pickup in an abandoned parking lot.

Emma closes her eyes as they both come down, taking in the sound of their heavy breathing and the delicious heat of their connection, wanting to luxuriate in the afterglow of a damn good fuck. But Otto pulls away and checks his watch. "I, uh, need to get going."

The cool night air hits her again and she shivers. Her heart clenches for a second. He's done with her that fast? Right. No strings. Those were her conditions, her rules. She looks around and spots a child booster seat in the back of the cab. Good God. Does he have to go pick up a kid? She hops out of the truck and pulls her dress down. Otto pulls her underwear from his back pocket and hands them back. She grins and steps into them, her bright yellow Chucks still on her feet. She runs her hands through her hair, trying to tame the waves into some semblance of order before giving him a nod and backing away toward the demon rental car. When the hot metal is against her back, she turns and slips into the driver's seat. With a silent prayer, she turns the key and the engine roars to life again and no smoke appears. She turns to say something, but he's already getting into his truck without another glance in her direction.

Emma pulls out of the parking lot and onto the street to head back to the ranch. Behind her, Otto turns the other way. An uneasy feeling takes residence in her stomach. She opens the window and breathes in the fresh air, hoping to chase it away. Trying to convince herself that she can act like it never happened, like some of the most amazing sex of her life has no more significance than anything else, like she can take it or leave it. And she definitely has to leave it. They made a deal.

No strings. Just once.

Now she has to live with it.

Chapter 10

OTTO

Otto glances toward the hill as the deep, loud roar of the ranch's four-wheeler cuts through the air. It's been modified of course thanks to Mario because the all-terrain vehicle wasn't loud enough when John first purchased it. Convincing Mitch to purchase the machine hadn't been hard at all. It made it easier to get around the land, hoist medium loads of equipment, and they could even attach a small plow to the front to help with snow removal. But who's riding it up here and why?

Speaking of equipment...Otto flings his hammer into the bed of the truck as Sawyer and Mario continue to install the woven wire replacement panel for the portion of the fence they're fixing. A tree had come down during a storm the prior week and ripped the fence apart. At least the posts held up and weren't damaged. Makes the job a little easier.

And he could use easier today. It's hot as hell out in the sun. With Addie accompanying them into the field and his mind still on his poor judgement the night before, Otto's nerves are frayed. He's having a heck of a time keeping his mind on the job and not on the fact he'd had sex in a parking lot with the boss's daughter the other night while his own daughter was at a freaking Girl Scout meeting.

After Emma had pulled onto the road last night, he'd rushed over to the nearest pharmacy and purchased a can of Febreze and proceeded to spray both himself and the cabin of his truck. Thank god for leather seats and the cool evening, otherwise everything might have stunk of sex and whatever that peach scent was that seemed to waft off Emma. He wasn't ready to explain to his six-year-old daughter what the smell was. Which is why he also made a stop at the bakery to pick up some fresh—and heated up—blondies, and left the bag open when he then drove back to the Girl Scout hall—where he should have stayed despite the predatory redhead—to pick her up.

What had he been thinking? He'd fucked the boss's daughter. In an abandoned lot. The daughter his boss just found out he had. Then left in a hurry. Sure he had a good reason to leave. But the rest…as a father, he'd kick his own ass. And Emma isn't some girl he isn't going to see again. No she lives—at least for the moment—on the same piece of property he does.

The answer is that he hadn't been thinking except about his own loneliness and need. The offer she'd made had been too good to pass up. No strings. No one knows. No reason for Veronica or Addie or Mitch to find out. But damn it had been good and not only because it had been too long for him. The way she'd bit his lower lip and said his name had set his blood on fire and then the way she'd opened to him, her sweetness, her warmth. He felt his brain clouding over just remembering it.

"Is there a post up that ass of yours we need to remove?" Sawyer flings a twig at him.

Otto glares then turns toward the tree about one hundred meters away where Addie is reading a book.

"She can't hear," Mario says. "Que paso?"

"Nothing." Otto grabs a water from the cooler, twists the cap off, and guzzles down every drop without stopping to take a breath.

"He's avoiding. Came home smelling like he rolled around in a dryer no less." Mario wiggles his eyebrows. "Wonder what he was trying to hide."

"Well, he was supposedly at a Girl Scout meeting, which was probably full of the moms of Girl Scouts. Maybe some of them are single. And he's new around here. Got that mysterious new guy vibe going. Maybe our boy got lucky." Sawyer leans against a post, crosses his arms, and quirks an eyebrow.

Otto turns his attention back toward the hill, the roar of the four-wheeler drawing closer as are a string of barks. *Please be John and Koda*. He would give anything for his other friend to save him from this inquisition. He's not saying anything to anybody about what happened. That was part of the deal. No one had to know but the two of them and damned if he is going to be the loud mouth that spills the beans.

The all-terrain vehicle comes into view and his heart lurches in his chest. No. Of all the people to be here, not her. Not now. But there is no denying that dark brown wavy hair flying out behind her. Or the bright yellow chucks that he'd last seen as he'd thrown her leg over his shoulder the night before. Just the thought of it makes him half-hard. It would be easier to forget if it hadn't been so damn good.

"Emma." Her name escapes his mouth before he can stop it.

It would be a comical scene if he wasn't so knotted up about what had transpired between them and how he can't get it, or her, out of his mind. Even through his regret, he can't help but smile as she chases after Two Bits and Nickel, screaming at the dogs to stop running.

"Dios mio. Did something happen with Emma?"

Otto jerks his head to face Mario only to find both men staring wide-eyed at him. But before the conversation can progress a high-pitched squeal fills his ears. Addie. Otto doesn't turn to see what's going on. He's running full speed toward his daughter, heart in his throat, before he even knows he's moving.

After cutting the distance between him and his little girl in half, he slows down to a jog as his brain registers Addison's squeal isn't one of pain but one of joy. Both dogs are showering his daughter in kisses. The thud of heavy footfalls comes to a stop next to him, Sawyer and Mario at his side. All of them are panting as they take a moment to catch their breath. They all exchange a glance. Sawyer puts his hand to his chest and Mario claps him on the back. They'd been every bit as terrified that something had happened to Addie as he had and had been every bit as ready to protect her. He's one lucky bastard and he knows it.

But then something else occurs to him. The roar of the four-wheeler is gone. As if in a slow motion horror movie, Otto watches as his daughter stands up to face Emma. No no no. As much as he doesn't want Mario and Sawyer to know about him and Emma, he wants Addie to know even less. He swallows hard.

"Hi!" Addie's voice rings out.

Emma swings a leg over the vehicle and heads toward his daughter as she waves. Emma's jeans and yellow tank top, which match her sneakers, are dusty, but her cheeks are pink and she seems to glow in the sun like a sunflower.

Fuck.

Otto shakes his head and stomps toward the duo, but not before his daughter holds out her hand to Emma. "I'm Addison, but you can call me Addie."

"Hi there. I'm Emma." They shake hands, both smiling at each other like long lost friends.

Otto's lips press into a tight line. Nope. He doesn't need his daughter interacting with Emma. The agreement is for no strings and if Addie forms any sort of bond with the woman, there will be strings. Lots and lots of strings.

And he doesn't need any of those.

"Addison, pack up your stuff. Time to head back." His voice is gruffer than he intends, the full impact showing when his daughter spins her head toward him all wide-eyed like a doe in headlights. Damn it to hell. It isn't Addie's fault he's an idiot.

"Otto?" Emma stares at him, blinking rapidly as if trying to chase away a mirage.

Otto nods. Curtly. "Emma."

He places a hand on Addison's shoulder, keeping his touch and his voice light. "Baby girl, we're heading in to get lunch. Your uncles are quite hungry."

"We are?" Mario asks as he and Sawyer finally reach the trio.

Otto gives his friend a stern look, an unspoken threat not to push the subject.

"Hey, Mario. I didn't mean to interrupt, but my dad asked me to round up the dogs since Linda's here. Guess they need to get some vaccines today. They don't seem to want to be rounded up, though." Even though Emma is speaking to Mario, her eyes bounce between him and Addie.

It must be quite a shock, but one he doesn't have to explain. His life is his. If only it could be that easy because instead of packing up her things like he's asked, Addison takes a step closer to Emma.

"I like your shoes. They're so yellow."

Emma smiles, but her body is tense. "Um, thanks. I have a couple of pairs in different colors."

"Really? Daddy only lets me have one pair. He says that's all I need." Addie pouts and gives her dad some side eye.

Emma looks over at Otto, too. "That seems unreasonable. Shoes are about so much more than covering your feet."

Addie throws her hands in the air. "I know! I told him. He doesn't listen."

"Addison, don't make me ask you again." Otto makes sure to keep his voice monotone. This isn't the first time Addie decided she preferred an audience other than him. She does it regularly when it comes to Mario, mostly because his friend spoils her rotten.

His little girl huffs and stomps off until her eyes fall on the dogs laying under the tree next to her book and backpack. Then she's down on her knees, rubbing bellies and scratching behind ears. Otto closes his eyes and rubs his temples. God help him.

"Looks like you and Emma are having quite a stressful day thanks to the young ones not minding too well." Sawyer looks over at Addie and the dogs and then back at Otto.

Mario rubs the back of his neck. "You know, Two Bits isn't young. Old man just has lots of spring to his step."

Otto scowls. "Thought you all were hungry and wanted to get back to the house."

"After looking at your sour mug all morning, Emma here is a ray of sunshine we're enjoying." Mario winks at him. "Gonna bask in it for a minute or two."

Otto's jaw ticks. He wishes his friend weren't so damn perceptive. Mario loves yanking his chain and is flirting with Emma in front of him because he knows it'll needle him. Otto shouldn't care. But dammit, he does. He's not crazy about the way Emma smiles back at Mario, either.

"Ready!" Addison comes bounding over to the group, backpack bouncing on her shoulders with each step.

Sawyer removes his Stetson and wipes the sweat from his forehead. "Emma, why don't you head back. We can load the dogs into the truck. That way you don't have to chase them around. Those two are quite stubborn."

Emma lets out a breath. "Thank god. Yes, absolutely. I can't even imagine how people run doggie daycares or walk multiple dogs at one time in the city. Trying to round two of them up has me needing a nap. Every time I came closer to them, they ran away faster. I think they might be in league with the cow and the chickens."

Otto snorts. Of course dogs run when you chase them. That's how dogs work. And how in the world does this girl expect to help her father out if she gets tired riding around on a four-wheeler? She definitely won't be able to handle the rest of ranch work, much less a child.

He straightens.

There are no children on the ranch. As far as he knows, Emma doesn't have any. So where did that thought pop in from? His stomach sinks to his feet when his eyes fall on Addie.

No.

It was one night, not even. One time. No strings. They both agreed.

"It was nice to meet you, Emma." Addie wraps both arms around the woman's waist, causing Otto to scowl.

Emma gives the girl an awkward hug and pats her shoulder. "Thanks again for handling the dogs." She starts to make her way back to the four-wheeler, but then turns and looks at him. "I'll see you back at the house."

He nods, then heads back to the truck. The roar of the muffler fills his ears but he doesn't look back. Instead he focuses on the two brutes with crossed arms waiting for him at the truck. Without missing a beat, Mario whistles loudly and the dogs bound over to the truck, then hop into the bed.

"So, you slept with my cousin."

Otto whips his head around, looking for his daughter. That is not a sentence he wants her little ears to hear. A second later he catches sight of her in the back seat of the truck. He dips his head. Of course Sawyer made sure Addie was out of earshot before he spoke. Sawyer is always careful. So much for no one but him and Emma knowing, though. "It was one time. Won't happen again. We were both in the same place at the same time and needing to blow off some steam and things sort of came about."

"Mmhmm," Mario adds.

Otto straightens. "Look, it can't happen again. I need this job and I doubt sleeping with Mitch's daughter is going to get me a good performance review. I need to concentrate on my relationship with Addison. This custody case is my priority. I'm not going to lose my little girl again. Veronica took her away once and it nearly destroyed me."

Mario shakes his head. "Emma's a nice person. She won't get in the way of the case. She could even help watch Addie."

"No." Otto's voice leaves no room for argument.

Sawyer sighs, then looks at Mario. "I saw some of the terms Veronica wants. She'd probably use Emma against Otto in some way based off the demands I've seen requested."

"She is spiteful. Not entirely sure why." Otto rubs his palms over his face and takes a deep breath. He isn't the one that left. "I also don't want Addie getting attached. Emma will be heading back to New York before we know it."

Truth is, he isn't just afraid of his daughter getting attached but of him getting attached as well. The night with Emma had been fucking amazing. He'd woken up hard that morning, thinking of her warm skin. She's sexy and smart and there's something in her eyes that calls to him. A deep longing she doesn't even seem to be aware of and he has a soul-deep need to make that flicker of sadness disappear.

He saw that longing in her eyes again today when she tried to wrangle the dogs. Totally out of her element. Not knowing what to do or how to do it, but trying to make the best of it. Otto rakes his fingers through his hair and heads to the driver's side of the truck. "I made a mistake. It's done. Let's move on."

"Fine." Mario taps the metal hood. "Just don't be a pendejo. She's trying to figure things out with a family she's just met and not all of them are happy to meet her. You're a parent. Imagine if it was Addison in her shoes. If your daughter had been alone her whole life and just found you again."

Otto groans. His friend's right. They need to help. It's the right thing to do. Emma's in over her head when it comes to helping on the ranch, but it gives her a reason to be here and bond with her family. "I'll step in where needed, but I'm standing firm on the Addie thing. I don't want my daughter getting attached."

Both men nod.

Now Otto has to make sure he doesn't let himself get in too deep, either.

Chapter 11

Emma

Emma fumes as she rides back to the main house. What is wrong with that man? She should have stayed away from him, let him fix her possessed rental car and waved while she drove away. She hadn't though and, if she was honest, her impromptu moment with Otto been what she needed at the moment. He'd shattered her. Driven out the worry and tension and loneliness with a hot kiss and a hard cock. Now, it didn't seem like such a great idea.

She slows the four-wheeler and looks up at the sky. She's never seen so much sky in her life. A few little puffy clouds float through it and, once again, she gets the weird sensation of being able to really breathe for the first time. The sheer expanse of space takes her breath away every time she stops to look at it. There's so much of it!

Sure, she's seen some great vistas in New York. There was one time she went to a launch party for a new moisturizer from a top skin care company on top of Rockefeller Center. The views had been amazing and the champagne had flowed like water. It had been fun and sophisticated and had left her feeling giddy. Somehow it hadn't quite hit her in the solar plexus like these views, though. A lot of stuff around here seems to hit her in the gut.

Stuff like Otto.

And he has a daughter. The booster seat in the back of the truck had been a bit of a clue, yet somehow it still surprised her to find the little girl under the tree with a backpack full of storybooks and a stuffed unicorn. But what was with the glower plastered on his face? Did he think she was trying to steal his daughter or something? Emma has no intention of disrupting his life or invading on his relationship with his child. She'd never try to step between a father and a daughter. If anything, she envies the little girl. No one has ever called her "baby girl" in that tone. Although, she has to admit, hearing Mitch – no Dad – call her EmmaBear comes damn close.

Emma shakes her head. She's here to get to know her family before heading back to New York. Getting attached to a cowboy isn't an option. Getting attached to the cowboy's daughter? Absolutely not.

She should have said something before leaving to go back to the house. Let him know she has every intention of keeping to their agreement. Although the way Mario's mouth twitched, as if trying to contain a smile, gave her the impression that maybe Otto hadn't stuck to their terms, that maybe Mario knew about what happened.

She guns the four-wheeler and drives onto the gravel path that takes her back to the house and parks by the barn.

Linda steps through the doorway wiping her hands on a handkerchief. "Couldn't find the dogs?"

Emma snorts as she dismounts the vehicle. "Oh, I found them. Then they ran away, though they seemed to enjoy being chased."

The older woman chuckles, making the laugh lines on her skin crinkle. "That they do." She adjusts her messy bun, trying to reign in a few gray strands. "Those two are like toddlers."

"Luckily, I ran into Mario, Otto, and Sawyer. They're bringing the dogs back with them. They should be here in a few minutes." Emma brushes some of the dirt off her jeans. "Anyway, I'm going to head inside and clean up a bit."

Emma heads to the main house, but stops mere yards from the steps. Matilda and her posse strut across her path and stop. Emma stares at them and several of the chickens cock their heads to the side to stare right back. "Let me guess. You wear pink on Wednesdays."

Matilda clucks in return.

"I've faced meaner girls than you." Emma had changed schools more times than she can count growing up. Perpetually being the new girl had taught her how to stand up to bullies. She stamps her foot and Matilda and company scurry away, clucking. Ha! She'll show that chicken who is Queen Bee. Staggering through the screen door leading directly into the kitchen, Emma lets out a heavy sigh. God, she needs a shower. Who knew a ranch could be so dusty? No time for that now, though. People are coming in for lunch and they're hungry.

No sooner has she pumped soap onto her hands at the kitchen sink when a low growl rumbles through the room. She spins to find Koda with her teeth bared and ears pricked high. Emma's heart thumps like an out of control drum machine and her mouth goes dry. She has no idea what to do. Koda is normally with John or Katie so their interactions have been few and far between. Emma doesn't think foot stomping will work the same way as it did on Matilda and she doesn't really want to find out. She's pretty sure chickens don't have teeth and Koda definitely does.

"*Stop,*" *her father's voice echoes from the hallway.* The dog's hackles go down and the growling stops as he waltzes into the room. "You're back. How'd it go?"

Emma lets out a breath and puts her hand to her chest. She keeps her eyes focused on Koda. "Um, why does she want to eat me?"

Her father scratches his head, heavy eyebrows drawn together in confusion, and then looks down at the dog, then back to her. "She's overprotective. Once she knows you are a friend, all's good. Forgot you two haven't formally met."

When the dog trots back into the living room, Emma slumps forward a bit as relief washes through her. She's never been around so many animals before. They're everywhere out here. Chickens and cows and dogs and horses. She can't turn around without something feathered or four-legged in her face and none of them seem to like her. She turns back around to the sink and washes her hands.

Her father saunters over and puts a heavy hand on her shoulder. "Were you able to round up Nickel and Two Bits for Linda?"

She groans and gives a rueful laugh. "Not exactly. Mario and the others helped. They're bringing them back."

"Then I guess I should get some sandwiches ready. I'm sure little Addison must be starving." Her father rubs his hands together and then moves in to wash them.

Emma grabs a paper towel and dries her hands, trying to chase away the lump forming in the back of her throat. She really missed out not having grown up in this house. If her father is so concerned about a child that isn't his, she can only imagine how much he would've taken care of her. Her fingers ball into tight fists. Her mother had robbed her of a loving childhood, but why? What had she done to deserve being abandoned like that? It's a piece to the puzzle that she might never find.

The stainless steel refrigerator door closes with a thunk and Emma lifts her head. Her father is balancing a stack of bread, cheese, and deli meat in his arms. She rushes over and grabs some of it. "Here, let me help you."

"Mind grabbing the tomatoes?"

Emma places the package of cheese on the counter and walks over to the table to grab some tomatoes from the bowl in the center. "I didn't know Otto had a daughter." She finds a cutting board and a knife and slices the tomatoes.

Her father smiles. "Neither did I until he came to speak to me one day to ask if it was okay if she stayed here whenever he had visitation. Wish he would've told me earlier, I would've set up one of the spare bedrooms for her to use in this house. Ever since Katie moved out, it's been quiet." He lays out five pieces of bread and then covers those with slices of cheese.

She offers him a weak smile. "Is that why you asked me to stay?" Is she just temporarily filling a Katie-sized hole in his life? Second best still?

Her father puts down the butter knife in his hand and turns to face her, his gaze strong and intense. "I asked you to stay here because you are my daughter. For whatever reason your mother kept you from me and I would like to make up for the time lost. Maybe I might have been a horrible husband, though for the life of me I could never figure out what I ever did that was so bad, but I take fatherhood very serious." He returns to his sandwiches, layering on turkey.

Her chest squeezes at his words. Yeah, her mother definitely fucked her over. "I wish I could have grown up here." She leans her head against his shoulder.

He plants a kiss on the top of her head and her heart nearly overflows. "You're here now and that's all that matters."

He's right. There's no changing the past. She plans to enjoy spending time with someone who actually wants to be her parent as much as possible.

"Is it weird having a child running around after so long?" She wants to ask more, but doesn't want to rouse her father's suspicions. The last thing she needs on her conscience is Otto getting fired because they slept together. All the same, she wants to know what she actually stepped into.

"It's kinda nice. Reminds me of when Katie was that age. Always running around getting into trouble. Addison sure seems like a firecracker. Definitely going to keep Otto on his toes."

"Fits right in with the dogs." She stacks tomato slices on top of the meat and cheese.

"Leave the tomato off that one." Her father points to the last sandwich on the line. "Linda doesn't like 'em on her sandwiches. Says they make the bread mushy."

He takes care of everyone. Emma puts the tops on the set of five sandwiches and stacks them on a platter. Mitch lays out five more slices of bread and they begin again.

"We'll help Otto out any way he needs. Nothing I admire more than a man doing right by his child." He gives her a quick sideways glance out from under his bushy eyebrows. "Come to think of it, we probably still have some of Katie's old toys and such up in the attic. Would you be willing to dig around up there and see if you can find any that Addie might like?"

"Sure," Emma says, grateful that there's a chore she can help with that doesn't involve an animal.

They finish off the next rounds of sandwich making in companionable silence. When they have twenty of them piled onto platters, Emma takes them out to the table. Her father is right behind her with a pitcher of sweet tea. "Will you teach me how to make that?"

He looks up. "The tea?"

She nods. "It's delicious."

He frowns. "They don't have sweet tea in New York City?"

"Not that I've run across." Just then her phone vibrates in her back pocket. She pulls it out and taps her security code onto the screen. Her email icon shows five new messages. Opening the app, she gasps when her eyes land on the second subject heading. It's from Tik Talk Media. With a shaky finger she scrolls through and reads the message. They want her to complete an online test that includes some copywriting. Holy shit. She's made it to the short list. Emma squeezes the phone to her chest and does a little happy dance.

"Good news I take it."

Emma spins around, completely having forgotten she isn't alone. She brushes a loose strand of hair that has fallen in front of her face. "Yeah, there's a job back in New York I was really hoping to get. Looks like I made it past the first round cuts."

Her father's smile fades a little. "Congratulations."

"Um, thanks. Anyway, I'm going to head upstairs. Looks like the next step is that I need to complete a test for them." She makes a mental note to add it to her to-do list. Her gaze falls to the counter with the sandwiches then back to her father. "I'll grab something to eat later."

"Sure. And you can tell me all about this dream job later. I don't quite know what a graphic designer does." Her father goes back to putting out plates and napkins.

A mix of joy and sadness fills her with each step away from the kitchen. Her dream job might be within reach, but she's only now getting to know her family. What happens when she goes back to New York? Will they stay in touch? Send the occasional email? She wants so much more than that. Just then Koda saunters into the hallway and Emma comes to a complete stop. The dog doesn't growl and continues past, briefly sniffing her hand before heading into the kitchen. Why is the dog here anyway and not wherever Katie and John are? Maybe Linda needs to treat all the dogs.

She shrugs and heads toward the staircase and up to the room she's staying in. If she lands the job with Tik Talk, she'll have a regular income again. And a bigger one than she's been used to. No more worrying about paying bills. No more buying generic at the grocery store. She's got a shot and her dream job and a father who wants to get to know her.

Her life is finally changing for the better.

Chapter 12

OTTO

Otto pulls the truck into a parking spot at The Pink Pony Ice Cream Parlor and turns off the engine. He glances over his shoulder to his little girl in the back seat and his chest clenches. Her feet, covered in pink sneakers, swing back and forth, her stuffed unicorn, Iris Twinklehoof, sitting beside her. In an hour Veronica will arrive to pick Addie up and his visitation will be over for the next two weeks. Every other weekend doesn't cut it, but Otto isn't going to fight his ex-wife right now. Not when she could easily close the door in his face, or not show up to their agreed upon meeting location just to mess with him.

He forces a smile when his daughter claps at the sight of the neon pink sign. "Daddy, I love this place!"

"I thought you might. That's why we came here." He unbuckles his seatbelt and exits the truck. Then he makes his way to Addison's side, opens the door, and unstraps her from the booster seat.

His little girl hops out, practically dancing on the sidewalk as he closes and locks the doors. She grabs his hand. "Come on. Let's go, slowpoke."

Otto chuckles and allows himself to be dragged into the shop. He just has to compartmentalize. Put the unwanted outcome that will occur in the next fifty-nine minutes out of his head. Enjoy the moment he has now.

Addie lets go of his hand and races over to the dispenser wall full of novelty flavors. Her little finger points at the one labeled Red Velvet Cake. "This one's my favorite."

He watches as his daughter crosses the room to grab an empty six-ounce container, then comes back and pulls the lever. His ex-wife must take their daughter here often. When the ice cream reaches the top, she passes it to the young girl working behind the counter. "Please add Gummi Bears, Unicorn Bark, and strawberries."

Otto shakes his head. What the heck is Unicorn Bark? He watches as the teenager behind the counter layers on some pastel-colored shards that he's sure aren't anything natural. What a concoction. His stomach turns at the thought of eating her edible creation. He grabs the same size container and opts for the Cinnamon Rice Pudding flavor. Following his daughter's lead, he hands his container over to the girl behind the counter. "I'll take some rainbow sprinkles."

After paying over twelve dollars for two small cups of ice cream, he sits down at an empty table with his daughter. She scoops a large helping of ice cream into her mouth and stares at him for a second. "Why were you mean to the lady?"

His brows furrow. He looks over his shoulder to the counter then back to his daughter. He hadn't been mean to the person handling their order, had he? "What lady?"

"The one chasing the doggies." She spoons another serving into her mouth and continues to stare at him.

Emma.

"I wasn't…um. Was I mean? I didn't mean to be." He scratches his head. This isn't a conversation he expected to be having. "Must've been cranky because I was so hungry."

Addie giggles. "Like the candy bar commercials?"

"Just like those." He shovels some ice cream into his mouth. Wow, it's delicious. Well worth the price, even if he hates to admit it.

"She's pretty." Addie picks up a Gummi Bear and pops it into her mouth. "Maybe she can be your girlfriend."

Otto nearly chokes on his food and begins coughing ferociously, knocking the center of his chest with a fist. Once he clears whatever had gotten stuck, he turns his attention back to his daughter. "Why would you say that?"

She shrugs. "Mommy has a boyfriend and I don't want you to be lonely."

Well, fuck.

No wonder Veronica has been going hard core with this visitation case. Probably wants the freedom to take off with her new beau. Replace Otto completely. Hell if that's going to happen. He'll fight tooth and nail for his rights to be in Addie's life.

"And I like her sneakers. Do you think I can get a pair? But not in yellow. It's not my favorite color. I like purple."

He rubs his temples and slouches in his chair. Why is she continuing to talk about Emma? Time to change tactics. "Your mom told me you have some sort of show in a couple of weeks. I'd like to come."

Addie rolls her eyes. "It's just ballet. I don't really like it so much, but Mommy says I have to stick with what I started."

Otto snorts. Coming from his ex-wife that's ironic being as she didn't stick through their marriage and had run off on him. But at least Veronica has enough sense to teach their daughter something of value. He should be grateful for that. Focus on the positive.

"Well, I'll be there."

Once they're done eating, they clean up and exit the parlor. They've got about fifteen minutes left. Otto holds his daughter's hand as they walk around town, looking in windows, but soon enough the chimes on his phone go off and the moment he's been dreading has arrived. It's time for Addie to go back home with her mom.

No sooner have they turned the corner to head back toward The Pink Pony Ice Cream Parlor, Otto spots Veronica's red Jeep Wrangler. He waves so his ex knows he's spotted her. She gives him a slight nod and waves at their daughter. At least she keeps things civil in front of Addie. He wishes she'd be as kind in front of the lawyers.

"Mommy!" Addie breaks away from his grip and bolts to her mother, and a piece of his heart shatters.

He watches as her tiny arms wrap around Veronica's neck, the ache in his chest taking over his entire body. He'll have to wait another fourteen days to get a hug from his little girl. His eyes grow wet but dammit to hell if he'll cry in front of his ex-wife.

He clears his throat as he walks up to the two. "I'll get her bag."

Veronica looks up at him as she stands. "Thank you, Otto."

There's no hint of remorse in her green eyes for the pain she causes him. No hatred either. It's as if he were a stranger. Maybe he is. He'd been deployed so often what else could he expect. Of the seven years they'd been married, he'd spent maybe a total of a year and a half actually at home. He makes his way over to his truck and grabs Addie's bag from the back seat, taking a minute to rein in his emotions before heading back over.

Veronica takes the bag from him and he bends down to hug his daughter. "Can't wait to see you again. But you know you can call me anytime."

"Okay, Daddy." She pulls back and places a big, wet kiss on his cheek.

Addie runs over to her mother who lifts the little girl into the Jeep and straps her in. Otto stays on the sidewalk and stares through the windshield, forcing himself not to blink in fear he might shed a tear. His ex-wife climbs into the driver seat, gives him a brief wave, then pulls out and onto the road.

Otto watches until the vehicle turns and is out of sight before he gets into his own truck. He sits there for a moment, jaw clenched tight. The emotions bubbling up inside are too much. How did he get here? To a point where he only gets to see his daughter bi-weekly? And the rest of the time he's so lonely his heart aches with every breath. Mario and Sawyer are like brothers to him, but there's a part of him they just can't fill. There's a well inside of him that feels like an empty chasm. He slams his palm on the steering wheel. "Fuck my life."

Taking a deep breath, he starts the engine and shifts into reverse to back onto the main street. Then changing into drive, he takes off toward the ranch, hoping the drive back will give him ample time to get his emotions in check. Focus on the future. Everything he's doing now is about paving the way for how things will be. He has to remember that.

But the moment he gets away from the lights of town the tears begin to flow. He wipes his eyes, his bottom lip quivering. If only he could turn back time maybe he could fix what went wrong in his marriage. Then he'd be able to be around Addie all the time.

Though he knows that isn't true. How would he have known re-enlisting wouldn't have saved his brothers-in-arms, that the war would've eventually killed them regardless of whether or not he was fighting by their sides? All he can do is move forward.

Chapter 13

EMMA

Emma shuts her computer and flings herself onto the bed. The copywriting test been grueling. It took her two hours to complete. She wanted it to be perfect. She proofread the copy she wrote three times yet still found a typo right before she hit send.

Something wet touches her hand and she jumps. Looking up at her, tongue lolling to the side is Nickel. "Seriously? You wouldn't come when I called you, but now you're giving me kisses? You're like the worst kind of girlfriend, those who only want you when you don't want them."

Nickel thumps her tail against the floor and Emma relents, giving the dog a scratch behind the ears while she looks out the window. No one is around. The yard is empty. They're all probably out doing something inexplicable to a cow or a horse. With any luck, her father is resting. Katie's right, he pushes himself too hard. Emma's starting to get a sense for when he's tired and needs a break. Which means she has an hour with nothing to do because if she starts putting dinner together in the kitchen, he'll hear her and come out to help.

A rustling noise makes her turn. Nickel has her head stuck in Emma's dirty clothes basket. "Get out of there."

She claps her hands and Nickel looks up, ears cocked and head tilted to one side, managing to look both guilty and adorable at the same time. "I'm beginning to understand why people have dogs. Come on. Let's go look in the attic for some toys for Addie." It's the next thing on her list. Might as well get to it.

Emma finds the attic stairs and climbs them, stopping once to bat away a cobweb she walks into. Creepy, much? She's glad to have Nickel at her heels. She edges up the stairs into a big open room and turns to take it in. It's the entire floor, broken up by a few posts here and there. Wood rafters above and wood floor beneath her feet and a thick coat of dust everywhere. She and Nickel sneeze in unison.

It's stuffy and hot. She pulls her hair up into a messy bun on top of her head. "Where should we start?"

Emma doesn't actually expect the dog to answer, but Nickel trots over to where boxes are stacked against the wall and sniffs at them.

"Good a place as any, I guess."

She grabs a box off the top of a stack of them. The tape is so old and dry it practically falls off on its own. She opens the flaps to find some children's books and a few very moth-eaten stuffed animals. The books are those cardboard ones for really little kids. Addison is well past that stage. Emma folds the flaps back in and pushes it away. The next few boxes don't yield much of interest either. Some blankets and baby clothes. She stops for a second to run her hand over a pastel crocheted blanket that must have been Katie's. It looks homemade. Had Isobel made it? Was there a time when she loved one of her daughters enough to sit for hours making a blanket?

Sighing, she tucks it back into the box and put it aside, too. The next box is bigger, more rectangular than square. She opens it and there are layers of tissue paper on top. She unfolds those to see beaded lace beneath it. Slowly, she pulls the item up and out of the box. A wedding dress. It has to be Isobel's. Who else's dress would be up here tucked away under all these other boxes?

She holds it to herself. Not that she has any need for a wedding dress. Still, how many little girls have played dress up in their mothers' dresses? What must that feel like? She shakes her head and folds it back away, settling the top back on the box.

In the next box, she hits gold. Well, gold trim at least. A delicate little tea set. Tiny cups with sprays of pink flowers and gold rims. Matching saucers. A teapot with a sugar bowl and creamer. It's all carefully wrapped. Addie might want to play with that. The box after that has some books. *Stuart Little. Charlotte's Web. The Velveteen Rabbit.* Oldies, but goodies. Addie might like them. There are a couple of dolls, too. The kind that close their eyes when they're laid down and open them when they're picked up. Emma can't decide if they're creepy or sweetly old-fashioned. She'll let Addie make the call. She stacks up her loot and heads back to the stairs. At the last minute, she adds the box with the wedding dress to her stack. She just wants to look at it in better light.

She leaves the box with the dress in her room and carries the boxes with the tea set and books and dolls down to the first floor, setting them on the kitchen table, but then she scampers back upstairs to her room to look at the wedding dress. She opens the box and unfolds the dress again. Holding it up against herself, she turns to look in the mirror. Nickel noses at the back of her knee.

"I'm just looking at it."

The dog curls up on the floor with a huff.

Emma twirls a little with the dress. It really is beautiful. The beaded bodice. The sweetheart neckline. It's tea length. No train. Not too fancy. Would it really hurt anything to try it on? Who would even know?

She looks down at Nickel, whose eyes are wide open. "This is between us, okay?"

Emma kicks off her shoes, pulls her tank top over her head, and drops her shorts to the ground. She steps into the dress and pulls it up, relishing the feel of the cool satin as it brushes against her skin. It slides up with a whisper. She slips her arms in and it settles on her shoulders, dropping into place as if it was made for her. She reaches behind and slides the zipper up. It glides smoothly. She opens the bedroom door to see herself in the full-length mirror, swishing the skirts this way and that. She hears a rustling noise behind her and turns to find Nickel with his nose once again deep in her dirty clothes basket. "Nickel, get out of there!"

Nickel's head comes up, a pair of Emma's panties firmly clenched in her teeth.

"Put that down!" She rushes to the dog who dashes around her and is out the door before she can grab her collar.

"Damn it! Nickel, come back here!" She charges after the dog down the stairs, skirts bunched up in her hands.

"Whoa there, buddy." Sawyer's voice echoes from the kitchen into the hallway as the back screen door in the kitchen squeaks open and bangs closed.

No, no, no.

Emma skids into the kitchen.

"What the—?" Sawyer stares at her, eyes blinking and mouth agape.

She leans over, hand resting on her thigh, to try to catch her breath. "The dog. Where's the dog?"

He points mutely to the kitchen door and she charges out.

And there in the yard is Otto, petting Nickel's head and holding her pink panties in one of his big fists, the big red truck he was driving when she first met him behind him. He looks up at her on the porch. His brows furrow, but he holds up the panties. "Were you looking for these?"

Her face is on fire, but she marches down the steps and grabs the panties from him. "Yes. Thank you very much." She looks down at Nickel. "Bad dog. Very bad dog." She turns to march back up to the house only to come face to face with Matilda who clucks at her and takes a menacing step toward her.

That, however, is the least of her problems. Katie and Sawyer now stand on the porch gape-mouthed. Her sister takes a step forward. "What the hell are you wearing?"

"It's... I found it up in the attic. I wanted to try it on... well, to see if it fit. Then Nickel grabbed my panties and I—" She sounds insane. One hundred percent out of her head.

Katie shakes her head. "Don't let Dad see you in that."

"Don't let Dad see who in what? What's all the ruckus about?" And now her father joins the rest of them. He takes one look at Emma, barefoot and bare legged, wearing a wedding dress and clutching a pair of underpants in the middle of the yard and he staggers back a step, hand to his chest.

"No!" Emma says, rushing toward him.

Katie cuts her off, glaring over her shoulder. "Stay back. You've done enough for one day, don't you think?"

"I didn't mean—"

Katie ignores her and takes him by his elbow to lead him back inside the house. "You okay, Dad? Come in and sit down. I'll get you a glass of water."

Her father clears his throat. "For a second, I thought it was her. I thought it was Isobel come back. She looks so much like her. So exactly like her."

Emma remains frozen in place as the door bangs closed, the tears gathering in her eyes spill over, hot and burning, and run down her cheeks. "I didn't mean..."

Otto's hand is on her shoulder, warm and rough. "I know. Mitch knows, too."

She shakes her head. "I just wanted to put on something that she'd had on once. I thought maybe I would be able to feel a little of what she must have felt when they first got married, that I could get close to that. Stupid." Her nose runs and without thinking, she blows it hard into her panties.

Otto stifles a laugh and she looks up at him, anger filling her eyes. "I may have caused my father to have another heart attack. How can you laugh?"

He schools his features, lips pressing into a straight line. "I'm sure Mitch is fine. Give him a minute."

"He shouldn't need to take a minute. Not because of me." Nothing she does here is right. She doesn't know how to call dogs or milk cows or ride horses. She's going home.

Emma shrugs Otto's hand off her shoulder and marches up the steps into the house and then up to her bedroom. She grabs her suitcase out of the closet and opens it up on the bed. Grabbing handfuls of clothing from the dresser drawers, she dumps them into the open suitcase, leaving out something to change into. She'll go back into town, get a room for the night, and fly out tomorrow or whenever the next flight is. Hell, she might go straight to the airport. She shimmies out of the wedding dress and puts on yoga pants and a t-shirt.

Her father walks into her room, brows raised and the corners of his mouth drawn down. "Hey, hey. What's going on here?"

She wipes the tears off her face with the back of her hand. "I'm packing. I'm going back to New York. I don't belong here."

"Let's talk first." He walks over to her and places his hands on her shoulders, gently moving her back from her suitcase. He sits down on the bed and waits until she takes a seat in the desk chair. "Now explain to me why you're leaving?"

She grabs a tissue of the box from the nightstand next to the bed and blows her nose. "Well, to start with, I've almost given you a heart attack twice and I've only been here a few days. Not a great track record."

He laughs. A big hearty belly laugh. And all she can do is stare at him.

He holds up his hands. "No. I'm not laughing at you, honey. And I suppose it's not really funny. It's just . . . do you have any idea how much you look like Isobel at your age?"

Emma shakes her head, pulling her legs up to rest her cheek against her knees. She's never seen a photo of Isobel except for the one the private investigator gave her and that was a recent one.

"Hold on. I'll be right back." Her father stands and exits the room.

Emma takes the opportunity to fold the wedding dress and places it carefully back into its box. What an idiot she is. What good could possibly come of trying it on?

Mitch comes back in with a photo album. Wordlessly, he hands it to her and then sits back down on the bed, folded hands between his knees. "I don't leave pictures of her out because Katie would keep looking at them and crying right after Isobel left. I thought it would be better for her to put them all away."

What did Katie have to cry about? Her sister had their father when their mother left. She'd had a house. No, not just a house. A home.

"Open it," Mitch urges.

She does and gasps. It's like looking at herself. "Wow."

"Wow. That's a very good way to sum it up. You gave me a turn today, like you did when you first arrived. That's okay. Burying Isobel's memory as deep as I have hasn't been all that healthy, I suppose. Sorta got stuck, unable to fully let go. You coming here, well, it's brought a lot of it back up. It might hurt a little, but it's kind of like digging out a splinter that's gone too deep and festered. The only way to get past it all is to get it out."

Emma traces her finger over the outline of Isobel's face in the photo. "I'm so sorry."

He stands and puts a hand on her shoulder. "Don't be. Please stay."

Emma shakes her head. "Every time I turn around I'm causing trouble for someone. Now that we know each other, we can email and talk on the phone. There's no real reason for me to stay."

Her father makes a funny noise. "You know that's not true. There's no substitute for time spent together. Besides, I want you to get to know the ranch, too. I want you to understand what that's about. And, of course, there's Katie."

Now it's Emma's turn to make a funny noise. She's pretty sure Katie would rather throw herself under a subway train than spend another minute with Emma.

He holds up his hand to stop her. "Give her time. You might have been even a bigger shock to her. Please stay. If you don't, I think I'll have a mutiny on my hands if I start doing the cooking again."

She laughs a little.

He puts his hands on her shoulders again. "Stay, Emma. Do it for your old dad."

And then he folds her in his arms and lets her sniffle against his big broad chest.

The next morning, Emma wakes to the sounds of voices calling out and doors slamming. She illuminates her phone to see the time. By now she should be used to everyone being up at four in the morning. Emma stumbles down the stairs to find her father out on the porch, barking orders and Otto, Sawyer, John, Katie, and Mario all saddling up.

Emma pulls at the light sweater she's thrown on over her pajamas tighter around her. "What's going on?"

He glances down at her. "Some cows got loose. Part of a fence must have come down that we didn't know about it. Sherriff called because they've moved onto the main road."

"Oh." She shivers a little and her father's arm drops down on her shoulder, pulling her close. He smells like soap and leather and she burrows in a little deeper. Warmth spreads through her. So does a sense of safety and security. Something she never truly had before.

In minutes everyone gallops off to tend to the escaped cows. Her father looks down at her. "You might as well go back to bed. They won't be back for hours."

"But they didn't even have breakfast."

"Better plan on feeding them a big lunch then."

Emma considers going back to bed, but she's up now. So she puts on a pot of coffee and peels some potatoes. She'll make a big hash that she can heat up and throw some eggs on top of when they get in. Along with some big slabs of bread and butter, it should fill them up. Once she's done all the prep work she can, she pours a cup of coffee and takes it over to her father in his office.

She sets the coffee down in front of him. "You hear anything from them?"

"Yep. They've got about half of them rounded up, but they still have a ways to go."

"I'm going to grab a quick shower and do some work." She catches him rubbing his sternum. "You'll let me know if you need anything?"

"Sounds like a plan, EmmaBear. Thanks." He returns back to the ledger in front of him.

She walks back to her room, setting each foot down in front of herself slowly, smiling. No one had ever given her a cute nickname, not her friends, and certainly not any of the foster parents she's had. Now she's someone's EmmaBear.

Emma showers and dresses, then opens the laptop to check her email. There's a message from a Ms. Doucette at Tik Talk. Both Emma's hands go over her mouth and she says a little silent prayer that she did all right on the test she took. Steeling herself, she takes a deep breath and clicks the email open and then does a fist pump in the air. She must have done okay because Ms. Doucette would like to set up a video interview with her on Tuesday. She's made it to the next round. She's one step closer to the job she's always wanted at the firm she's always wanted to work for. All the years of pushing herself to get the best grades, of hustling to get the best jobs, of striving to do the very best work could be paying off. If she gets this job, it will have all been worth it. She'll be able to relax a little.

She shoots back a quick email confirming the time and date. She also has a request in her email from a former client to put together some presentation slides. She can knock that out and have a little extra in her bank account when she gets home.

She barely notices that a couple of hours have gone by when she hears the creak of the kitchen door swinging open and banging shut. She saves her work and goes downstairs to see who's come back. She rounds the corner into the kitchen to find her sister taking off her boots.

Katie looks up at Emma. "Smells good. Did you finish cooking already?"

"I got a jumpstart. Figured you'd all be hungry by the time you got back. It's the least I can do."

"Thank you. I appreciate it." Her sister pauses for a moment. "And I appreciate all the help you've been around here with meals and with Dad."

Emma blinks rapidly. Did she hear correctly? She swallows and takes in a deep breath. "You're welcome, but it's been a real privilege for me. I've never been part of anything quite like this."

"I'm beginning to understand that." Katie looks at her, head cocked slightly to one side, as if she's really looking at Emma for the first time.

A lot of Emma's questions have been answered since arriving at Three Keys. But there are a few she hasn't been able to bring herself to ask. Maybe now is the time. "Do you remember Isobel at all?"

Katie's head shoots up, bright pink circles high on her cheeks. "A little."

Emma plays with the hem of her sky-blue t-shirt. "Why'd she leave?"

Her sister pulls the pitcher of sweet tea out of the refrigerator then, she pulls out two glasses and pours one for each of them. "I think I've spent half my life trying to figure out the same thing. I was only five when she left. I used to think she left because of me."

Emma takes one of the glasses and both of them sit at the table across from one another. "Why would you think that?"

"Didn't help when my classmates in elementary school would say she left because she didn't want me. Not that anyone knew her, but it was something to say to get under my skin. Dad never speaks about it either. Truth is, I don't really think he knows either." Katie turns her glass in a slow circle on the table.

"But you know that's not true now, right?" Emma is well aware of what it feels like to wonder why your mother doesn't love you. She hopes her sister has found a way past it.

Katie nods. "As I got older and Dad told me how he searched for her, I started to learn more. People at the Tongue River reservation who knew her were taking bets how long she'd stay when they got married. Dad was apparently the only one who thought it would be forever. Seems our mother had a history of not wanting to stay in one place too long." She looks off into space for a second. "I don't think our mother ever wanted to be a mom."

Emma snorts. "I came to much the same conclusion when she slammed the door in my face and told me to get off her property."

Katie's eyebrows go up. "Are you serious? Why didn't you say something?"

Emma shrugs. "It's not something I like to advertise. It was—"

"Humiliating? Horrifying? Devastating?" Katie attempts to finish Emma's sentence. "Left you wondering what could be so wrong with you that your own mother didn't want you?"

Emma winces and then laughs a little. Amazing to find someone who truly knows exactly how she feels. "Yeah. Pretty much all that."

"The legacy of Isobel. Anytime one of the mean girls in junior high wanted to get to me, she'd ask me where my mom was." Katie finishes her sweet tea and then stands. "Going to wash up and then I'll be down to help you get lunch on the table."

As Katie walks past, her hand drops onto Emma's shoulder and she gives it a soft squeeze. Tears gather in Emma's eyes. She'd wanted to connect with her sister, and her father had been right. Katie had just needed some time. Emma's glad she waited.

Chapter 14

OTTO

It has been a day. Hot, sweaty, and hard. Why those cattle chose a day when the temperature and the humidity were both in the nineties to get out and run amok, Otto cannot understand. He sure as hell would rather be in a cool shady barn munching on hay than running all over the hillsides with the sun beating down on his back. The air's like a wet sponge and there isn't even a hint of a breeze to cool it down.

Otto pulls off his sweaty t-shirt and tosses it into the laundry basket and tries to mask the worst of the stench with a stick of deodorant with a peppermint and lime aroma. Good luck with that.

"You ready? I'm starving over here," Sawyer calls out from down the hall.

Otto grabs a clean shirt and throws it on. Sawyer and Mario are as hot and sweaty as he is and he's as hungry as they are, but he's maybe a little more aware of how they smell. His stomach lets out a growl.

"Cabron, ándale!" There's a hint of frustration in Mario's tone.

"I'm coming." He rolls his eyes, but a good-natured smile blooms on his lips. Those two could walk over to the house without him. They don't have to wait, but they're not going to budge until they know he's by their side. He didn't know if he'd ever have the feeling of being in a group of people who all had each other's backs when he left the military. He'd been ready to give up that camaraderie to be a father to Addie. He feels damn lucky to have found it here. Talk about having your cake and eating it, too.

The three men nearly jog the distance to the main house, the thought of sitting down to a meal moving their feet. They'd found out about the cows early and no one had had time for breakfast. At one o'clock, they'd already put in a seven-hour day and done it without even a cup of coffee in their stomachs.

John, hair wet from his shower, smiles as the three of them pile into the kitchen. "Took ya three long enough. Thought I might've needed to send Koda to search for you guys."

"Just wanted to clean up a bit." Easy enough for John. He gets to shower in the main house instead of the building across the way where the water pressure sucks.

Sawyer claps a hand on his shoulder. "Koda woulda found us real fast."

Otto side-eyes his friend. "It's not like you smell so great either, sweet pea."

Sawyer sniffs at himself and makes a face. "Good point."

John laughs and gestures for them to get to the table. "You all can shower after you eat. Emma's got a pile of food out on the table ready for us."

Otto doesn't wait to be told twice. He gets into the dining room and stops for a second to take in the spread on the table. Hash with fried eggs on top. Big slabs of bread. A bowl of fruit. He nearly groans, he's so hungry. Emma and Katie chat as they dig into the casserole, Koda lying on the floor between them. For a moment, Otto stares at Emma. She hasn't noticed him yet, and there's a real smile on her face that causes her cheeks to pinch upward. It's beautiful. There also happens to be a spot next to her that's empty. Otto hesitates. Bad choice. His friends eye one another as if relaying a silent message, then hurry to sit leaving the only chair available the one next to Emma being that John would want to sit next to his wife. Can they make things any more obvious?

Emma glances up at him and damn if his heart doesn't stutter. He sucks in a deep breath, walks around the table and takes the only remaining seat next to her. He pulls his chair closer to the table. But too close that he lets out a gasp when the edge hits just under his sternum. Yup, nothing like making a fool of himself. Reaching for the hash, he purposefully avoids Emma's stare, even though he can feel it on his profile.

He shovels a pile of food on his plate and then passes it on. The smell of potatoes and sausage and onions making him salivate so much he worries he'll choke before he can get it in his mouth. He manages, though. Groaning, he barely takes a second to chew before cramming in the next mouthful.

Emma giggles. "Guess you worked up a big appetite."

"Yep. I'm sure that's what it is." Katie sits back and crosses her arms, staring at him as if a detective waiting for him to confess to a crime. Damn woman had eyes that saw through walls. He doesn't want to admit it, but her stare makes him squirm.

Is his interest in Emma that obvious? Or did someone snitch? His eyes fly to Sawyer and Mario, both too focused on their plates for the action to be natural. He clenches his teeth and lets out a groan. How much did Katie know? And did Mitch catch wind of the gossip?

He swallows and looks at Katie. "Didn't really have time to eat this morning. Why aren't you bothering the other two?"

John quirks an eyebrow at him. He knows the look, the one that signals he needs to tread carefully or he'll be dealing with John. Fair enough.

Mitch strolls in with Nickel and Two Bits on his heels and takes a seat. "Y'all must be exhausted. Take the afternoon off. Summerfest in Billings starts today. Maybe head in and check it out."

"Summerfest?" Emma looks around the table. "What's that?"

Sawyer takes a big gulp of sweet tea, then sets his glass down on the table with a thunk. "It's a music and art festival they hold every summer. Plus, there's food booths and dancing. Stuff like that."

And a special area for kids. Otto had wanted to take Addie, but Veronica vetoed the request. He looks down at his plate, his appetite waning.

"Sounds fun," Emma says.

"You should go." Mitch waves his fork at Sawyer, Mario, and Otto. "I'm sure these three are going."

Otto swallows hard, poking at his food and hoping the conversation will move on to something else. He's thankful when Linda walks in from the kitchen. "Everything okay with the herd?"

"Everyone looks fine. I stitched up a scrape or two, but nothing major."

"Thanks, Linda." Mitch reaches up to pat the hand Linda still has on his shoulder. "Grab yourself a chair and a plate and get in here. We've got plenty."

"Got some other clients I need to tend to." She looks over at Katie. "You and John heading into Billings? I can take Koda with me if you want."

"We're going to head in later. Have some stuff to finish up at our house first." Katie looks over at Emma. "If my sister is heading over to Summerfest as well I'll leave Koda here with Dad."

Linda nods then waves good bye before heading out. Otto clenches his teeth. Guess he'll be heading into Summerfest whether he wants to or not. He shovels more food into his mouth and chews.

Mitch clears his throat and turns to his younger daughter. "So how'd that test go?"

Otto's brows furrow. Didn't know she had a test to take. What could it be for?

As if channeling his thoughts, Katie looks over to her sister. "What test?"

Emma sets her fork down. "A firm I applied to back in New York has a complicated interview process including an online test. Pretty sure it means I made it past the first screening for the job."

Otto's stomach drops at the mention of the east coast state. Time to make a better effort into getting his emotions in check. Long distance relation.... Nope. No need to go there. They didn't have a relationship. They'd had one time. They'd made a deal.

Mario pours himself a glass of water. "What kinda job? When does it start?"

"Graphic designer. And it's hard to know. Could be a few weeks. Could be a few months."

Weeks or months, doesn't really matter. She's leaving. This isn't her home. Otto's upper lip twitches and he stabs at his food.

Katie clears her throat, loudly. "Emma, what size shoe do you wear?"

Emma's head tilts the slightest bit, lips puckering and brows drawing together. Odd question for her sister to ask. "Eight and a half."

"Could I borrow the blue shoes you wore the other day?" Katie bites her lip in the exact same way Emma does when she's unsure.

"The blue Chucks? Of course. You want to wear them tonight?"

Katie nods. "If you wouldn't mind."

"Not at all. I was going to wear the yellow ones." Emma picks up a piece of bread and tears the crust off one side.

"With that sunflower dress you were wearing the first day you came here?" Katie smiles. "That'll look so cute."

Otto groans. He remembers the sundress all too well. The room goes quiet and he looks up to find everyone looking at him. Emma, in particular, stares daggers at him. "What?"

"You don't like my sundress?" She blinks a few times.

Shit.

Now what's he supposed to say? That the flutter of the sundress in the breeze haunts his dreams? That he'll never forget seeing her on the side of the road, talking about bunnies, and wanting to tow her car out by the bumper. "Sorry. Thinking about something else. Just remembered something out in the barn I need to check."

He takes a last bite of food and stands, picking up his plate to carry it back into the kitchen. True to his word, he heads out to the barn and finds Bayberry. The horse nickers a greeting to him and Otto takes a moment to press his forehead against the horse's long nose, breathing in his breath. He steadies himself.

What happened between him and Emma was a one-time deal. They both agreed. So why does he care if she's applying for some job back in New York City? It's no business of his. Yet it feels like a sucker punch all the same. It makes no sense.

He strokes Bayberry's nose. This makes sense to him. The horse. The barn. The work. He'll focus on this. The open sky. This will get him through.

Chapter 15

Emma

Working in tandem like they've been doing it for years, Katie washes as Emma dries. Emma glances sideways at her sister. "So is Linda going to be our new *mom*?"

A glass shoots out of Katie's hand and she just manages to catch it before it hits the stainless steel sink and shatters. "Not you, too? Why does everyone think something is going on between them?"

Emma picks up a plate and dries it, setting it down on the stack that's already done. "Oh, little things. The way she makes sure Dad's plate is full and the way he looks at her when she touches his arm."

Katie hands her the clean glass. "Linda's been a lifesaver. Not only for Dad, but for me, too. She was the closest thing I had to a mom after Isobel left."

Emma's chest tightens a bit. Even though neither of them had their mom, someone caring stepped into the role for Katie. Once again Emma appears to have drawn the short end of the stick. But at least her father had help. She couldn't imagine what it would be like to have a spouse not only run out, but leave a person a single parent at the same time with a heartbroken child. "There seems to be some chemistry between her and our father. They never dated?"

Katie chuckles. "You'd know about chemistry."

Emma freezes. "What's that supposed to mean?"

Katie shrugs and bends over the casserole dish to scrub off some stuck-on food. "The air practically crackles when you and Otto are in the same room."

So, it's as obvious to everyone else as it is to her. "It crackles and then he acts like I'm the biggest annoyance he's ever encountered. I'm not sure what to make of it."

Katie sets the clean casserole dish on the counter and turns, drying her hands, and leaning back against the sink. "Really? How much do you know about Otto?"

Emma picks up the casserole dish "Not much. It's not like he's particularly forthcoming."

"He's got a lot of stuff on his plate especially with trying to get joint custody of his daughter and his ex-wife fighting him tooth and nail. He also hasn't been out of the service for long and that can be difficult." Her sister sighs and pauses before continuing on. "John had a difficult time at least. We're through the worst of it, but he says most everyone goes through something when they leave."

Emma picks up the stacked dishes. "I'm sorry. That sounds like it was hard." Mario mentioned Katie needing to help John, too. Maybe her big sister hadn't had it so easy. Just because she had a home didn't mean everything was always rosy.

Katie looks down into the sink for a moment, then blows out a breath. "It was. It was really hard for a while."

Emma puts the dishes into the cupboard. "And you think Otto might be having the same kind of hard time?"

Katie turns and leans her back against the counter. "Maybe not the exact same, but definitely related."

"Thanks for telling me. It makes it easier to understand." She wants to ask what she can do to help, but it's not really her place, is it? It's not like she and Otto are in a relationship. They're barely even friends. Now her sister, on the other hand, might be becoming a friend. That is definitely her place. "Let's head up to my room so I can grab the sneakers for you."

Katie follows her out of the kitchen and up the stairs and pauses at the doorway, looking in. "Your room, huh?"

Emma looks around. Wow, she's really made herself at home. A scarf draped over the bedside lamp to soften its light. Her shoes a crazy jumble on the closet floor. A bowl she borrowed from the china closet in the dining room filled with her jewelry on the dresser. Has she overstepped?

Katie smiles and quirks a brow. "You really made the space your own. I like it."

Emma bites her cheek, happy Katie isn't angry. She heads over to the closet and grabs the blue Chucks from the pile, then turns to her sister. "Here. Try 'em on. I'm sure they'll fit."

Katie grabs them and plops onto the bed then kicks off her boots and tries on the shoes. She holds her feet out in front of her, turning them this way and that. "I've got this blue sleeveless top that's got a little lace on it. You think the shoes will go with it?"

"I'm sure. Hey, it's almost like we're real sisters, borrowing clothes and asking for advice." Emma smiles, but Katie stiffens.

Her sister takes off the Chucks and puts her boots back on. "I'll bring 'em back right after the festival."

Emma laughs. "Take your time. I know where you live."

"Yeah, you do. See you at the festival. You okay riding in with Sawyer, Mario, and Otto?" Her sister stands and wiggles her eyebrows, a tiny smirk on her lips.

"I'll be fine." She tosses a pillow at Katie.

A few hours later, Emma runs out of the house to catch her ride into Billings. She's wearing the sundress Otto apparently hates and her camera bag is bouncing against her hip. All three of the men are leaning against the side of the truck, all wearing jeans and boots and cowboy hats, all dust and dirt-free. Sawyer has his shirt buttoned all the way up to his neck, just the way her father wears his, but Mario and Otto both have theirs unbuttoned at the neck.

Matilda is scratching in the dirt nearby, but only gives Emma a glance and goes back to pecking at the ground. Perhaps they've come to some kind of détente. The humidity has eased up and the temperature has started to drop. The air is still warm and scented with the aromas of fresh cut hay and sunshine. She barely notices the manure smell anymore.

Sawyer puts up a hand. "Whoa, there. No need to run. The festival goes for a couple days."

"Yeah, but tonight's the cornhole championship." Mario opens the door to get into the back of the truck's extended cab. "We don't want to miss signing up for that. I think we've got a shot at winning the doubles tournament."

"The *what* tournament?" Emma's not sure she heard right. She starts to climb in next to Mario.

Otto puts his hand on her arm and shakes his head, getting in instead. "Cornhole. And ladies get to ride shotgun."

"But my legs are so much shorter than yours. You'll be all squished and what is a cornhole?"

"Otto and Mario will be fine." Sawyer walks around to the driver's side to get in. "We'll explain cornhole to you on the way there."

It's a long enough drive that she's thoroughly confused about how to play cornhole once they get there with all three men chiming in with their thoughts on strategy and techniques. They pull into the dirt lot and she steps down from the truck onto the gravel, smoothing her dress. "Go ahead, you three. I'll meet you back here at the truck at ten if I don't find you sooner."

Mario looks over at Otto with a raised eyebrow.

Otto rolls his eyes. "Go ahead. I'll make sure she doesn't get lost."

"I don't need a babysitter." Emma arranges her camera bag so it doesn't bounce as she walks.

Otto points to the bag. "What's in that?"

She looks up, surprised that he's interested. "My camera. A couple of lenses. A collapsible monopod."

His forehead furrows.

"It's like a tripod, but it's got one leg. It helps hold the camera steady for long exposures. I think I can get some great shots with all the lights when it gets dark."

"That won't be for a while. This time of year, sun won't go down until close to nine." He looks up at the sky as if checking the position of the sun.

"I'm aware. I'm sure there'll be something worth shooting before I leave." She never knows what she might stumble on that will be helpful in an ad or a brochure. There's sure to be plenty here, though.

"Thought you were a graphic designer, not a photographer."

She smiles. "I'm a little of both. It's handy to have my own library of images and not have to use stock photos, especially when I'm working freelance. Cuts down on my costs and clients seem to like it."

"I'm sure they do." He nods. "Hungry?"

She blushes. "Starved, to be honest. Lunch seems like a long time ago."

"Let's go."

He offers her his arm and, after hesitating for a moment, she takes it. Good Lord, he's strong. The corded muscles stretch the fabric of his shirt.

She lifts her head, sniffs the air, and catches a heady combination of fried food, sunscreen, dust, and horse manure. When had that last thing stopped making her wrinkle her nose? She almost thinks it smells good, like home. Almost. "Will there be food on sticks?"

He falters for a step and looks down at her, brown eyes intense and searching. "Food on what?"

"On sticks. Like you read about in the paper about state fairs. Corn dogs and popcorn balls and bacon and bananas." She's almost skipping in anticipation.

"There's sure to be at least some things on sticks." He tilts his cowboy hat back a little on his head. "Why?"

She shrugs. "I've never had any. None of my foster families ever took me. I've always wanted to try some of it, though." She looks up at him, smiling, feeling her cheeks go a little pink. She brushes a few strands of hair that the breeze has blown across her face away.

He gives her a nod and pulls her arm closer to him. "Well, then let's go get some food on a stick."

Chapter 16

OTTO

Otto and Emma sit at one of the wooden picnic benches. Around them people play games like popping balloons with darts and ring toss. The salt and butter aroma from popcorn fills the air. But instead of the crowd, Otto's full attention is on Emma, who has a deep-fried Twinkie on a stick that she waves around like a wand as she talks, illustrating her points.

Otto's own upbringing isn't what anyone would call privileged. His mom worked part-time as a cashier at a local grocery store while his dad worked maintenance at the junior college. He'd never thought about what it might be like not to have had that solid ground beneath his feet growing up. Although, isn't that exactly why he's here in Montana? So he can make sure Addie has solid ground? So she knows she can trust the adults in her life to be there for her?

Emma is about to chomp into her Twinkie and without thinking beyond not wanting the greasy treat to leave a blotch on his favorite dress, Otto tucks a napkin into the neckline of her dress. He swallows hard, his hands so close to her beautiful breasts. "One of the things you should know about food on a stick is that it often falls off."

Emma looks down and then back up with a brow arched. "That wasn't just a chance to cop a cheap feel?"

He jerks his hands away. "No! Of course not! Just didn't want you ruining your clothes."

She laughs. "I thought you didn't like this dress."

He shakes his head. "Never said that. Never thought that. Kind of the opposite to be honest. That's what you were wearing the first time we met. Made quite an impression."

She's silent for a moment, chewing on a bite of her Twinkie. "Is that why you call me Sunflower?"

"Part of it." He's not sure how to explain the rest like the way she stands up and faces everything reminds him of the way sunflowers stand sentinel in the fields.

A horse from a small corral to their right whinnies and Emma jumps a little. "You know, I've never ridden a horse. I sort of daydream about it whenever I see y'all riding around."

Otto sits up straight. He didn't grow up in Montana, but he'd been about seven-years-old the first time he learned to ride. "Really?"

"Back in New York, especially in the city, it's more for those who have money to spare. A luxury if you will. Though, the saddles are different." Emma nibbles more of her Twinkie off the stick, a drift of powdered sugar raining down.

"English saddles." Western riding isn't what most of the east coast does. He remembers when he was stationed in Virginia Beach how most people rode dressage or jumping. An old buddy of his had a sister who played polo even. Lots of horses, but no one was really into western riding.

"You want to learn?" The words are out before he can stop them.

She hesitates. "I'd like to at least try."

"I think we can make that happen." He turns the beer he holds between his fingers in a circle and then takes a long swig.

From what he's witnessed, Emma is always up to try something new. And when she fails, she gets back up and tries again. And again after that if she needs to. Like with milking a cow. Hell, she hadn't even balked at needing to use the internet to figure it out. Emma is the kind of woman he hopes Addie turns out to be some day.

Fearless and determined.

Emma finishes her Twinkie and brushes the powdered sugar off her hands. When the distant sound of revving engines reaches them, she cocks her head. "What's that?"

"Most likely the vintage cars and hot rods."

She claps her hands and picks up her camera bag. "Ooh. Let's go."

"You want to see old cars?"

"Absolutely. C'mon." She bounces on the toes of those yellow Chucks in anticipation. He tries like hell not to remember what it was like to have them kicking at his back as he made her call out his name.

He stands and she takes his arm again, her touch ignites something in him. Lust for sure. Passion definitely. But something more, too. Something tender that he doesn't want to look at too hard. She'll be heading back to New York at some point, after all. Maybe sometime soon even.

As they approach the area with all the games and rides for young kids, a pack of little boys splits to race around them on either side. A harried man chases after them. "Boys! Boys! Slow down!"

Otto laughs, the kids' enthusiasm almost catching. But as a little girl with brown hair in a ponytail skips past him, his smile dies. He can't help but think about what it would have been like to bring Addie.

Emma looks up at him, concern on her face. "You okay?"

He sighs. "I wanted to bring Addie to the festival, but her mother wouldn't allow it. And because I just got a one word answer I don't know if she is taking our daughter or if she just doesn't want Addie to go."

Veronica is doing everything she can to frustrate him and get him to lose his temper. He won't, though. He's not doing anything to give her any ammunition against him.

He points to a little girl, a look of both terror and anticipation on her face, as she pushes off to go careening wildly down the slide, arms in the air, shrieking the whole way. She shoots off the end of the slide, barely managing to land on her feet. Then she's jumping up and down. "Again! Again! Again!"

Emma laughs. "Pretty cute."

"Now imagine that's a little girl that you know, that you love. Imagine her joy is your joy and you get to feel proud on top of it for bringing her to a place where she can feel that." He looks down, kicking a little at the dirt under his boot, not wanting Emma to see the hurt on his face.

When he looks up, she's leaning against the fence facing him, elbows braced on the top rail and one foot hooked on the bottom one. "You're pretty much head over heels crazy about your daughter."

He looks at her from under the brim of his hat. "Yep. Since the first moment I held her."

Kind of like I feel about you.

"When is she coming to visit again?"

"In a few days." He hates that they're only visits.

"Who watches her while you're working?"

He grabs the top rail of the fence. Is he doing something wrong taking Addie out with him all the time? No one has said anything, but he can't afford to make a single misstep. "She comes along with us and reads or colors or plays with her stuffed animals while we do what needs doing. Same as when you first met her."

Emma's brows go up. "And she likes that?"

"She doesn't complain. Much." Every once in a while if it's hot or the day's been long, she's gotten cranky, but she seems to mainly be happy to be near him and Mario and Sawyer. Happy is good, right?

"Well, if there's a time you don't want to take her out in the fields with you, she can hang around with me at the house as long as I'm here." She straightens up and then falters at the look on his face. "I'm sorry. I didn't mean to overstep."

"You didn't." He tries to make his face look neutral. "Just trying to get to know my daughter better. Between deployments and everything else haven't gotten much time with her."

"I'm sure she treasures ever minute she has with you."

There's a wistfulness in her voice that makes Otto's heart twist. He hasn't missed how she looks at Mitch or the way her face brightened when Katie asked if she could borrow a pair of shoes. He can see how much she treasures having a family. How will having a family stack up against a job she's been working toward for years? Maybe it won't be an issue. Maybe she won't even get the job and she'll stay here in Montana. "Let's go and see your old cars."

She takes his arm again and they walk on, making their way to where the vintage cars gleam in the late evening sunlight.

Emma's big eyes get even wider. "Wow! These are amazing!" She digs in her camera bag to pull out a camera body and a lens, then struggles to get everything together with the bag slung over her shoulder. Finally she holds it out to Otto. "Would you mind holding this?"

Holding a woman's camera bag is slightly more dignified than holding a woman's purse. Otto still feels a little ridiculous standing there while Emma crouches and leans and moves in and out. "What is it you're trying to take a picture of?"

She stands, cheeks pink and eyes bright. "I'm trying to – I'm not sure how to say it – to get the essence of the cars?"

"The essence?" He's not certain what she means.

"Yeah. So there are tons of photos of these cars." She gestures to the fleet they've been walking through, full of old Corvettes and Thunderbirds and El Dorados and Roadsters. "Or ones just like them. Those photos look like the cars look. They're representational. You can look at the photo and feel like you've looked at the car. You understand physically what it is. Sometimes for an ad or a brochure, though, I don't so much want what the car looks like as what it feels like."

Otto shakes his head, still not quite following. "How do you know what that is?"

"So, that one over there." She points to a baby blue Buick Electra with fins that she'd spent ten minutes shooting from every angle imaginable. "It's all about those big round headlights and those fins, right? But it's also a little about optimism and adventure and discovering the thrill of the open road."

"I guess so." He draws each word out.

She takes her camera and turns the display of the camera toward him. He leans in to look at the photo taken from close in by the headlights so they're large and in the foreground with the fins stretching out behind because of the foreshortening and looking like they go off into the horizon as they blur. There's a sense of motion as if the car is launching out of the photo, anxious to be out in the world.

He's starting to get it.

Then she thumbs to another set of photos of a Dodge Charger. "This one's all about power and strength."

The photos have the car at an angle, filling the screen at a diagonal and looking like it's going a million miles an hour even though it's standing still. He smiles, fully getting what she's saying. She's captured something more important than what the cars look like. She sees beyond what's there to what things really are. Maybe she sees what Otto is, maybe she knows his essence. He's starting to feel like he knows hers.

She smiles back, tucking the camera back into her bag. "What now?"

What he really wants is to hold her, to take her in his arms, to feel her heartbeat against his chest and there's a place nearby where he can do that in a socially acceptable way. "How about we go dance?"

Chapter 17

EMMA

Every time Emma turns around there's something she doesn't know how to do. Milk a cow. Round up dogs. Evade packs of possessive chickens. Dance to country-western music. She looks over Otto's shoulder at the pavilion. Her heart palpitates as she rubs her forearm. "I don't know how."

"You don't have to know." Otto holds out his hand. "I know how to lead."

Of course he does. Hell, he'd led her through the most amazing orgasms of her life. She takes his hand, liking the way his calloused palms feel against hers, wanting to feel them slide up her legs again. She shivers a little despite the heat.

Otto leads her to the middle of the dance floor and as she begins to succumb to self-consciousness, he twirls her out, then brings her back into his arms. Emma squeaks, then giggles. With one hand on the small of her back and the other in her hand, he leads her around in effortless steps and she follows as if she's been doing it her whole life. They float around the floor in tandem, as in sync with each other as they'd been in the front seat of his truck and it's damn near as sexy.

Otto spins her out again and brings her back. His minty breath brushes over her lips and she looks up to meet his eyes. "Wow, you're beautiful."

The words hit her hard, but more jarring is the look on his face. His brows knit and his voice rasps, as if he really means it and it almost pains him to say. Men have told her she's beautiful before, but no one has ever made her feel their words. She does now. All the way down to her toes. She looks away, leaning in to rest her head against his chest, not quite willing or able to hold his gaze. "You mean when I'm not covered in chicken shit complete with frizzy hair because I'm completely a fish out of water. Or whatever you say here in Montana. A cow out of her pasture? A chicken out of her coop?"

He laughs. "Sunflower, you might be green as hell, but you never stop trying and are too stubborn to give up. Your heart's in the right place. I admire that."

Her cheeks warm and goosebumps flare across her skin. No one's really acknowledged what she's been doing or how she's been struggling. Sure, her father is grateful. He did express his gratitude as well, but he mostly sees her cleaning up in the kitchen. No one really struggles washing dishes or getting food ready, unless done on purpose. Like how one of her foster siblings would purposely break plates or cups so they were never asked to clean up again.

The lack of acknowledgement is nothing new. It's been that way her whole life. Except not now with Otto. He sees her. He knows she's struggling and instead of thinking she's an idiot, it makes him admire her.

The song ends, and on the final chord, he dips her and brings her back up tight against him. She's way too aware of the breadth of his chest, the muscles of his thighs, the thick evidence of his attraction to her. Every part of her body hums. Her own breath becomes shallow and her heartbeat picks up speed.

His eyes darken as he slides his hands into her thick brown hair. "I want to—"

She doesn't wait for him to finish the sentence. She goes up on her toes and her mouth comes crashing against his. Teeth collide, her hand cradles the nape of his neck, their tongues passionately dance together.

Otto tastes like beer and mint and smells like sweet hay and soap. He fills her senses completely, overwhelming her, making her lose herself in the moment. A low growl erupts from deep within Otto, vibrating over to her. Emma deepens their kiss, wondering what else the night has in store because she isn't quite ready to end her time with the cowboy just yet.

And then he breaks away and steps back, leaving her off balance. He's staring over her shoulder, color draining from his face. She turns to see what he's looking at.

John and Katie.

Emma almost laughs. Not that the situation is funny. But it sort of is, because her sister *would* have to be here, interrupting the most passionate kiss she's ever had in her life. Luckily the two are completely absorbed in each other, Katie's arms around John's neck and John's around Katie's waist. Emma turns back to Otto. "I don't think they saw anything."

He rubs the back of his neck. "I hope not. Think she suspects something happened between us."

Katie's aware of their chemistry, but Emma doesn't believe her sister suspects they'd acted on it. Could there be more to it? Their conversation in the kitchen couldn't have come from out of the blue. "Did you tell someone?"

His gaze jerks back to her. "No one. Well, didn't deny anything either. I'm not the best liar. Kinda easy to read."

She buries her face in her palms. "So, everyone knows."

"Most everyone suspects I have an interest in you. None know whether it's returned."

Did he just say he's interested in her? Her mind whirls. She's never been so instantly attracted to anyone in her life. It's not only his body. From the second she first saw him, emerging from the truck, clearly on his way to something important but unwilling to leave her there on the side of the road, he's made her feel things she hasn't felt before. Safe. Protected. Cared for. Of course his daughter adores him. What little girl—what woman—wouldn't?

This is temporary, though. She's not here forever. Family or no family, her life is in New York. She's scrimped and saved, worked two jobs while going to school and pushed herself to be at the top of her class to get where she is. She only came to Montana to get some questions answered. She only stayed to get to know her family a little. Eventually she's going back to New York, hopefully to a job at Tik Talk.

Living here permanently isn't an option. And neither is falling in love.

A two-stepping couple bumps into them. They're only making themselves more conspicuous by standing here in the middle of the dance floor staring at each other. She grabs his hand and leads him away. "How about you buy me a beer?"

Chapter 18

OTTO

Otto tosses and turns under the covers. No way is he getting any sleep tonight. Emma's kiss had done all kinds of things to his insides, to his emotions. Never has anyone kissed him like that. Set his blood on fire like that.

Sawyer had pulled the truck up to the steps of the house to drop her off and then driven on to the bunkhouse. He'd barely gotten to say good night and then she was gone. Physically at least. Because mentally he's reliving every second of walking with her, dancing with her, kissing her.

"Fuck it." With a groan he rolls over until he's sitting up resting his head in his palms, elbows against knees.

After grabbing two beers, they'd headed over to watch Mario and Sawyer compete in the cornhole competition, Emma catching photos of Mario clowning around, but still nailing almost every shot. His friends ended up taking third place. Mario was still grumbling about being robbed and that the kid on the winning team had to be a ringer when they'd piled back into the truck. This time, Emma had insisted on sitting in back with Otto. She'd fallen asleep on his shoulder, a sweet weight against him as Sawyer had driven them home.

She'd looked disappointed as she waved goodnight and headed into the main house. Part of him hated watching her walk away. But then his brain, the logical side, whispered and reminded him soon she'd be leaving, and not just to the main house, but all the way back to New York. Then what would he do? Better not to get in too deep. Better to remember their pact. No strings. One time only.

Otto stands and walks into the small kitchen area and grabs a glass before filling it with water from the sink. He takes a swig and stares at the stainless steel faucet. Finishing his drink, he sets the glass down in the sink, then heads over to the loveseat and clicks on the TV, hoping there'll be something mindless that will distract him from thoughts of Emma but still lull him to sleep. If he doesn't get at least a few hours, tomorrow will be hell on his body.

He settles on an old black and white movie that seems to involve an opera singer and a Canadian Mounty looking for someone's brother. He lets himself drift until a knock at the door jolts him. For a second, he wonders if he's hallucinated the sound or if it's in the movie soundtrack, but then there it is again.

Thunk-thunk-thunk.

Has to be Mario. Maybe even Sawyer. Otto hoists himself up, his feet dragging as he makes his way to the door. Twisting the handle, he pulls the wooden slab open. "What the hell."

Emma.

Shit.

He closes the door and leans his forehead against it.

"Uh, hello? Thanks for shutting the door in my face." Her muffled voice comes through the closed door.

Shit.

"Sorry. I just...wasn't expecting you." He'd been thinking about her, maybe even fantasizing a bit about her, but expecting her? No.

"So who were you expecting when you answered the door half-naked?"

He has no answer for that. He waits for a second. Maybe she'll leave. Maybe if he tiptoes back into bed she'll disappear. He takes a tentative step backward, bare feet cold on the tile floor.

She knocks again. "How do you know there isn't some emergency at the main house?"

He swings open the door. "Damn. I... hell...is everything okay? Let me get dressed."

Otto practically runs to his bed, reaches down, and starts doing the one-legged hop as he shoves his legs into a pair of jeans. Why hadn't he thought there might've been trouble? That something could've happened to Mitch? Had he had another heart attack? But when he looks up, Emma has a hand covering her mouth as she laughs.

He drops the waist of his jeans sending the pants to pool around his ankles. "Are you kidding right now?"

"If there was an emergency do you think the first thing out of my mouth would have been about how you're dressed?" The corner of her mouth curls up into a lopsided grin when her gaze travels to his groin. "Or rather, undressed."

And at that moment his dick has to twitch. Yup, because it likes her gaze and definitely enjoys making him feel awkward. Otto mumbles a string of curses under his breath as he bends over to pull his jeans up.

Emma steps into his apartment and closes the door. She leans back against it, teeth sunk into that lower lip. She's wearing yoga pants and a loose tank top. He's pretty sure there's no bra beneath it. Her hair tumbles around her shoulders. She looks soft and sweet and a little bit rumpled. The twitch turns into something closer to a leap.

"Sorry if woke you. I, uh, couldn't sleep and decided to take a walk and ended up here." Her gaze travels down his chest, leaving a trail of heat. She doesn't even have to touch him to turn him on.

Uh huh. Right. Because that's what people do. They wander around in the dark and randomly end up on other people's doorsteps. Otto scratches the top of his head then strides past the beautiful woman to the fridge and opens it, hoping for a distraction. "Want water or beer? Got some juice boxes, too."

Emma's nails drag lightly down his back, setting off every nerve ending in his body. His fingers grip the door panel as his muscles tense, abdomen flexing. She presses against his body, her lips against his ear, the peach scent that's been haunting his dreams tickling his nose. "I thought maybe we could renegotiate our deal. Maybe it doesn't have to be one time only."

Otto clears his throat and turns around backing up into the fridge until he's practically folding himself into the shelves. "Not sure it's such a good idea."

Emma takes a step back, her shoulders slumping forward. "Oh. I, um, sorry."

She spins and heads toward the door. But Otto is faster and gently grabs her elbow. Fuck, he hadn't meant to insult her. He takes a deep breath to gain some control over his libido, trying to do the right thing. "Emma, I'm attracted. Believe me. Just not sure it's the right thing to do."

She turns, hands on her hips, eyes snapping. "Then why'd you kiss me? And don't tell me that it was me that kissed you because you kissed me back. And that kiss went on forever. Or at least it felt like forever."

He shoves his hair back with both hands. "Which is why I'm not sure this is such a good idea. That kiss. The other night in my truck. It's too much, especially since you're leaving. Not to mention my own shit with the custody battle." Veronica and her lawyer would make mincemeat out of him if they thought he was having casual hook-ups.

"Otto, I didn't come here looking for a diamond ring. I enjoy being around you." She erases whatever distance is between them, looks him straight in the eyes as she licks her lips, then traces her index finger down the center of his chest and hooks it into the waistband of his jeans. "And I definitely enjoy being with you."

Rational thought disappears. Her finger leaves a trail of fire and ice. His dick stiffens even more, straining against the zipper of his jeans. She's here now. So what if she's gone tomorrow? They're adults. Whatever control he has evaporates.

He sucks in a deep breath and locks eyes with her. "Touch me."

Emma reaches out, her palm pressing against the zipper of his jeans. Her lips part as a small gasp escapes. God, it feels good to be touched by her. She rubs his length causing his hips to jerk forward, a long groan rumbling from deep in his chest. He backs up until they're in his room.

Otto swallows hard, fighting to remain still as he offers her control of the situation. He'd taken her the last time. In the parking lot. Devoured her. Ravaged her. Plundered her. And right now, more than anything, he wants her to take him.

Emma keeps her eyes locked with his as she unbuttons his jeans and reaches inside gripping him. Stroking him. His eyes close at the sensation—the ache too good, too much. He sucks in a sharp breath and keeps his eyes closed as she pulls down his jeans...until her soft lips and warm mouth engulf him.

His eyes shoot open. "Oh, fuck, Emma."

She sucks him in deeper, adding more pressure, and his knees buckle slightly. The way her tongue circles around him, how her hands fondle his balls, he isn't going to last much longer. Her nails drag across his ass as she takes him in deep and sucks.

"Emma. Now. I'm gonna…" He tries to pull away, to not come in her mouth without her consent. But she grabs his ass and pulls him back to her. He laces his fingers in her hair as his hips jut forward, his orgasm hitting hard. "Oh, fuck."

As he struggles to catch his breath, Emma rises to her feet. Her chest heaves, her pupils dilated, and while every part of him is aware of her arousal, Otto still can't help but focus on the triumphant grin spread across her face.

A tingling sensation ripples down his spine. Emma makes him forget the stress in his life. She is his sunflower, his happiness. And damn can she make him weak in the knees. But that cocky grin is a challenge. One he's about to accept because he won't be the only one moaning someone's name tonight.

Otto hoists Emma into his arms and carries her over to his bed. When he kisses her neck, she lets out a pretty sigh that tightens his chest. He fights to go slow, to take in every part of her. He kisses the soft skin of her pert breasts above the neckline of her tank top as he eases his hand between her legs.

A low moan echoes into the dark room as he strokes his fingertips through the yoga pants she wears. Heat and satisfaction filling him as she moves against his touch, her breath becoming raspy. "God, you're so beautiful Sunflower."

He slides his hand inside her pants only to find she isn't wearing any panties and a low growl rumbles through his chest, his dick starting to become hard again. Emma grabs at his hair, her nails scratching at his scalp when he gently closes his teeth around her nipple over the thin cotton top she wears.

Otto glances toward her face only to find her watching him, eyes open, and it sets him on fire. But he also notices the way she bites her lip as if to keep from calling out his name. The corner of his mouth curls up into a lopsided smile as he decides to erase that last modicum of self-control.

When her breath grows short and choppy, and the lifts of her pelvis against his hand grow more desperate, Otto nips her earlobe. "Come for me, Sunflower."

"Oh, God," Emma cries out as her body lifts and her sex clamps around his fingers.

He gently kisses her as she comes down, completely shocked when her tongue demands more. Claims more. "Otto. More. Please."

She grabs at the waist of her pants and pulls them off. He sits up and helps, his dick hard as steel and throbbing. He reaches over to the nightstand and grabs a condom. He chuckles at her impatient huffs then moves between her parted legs and presses himself inward slowly.

"Otto, I swear..."

His Sunflower needs more and he is happy to oblige. When her legs wrap around his hips, he increases his strokes until he's driving into her, hard and fast. "Sunflower. So good. So tight."

"More. Otto. Harder."

Otto lets himself go as she meets each of his strokes. The bed creaks beneath them. He hopes it holds. He plunges into her faster and faster, planting his palms at either side of her head. Her hands are everywhere on him, and their eyes are locked on each other as their grunts and moans fill his dark bedroom.

Emma's back arches and her eyes roll up as she cries out when her orgasm hits, pushing Otto over the edge. His climax is explosive, reverberating through his entire body. And when it's done, it leaves him drained.

For a moment, he stays right where he is, poised over her, belly to belly, both of them breathing hard. Shock waves continue to pass through them and he has trouble figuring out where she ends and he begins. Finally, he lifts his weight and rolls to the side then gathers her in his arms.

"That was . . ." Her words drift off as if she can't find the right ones to describe what just happened between them.

He understands. He doesn't have words for it either. "I know."

"Not ever before," she whispers, snuggling her head down on his chest.

"Me neither." He tightens his arm around her and kisses the top of her head.

They float together, sated and spent, their breath and heartbeats gradually slowing. She starts to get up and he tightens his arm around her, not wanting her to leave, wanting to stretch this moment for as long as he can. She may leave soon. Back to New York and he may never see her again, but he can have this. He can have this moment. "Stay with me tonight?"

She relaxes a fraction. "You sure?"

He nods and kisses her forehead. When she snuggles up against him, he pulls the blanket over them both before tightening his arms around Emma. He's never felt so…at ease, so complete before. He's going to treasure it. Even if it's just for tonight.

Maybe it isn't, though. Every day Emma gets more entwined with her family, closer with them, more connected. Maybe Emma might stay in Montana longer. Either way, he plans to make the most of whatever time he has with her.

Chapter 19

EMMA

Emma loads the last of the coffee mugs into the dishwasher, hyperaware of the people moving about the kitchen. Like her father. And her sister. And her brother-in-law. The exhaustion of yesterday's cattle emergency has faded and now her father and John are discussing stuff Emma doesn't quite understand, but is beginning to get a gist of. Like how cows get moved from one pasture to another.

    The nervous energy coursing through her body won't dissipate, though. Did they know where she spent the previous night? Otto had gently jostled her awake long before the sun streaked the sky and walked her back to the main house, leaving her with a soft kiss at the door. She'd almost dragged him in after her, but hadn't.

She'd slipped in, easing the door shut and avoiding the third step on the stairs that creaks.

Plus, Katie and John live in another house over a mile away. No way could they know.

Snuck over. Like she's sixteen instead of twenty-five. Well, almost twenty-five.

Emma can't help but smile to herself. Is this another thing she missed out on? Would Katie have covered for her if they'd grown up together? A few weeks ago, she would have believed her sister would throw her under the bus without even looking. Today? She's not so sure.

"What's up?"

Emma spins around to find Katie staring at her. "Um, huh?"

Her sister cocks a brow and leans one hip against the sink, pulling her long braid over her shoulder. "You're staring at the dishwasher like it's about to do a magic trick. Is everything okay? You feel all right?"

It's that damn kiss. She hasn't been able to stop thinking about it. The way the world had fallen away as her lips met Otto's and how their tongues tangled was unlike anything she'd ever experienced before. Not to mention what came after. Her cheeks heat at the memory. Emma fidgets with the sponge in her hand and turns back to the sink. "Yeah, I was just thinking about what I need to get done for the day."

"You sure? You look flushed." Katie is quiet for a moment. "Let me know if you need any help. Really. Let me know. I know I've kind of been letting you sink or swim on your own. I'd . . . I'd like to change that."

Emma smiles, a hot rush of emotion nearly choking her and some of that tension fading away. She feels . . . seen. By her sister. "Thanks. I appreciate it."

She rinses off her hands, then dries them with the towel as Katie heads into the living room. Maybe it hadn't started out pretty. She still remembers the look on Katie's face when their father told her who she was. Now she imagines what Katie might look like when Emma gets off the plane at Thanksgiving or Christmas. It will be nice having some place to go for the holidays, instead of spending them alone in her tiny Brooklyn apartment.

Just then the backdoor opens and Otto walks in, causing the ball of nerves that had temporarily disappeared to reappear. He tips his Stetson. "Mornin'."

A slight pink tinges his cheeks even though his features are schooled to almost non-expression. Are they back to those first days when she couldn't figure out if he hated her or not? A pang rushes through her. Does he regret having her stay the night? But before she has time to think about how to address her question, a tiny figure pokes her head around the doorway and waves at her. "Hi."

Oh. His daughter's here. Emma tucks a strand of hair behind her ear and waves back. "Hi."

Otto clears his throat. "I, uh, have a favor to ask."

Addison frowns and places a hand on her hip. "Dad, you said you asked her already."

Emma blinks. "Asked me what?"

Addison walks over to her. "If we can hang out instead of me going with Dad to do his chores."

"Veronica called this morning early. She has some kind of work function she needs to go to and so Addie's here with me today. Normally I can plan so she can come along with us, but we're moving the herd out of the North pasture. It'll be all day and I'll be on horseback for most of it. It's hot and I can't figure out where Addie can be so I can keep an eye on her and the herd at the same time and last night you said you could maybe help out." Otto stops, looking as stunned as Emma feels at the torrent of words that just poured out of his mouth.

Katie walks back into the room at that very moment. "I was going to go into town to get a manicure. We should all go."

Addison bounces on her toes. "Can I go, Dad? Please? Please?"

When Otto stands there silently, Emma jumps in. "I told you I'd help whenever you needed. If it's okay with you, I'd be more than happy to take Addison on a girls' day with my *sister*."

Otto's eyes widen at her last word and she's glad he caught the title. "Maybe later you can give me that horseback riding lesson in exchange."

"It's a deal." He nods, then turns to his daughter. "Addie, you listen to whatever Emma tells you. No sass."

"Okay," the little girl replies, clasping her hands under her chin in a semi-successful attempt to look angelic.

He looks back up at Emma, his hands slowly turning his cowboy hat in front of him. Emma can't help thinking about what those hands had done to her the night before, how they'd teased and coaxed her. His whisper in her ear asking her—no commanding her—to come for him. Heat rushes through her and she's about to come again just thinking about it.

"Why are you staring at each other like that?" his daughter asks, looking between them.

Crap. Addison, Katie, John, and her father are all watching them stare at each other.

She spins back to face Otto. "Is there any time you want us to have her back by?"

Otto rubs the back of his neck. "Not sure what time I'll be done by, but she has some homework to do. So, don't want her out all day."

Katie walks over to stand next to Emma. "We'll take care of it. We've got it."

We.

Her sister talks about them as a united front. Emma smiles at her and mouths a thank you.

Otto nods at both of them before heading out the door. Once he's out of sight, she turns and claps her hands together. "All right, so I'm gonna head upstairs and grab my bag. Then we'll head out?"

A couple of minutes later they all pile into Katie's Prius and head into town. There isn't a cloud in the sky and the sun beats through the windshield, warming up the already hot car. And of all things, Katie not only drives with the air conditioning on but the windows rolled down and pop music pumping from the stereo. They all sing along. It's like the start of a road trip movie.

Emma closes her eyes and rests her head back. "I could get used to this smell. What is it?"

"Fireweed mostly. Maybe a touch of yellow bells and lupine. Must be a lot different than New York," Katie says.

Emma snorts. "You have no idea. The only time you smell flowers is when you walk by a flower shop or accidentally stumble into someone's wedding in the park." It's part of why she always brings flowers into her apartment. Perfumes and air fresheners never quite capture what nature provides.

From the car seat in the back Addie chimes in. "What's New York smell like?"

Good question. Emma has never really thought about it. "Well, car exhaust, of course, with maybe an undertone of garbage on a hot day. But also it depends where you are. Sometimes pizza. Soft pretzels. Halal."

"What's . . . halal?" Addie asked.

"Mainly, it's delicious." Every Thursday was halal day for Emma. She'd grab either a gyro or rice dish for dinner to bring home while she watched TV. She's a little sad that Addie has never tasted it. She's probably never had a decent slice of pizza either. Or a real bagel. "It's a type of Arabic food. There are lots of vendors with food carts around New York selling it, and it's really popular."

"Maybe Daddy can take me to New York one day. I want to try that kind of food," Addie says.

Emma blinks, unsure of how to respond and when she looks to her left Katie shoots her a questioning look. So, she turns to look over her shoulder to the little girl in the back seat. "You would have a lot of fun. There's so much to see. Tons of museums and parks and stuff. And a lot of people."

"Do they have horses too?"

Emma considers. "Sort of. There are horse-drawn carriages in Central Park and some police officers ride horses. But it's not like here where almost anybody could ride a horse."

Addie's feet swing and her heels bounce against the booster seat. "That's too bad. I love horses."

"It's hard for one place to have everything that you want," Katie says with a sidelong look at Emma.

For Emma, New York has only been the place that has everything she wants. She loves the energy of the place. The fast pace. The noise. The people. The culture. The food! It's a tough place to make it, but like the song says, if you have, you can do it anywhere. To her, getting a job as a graphic designer for Tik Talk will mean that she's made it in one of the biggest and most competitive markets in the world. Once she's done that, she can relax a little. She can be happy, especially now that she's putting a button on the whole finding her family thing. Her questions are being answered. She can move on.

Twenty minutes later, they're in town. It's still warm, but the humidity has lessened. Katie drives past the parking lot where Emma and Otto had sex the first time and Emma's cheeks get a tiny bit hot. They park on the street in an angled space, one of many open. Emma looks around amazed at the spaces. No parallel parking here.

"Should we have made appointments?" Even with an appointment, she often waits thirty minutes or more in New York. Will Addie be able to sit still that long? It seems like a lot to ask of a little girl.

Katie shakes her head. "We should be fine."

And they are. There are chairs open in the cozy salon and Emma relaxes the second she steps into the shop. The neutral beige stone tile floor extends a quarter of the way up the wall, which is painted a light pastel yellow. Flower arrangements sit next to each pedicure chair, filling the space with their perfume punctuated by the occasional whiff of acetone. Some kind of new age music plays soft enough that she can barely hear it. And it's clean. So clean.

"Do you have room for three?" Katie asks.

"Of course." A young woman with jet black hair and brown skin comes out from behind the counter. She crouches down to talk to Addie. "Want to pick your color?"

Addie nods, eyes wide at the array of nail polishes on the wall before her. She points to a purple one. "That one."

Emma plucks it off the shelf and looks at the bottom. "Va-va-voom Violet?" She glances over at Katie who gives a tiny headshake. Yeah. Maybe a little much for a little girl. "How about this?" Emma hands her Made You Blush. It's a pale pink.

Addie scrunches up her face and shakes her head.

Emma puts it back even though Katie looks at it longingly.

"Can I have this one?" Addie points to a periwinkle color called Be My Boo-Berry.

It should be fine. Otto can't object to that, can he? Maybe he'll even like it. "Wanna do our toenails the same so we can match?"

Addie jumps up and down. "Yes! Yes! Yes! You, too, Miss Katie? Please?"

Katie looks back from where she's picking Made You Blush back up and laughs. "Sure. What the heck? It'll match those Chucks you lent me, Emma."

The nail tech ushers them to three pedicure chairs, placing Addie in the middle between Katie and Emma. Emma helps her climb into the big chair.

"You and Katie are sisters?" Addie asks.

"Yup," Emma says, enjoying the feeling of getting to say yes to that question and seeing a smile on Katie's face, too.

"What's it like having a sister?"

"Well..." Emma unties Addie's shoes and takes them off as she considers her answer. The truth is, Emma isn't sure what it's like having a sister. She's only just met Katie. However, she can't help but be glad her sister is here, trying to build a relationship. "Katie and I are kind of new at being sisters. We only just found out about each other. I think that having a sister is kind of like having a friend. You know how sometimes you might fight with a friend? Or not see them for a while? Maybe they're not your friend for a while?"

Addie nods as Emma pulls off her socks for her. "I got really mad at Jenny for using up all the purple glitter on her drawing before I even got a chance to put any on mine."

The nail tech hits the controls to start filling the well beneath Addie's feet with warm water.

"Exactly, but a sister is always your sister. It doesn't matter if you're mad at each other or fight over something. She's there, even if she doesn't know you exist." Emma stands up to take off her own shoes and looks over at Katie who reaches out a hand. She takes it and Katie gives Emma's hand a little squeeze before she drops it. Emma swallows hard. It's a small gesture – only a little hand squeeze – but it means so much to her. She's never had a person she could really rely on, someone who would be there no matter what.

"I wish I had a sister," Addie says. The little girl has to sit at nearly the edge of her seat for her feet to hang down low enough to get in the warm water. She drags her big toe through the water, making a little wake.

Emma looks over Addie's head to Katie for some kind of clue of how to respond and gets a bemused shrug. Great. She's on her own. She turns on the massage function in Addie's chair and watches the little girl's eyes go wide. Good. That'll distract her for a few minutes.

"Why do you think I don't?"

Maybe not then. Damn. "I'm sorry?"

The nail technician has taken one of Addie's feet and is using a small scrub brush on it. The little girl starts to squirm. "That tickles."

"You'll get used to it," Katie says, but she jumps a little too as another nail tech starts working on her feet.

Emma climbs into her own chair and starts the massage function, closing her eyes to relax back into it. Something pokes her arm in a rapid staccato. She opens her eyes to see Addie tapping on her forearm with her little index finger.

"I asked my dad if I could have a sister once, and he said that that wasn't something that was going to happen any time soon because I guess him and mom both agreed that having me was enough. But now they have to share me, and since I live more with my mom, having a sister so my dad won't be alone might be good."

The pedicurist massages Emma's foot, which allows her another moment to settle in. Who knew taking a little kid for a pedicure was going to make her do mental gymnastics like this? It's exhausting and she so doesn't want to say anything that she shouldn't or not say something she should. "I don't think it was part of their plan to do that."

When Addie doesn't respond, Emma turns her head. Her heart stutters, afraid she said the wrong thing, that Addie is on the brink of crying. Instead, Addie is looking down at her hands in her lap, tugging on her bottom lip as if she's considering what Emma said. Maybe Emma will luck out and that will be the end of the questions.

"Are you part of my dad's plan?" Addie asks after a moment.

Emma's so surprised, she nearly chokes on her own saliva. Katie chuckles, but smothers it behind her hands when Emma shoots her a glare.

"Honestly, Addie, I don't know," Emma says. "I don't really know what your dad's plan is." She had a plan, with bullet points and short-term and long-term goals and all the rest. Beyond being Addie's dad, Emma doesn't know what kind of plan Otto is working on.

"Do you think you could give me a sister?" Addie asks.

Again, Emma isn't prepared for that question. This time, Katie doesn't even bother to hide her amusement. She laughs, a deep sound that consumes her entire body. Emma wants to feign offense, but she can't. The sound is too contagious. She ends up laughing, too. Addie looks back and forth between them, eyes squinted, trying to figure out what's going on.

"You have to stop squirming or I'm going to paint your entire toe," the pedicurist says.

"Sorry," Emma mumbles. She looks over at Addie, who stares. It's obvious she wants some sort of answer.

"Having a baby is a big decision between two people who care about each other very much," Emma says. "You may get a sister or a brother in the future, but that's up to your mom and dad. And while we don't know the plan, I know that they love you very much and are lucky to have you."

Addie rolls her eyes, apparently having heard that all before. "Yeah, I guess. It's just, I know Daddy cares about you. So I figured, since you said sisters come from two people who care about each other, why can't my sister come from you?"

Emma opens her mouth. Katie keeps laughing so hard that her pedicurist has to tell her to stop squirming as well. Finally, Emma smiles. "You know what, Addie? That sounds like the perfect question for your father when we get back."

Chapter 20

OTTO

Sawyer parks the truck next to the barn and Otto gets out, wiping the sweat from his brow and heads toward the main house. The day has been long and grueling, even with Mario and Sawyer assisting. The weather doesn't help much with the sun beating down on them and the dirt kicking up. All he really wants to do is take a shower and crawl into bed to sleep for the next week.

But he has Addison. Otto hadn't been prepared to have Addie on such a long hard day on the ranch. But there was no way he was going to say no to Veronica, even when she gave him no warning. Nope. That would be one more thing she'd use against him with the lawyers. So he scrambled and asked Emma.

He swallows hard.

If Addie gets attached to her and then Emma goes back to New York, his daughter's little heart might get broken. He knows his heart is on the line, too, but he's a big boy. He can take it. The thought of Addie hurting, though? That is too much.

But it's only one day. How bonded could they get in a few hours?

Brushing dust off his Stetson and jeans he bounds up the steps toward the screen door to the kitchen. He pulls the door open and enters the kitchen. On the counter are three Tupperwares of food, a routine Mitch created for the days when the workers were out most of the day. This way they can take dinner back to their quarters and relax rather than all sitting at the table. A routine Otto is grateful for with the exception that tonight he would've loved to have dinner with his daughter after spending the day away from her.

Mumbling voices drift into the kitchen from the dining room; the soft giggle of his daughter cuts through the air. What the heck are they up to that's so funny? Otto steps softly toward the sound, glad that she sounds happy. That's one worry off his shoulders.

When he gets to the archway of the room he finds Emma and Addie sitting at the table with a big poster board, glue, construction paper, and glitter. Ah. Addie's homework. A presentation on dolphins. He leans against the archway, content to watch them work together.

Addie's tongue pokes out the side of her mouth as she uses a glitter marker to color in a shape while Emma glues down a picture of some sort.

"What's your favorite animal?" his daughter asks.

Emma picks up another picture and squeezes glue on the back of it. "Um, I think cheetahs are cool. Their spots are pretty and they can run so fast."

His daughter looks up at Emma. "Have you ever seen one?"

"When I was a little girl our school took a trip to the zoo and they had two there. But they don't have them anymore."

Addie bows her head to return to her coloring. "You're lucky. I hope one day I can see dolphins."

Emma flips the image over and places it onto the posterboard. "Maybe that can be part of your report. You could talk about places that dolphins live and pick a place you want to go visit someday. Set it as a goal."

"My teacher might even give me extra points for that! Do you think we can print up some pictures of places to put on the poster?" Addie points to a blank space. "Right here might work."

Emma straightens up and looks at the spot Addie indicates. "It would totally work. When your dad comes back I can zip over to the barn office and print some up."

Otto clears his throat at that moment. "I'm here."

Both Emma and Addie spin around and stare at him. Addie gets off the chair and runs over to him, squeezing him tight around the hips. "I missed you."

Otto reaches down and picks her up into his arms, then places a kiss on her cheek. "Missed you, too, sweetheart."

"Look, Daddy." Addie holds up her hand to show him the bright blue nail polish. "Emma, Katie, and I all got the same color."

Otto smiles and looks over his daughter's shoulder toward Emma who flashes him her own hand. His heart warms. Though he shouldn't be completely shocked. After all, his daughter has managed to con both Mario and Sawyer into letting her paint their nails with glitter polish, but Emma is showing off the matching color as if it were a badge of honor.

Otto turns his attention back to his daughter. "How much left of your homework do you have to finish?"

"We're almost done. Emma has to print some pictures for us to glue."

Emma stands from the chair and makes her way over, placing her hand on Addie's back. "I can go to the office and do that and your dad can help you glue down the rest of the pieces."

Addie shakes her head. "Nooo. I don't want help. I want to do it myself."

The girl has an independent streak that he loves and he's not going to squash it. "Well, how about you do that while I eat dinner and if you need help, then I'll jump in?"

His daughter nods. He sets her down and Emma makes her way past them, then into the kitchen and out the back door. His heart sinks a little at her absence even though he knows she's coming right back. What the hell is that about? If he's getting worked up over her going to the office, how's he going to react when she leaves to go back to New York?

Pushing the question from his mind, he returns his attention to Addie who is scrambling back up into her chair. "Okay, you start while I heat my food. I'll be right back."

Addie barely gives him a glance. She's already spreading glue on something. Otto heads back into the kitchen. He grabs the Tupperware and puts it into the microwave, then looks out the window over the sink to the barn where the office is, hoping to catch even a glimpse of Emma. Dammit. He wants to be able to look at her all the time.

He shakes his head and walks back to the microwave waiting for the time to run out. Then his attention turns back to the counter where two other Tupperwares sit. Sooner or later Mario and Sawyer will be over. Both had gone back to the bunkhouse to clean up before they headed over. He and Addie should be done by then and heading back to his apartment.

Hopefully.

Mario and Sawyer had a lot of questions and had peppered him with them the whole day. His fault. Well, no one's fault really. Apparently, he and Emma had been quite *loud* the previous night. A smile tugs at his lips thinking about the way he made her call out his name.

The microwave dings and he opens the door and pulls his food out. After he grabs a fork from the utensil drawer, he heads into the dining room. "Did you have fun today?"

His daughter looks up, a huge grin on her face. "YES!"

He quirks a brow. "Oh, really? What else did you do?"

"After we got our nails done, we had lunch at Willow Bistro. I had chicken fingers and Katie got me a special drink that had a tiny umbrella in it." She paused as if still in awe of the tiny umbrella. "Then we went to Mountain Boutique. We looked at dresses for Katie and tops for Emma and I even got to try on a skirt. Shopping is so much fun. We should go more, Daddy. I can show you how."

Oh great. If his daughter ends up falling in love with shopping he may have to take on a second job. He scoots into a chair and scoops up some mashed potatoes. "Sounds like a full day."

Addie looks up and meets his eyes. "It would have been more fun if you were there."

His heart tugs. If he loses the custody battle...no. That isn't an option. He will move planets if he has to so he can remain in Addie's life. She's his little girl and the fact she wants him around has to mean something.

A moment later the back door to the kitchen bangs shut and when he looks over his shoulder Emma is walking into the room with a bunch of papers in her hand. She smiles at him, then makes her way over to Addie. "Okay, so I printed up some famous zoos and some of them even have dolphin experiences where you can feed them and swim with them."

Addie's eyes go wide. "Really? People can do that?"

Emma nods as she sits down in the chair and grabs the child scissors from the table. She cuts the pictures as Addie scatters the papers around. "This place looks cool. Dad, do you think we can go one day?"

He reaches over and turns the picture toward him. Florida. Could have been worse. Could have been somewhere in the Caribbean or something. "I think I can make that happen."

Addie claps her hands together and smiles wide.

"But first we should finish your collage," Emma says as she hands Addie the cutout.

His daughter takes it and flips it over before taking a glue stick to it. Once she's done she presses the picture down on an empty space on the posterboard. Otto shoves a spoonful of mashed potatoes into his mouth as he watches his two girls. He coughs as the potatoes go down his throat the wrong way.

His two girls.

Since when does he consider Emma his girl? They've had some fun. That's all. Okay. It isn't all. That fun has been seriously mind-blowing. She's being nice to his kid. That's always a plus. But his girl?

He chases away the thoughts and finishes his meal while his daughter finishes her project.

Addie smacks the last picture down and picks up the posterboard to show it to Otto. "What do you think?"

Otto cocks his head to look at it. "That's real nice, honey. Outstanding, in fact." And it is. He's not quite sure what it is, but it looks so balanced and like it all flows together.

Addie peeks out from behind the posterboard. "Emma showed me how to look at the paper like a . . . like a . . ." Her words trail off and she looks at Emma.

"Like a grid," Emma offers, eyes on Addie.

"Like a grid. And that helps you put things in places that look good to people and helps them understand what they're looking at." Addie sets the board down and looks up at Emma, who smooths the little girl's hair back.

Otto looks up at Emma, not quite sure what he's hearing.

Emma shrugs, hair tumbling off her bare shoulder. "It's what I do for a living."

He frowns. "Move pieces of paper around on a board?"

She punches him lightly in the shoulder. "It's a little more than that."

He pretends to be knocked sideways by the force of her punch. "Well, okay, then. Pardon me."

Emma turns to Addie. "It's beautiful. Your teacher is going to love it," Emma says, looking it over with her hands on her hips.

"Couldn't agree more." He looks at Emma. "Thank you for helping."

Addie gives Emma a huge hug. "Thank you. I had so much fun today."

Emma runs her hands through Addie's hair. "Me, too."

Otto's chest swells. His daughter likes Emma as much as he does it seems. He hopes that doesn't spell heartbreak for both of them.

"Addie, it's time for bed. Let's clean up, then we have to head home."

His daughter nods and starts gathering the markers on the table as he goes into the kitchen. Emma comes up behind him. "She really did have fun today. Thank you for trusting me with her."

"I appreciate you watching her." He grabs the sponge and she reaches out to take it. Her touch feels like an iron brand on his skin.

"Otto, I can clean up. You had a long day."

When he turns he meets her gaze, her soft eyes comforting and inviting. He lets go of the sponge and she takes the Tupperware from him. He shakes his head. His dish. His responsibility. At least, that's how things always were with Veronica. They never did manage to create a united front. There was what she wanted and what he wanted and, outside of wanting Addie, those desires never seemed to be the same. They never had each other's backs.

He looks over her shoulder toward the dining room. Addie is still busy cleaning up. So he turns back to Emma and steps closer, leaning down and pressing his lips to hers. His tongue gently brushes her lips before he pulls away. "Thank you for helping me today. It means a lot."

Emma's cheeks are tinted a light shade of pink and she looks up at him from beneath hooded lashes. "Anytime."

He bends over and kisses the tip of her nose right before Addie walks into the room carrying her bag and poster. "All set, Daddy."

Just as they are about to exit, Addie turns toward Emma. "Do you think you can come to my dance recital on Friday?"

Emma straightens. "Oh, um, sure. I don't really have much going on." She looks over to him. "If you don't mind that is, I would love to go."

Otto tenses. He'd love to spend more time with Emma. But he's unsure how his ex-wife might react. Not that the other woman would be there. Addison's mom has plans to be out of town, but he's sure other moms will mention Emma's presence. But when he looks at his daughter's hopeful eyes, he knows there is only one answer. "If that's what my daughter wants, then I guess you're coming with me."

Addison jumps up and down and leaps at him, wrapping her tiny arms around his waist. "Thank you, Daddy."

He rubs the center of her back. "Now, say goodnight and let's get going."

With that, his daughter says farewell to Emma and then walks with him through the kitchen and out the back door toward the employee building. The last half hour was one of the best of his life, sitting at the table and eating dinner while his daughter and Emma worked on a school project. It was a real life manifestation of the way he pictures a home should feel like, what a family should feel like.

And it's something he wants more of. He just isn't sure how to make that happen.

Chapter 29

Emma

It hadn't been easy to fall asleep. If she wasn't thinking about Otto, she was thinking about the day she'd spent with Katie and Addie. It had been the quintessential girls' day out. Mani/pedis, lunch, shopping. And Addie was just so darn cute. Too excited about the adventure to be on anything but her very best behavior. Emma had even enjoyed helping Addie with her homework.

    She chuckles. Dolphins. Who'd have thought they could be so much fun? Of course, the assignment played right into Emma's strengths in layout and design. She actually had something to offer, something that would help. She was needed. She likes the feeling. It's not one she's accustomed to. Nobody actually needs her in New York.

Regardless of whether or not she's slept, though, ranch life starts early. Her alarm goes off at four-thirty and she wipes the sleep from her eyes, pulls her hair back, gets dressed and goes downstairs to start a batch of biscuits.

Her father comes in, yawning and stretching. He stands next to her at the stove. Emma freezes as he plants a kiss on top of her head the same way Otto kisses Addie on the top of the head. "What's for breakfast today, EmmaBear?"

It's like the little hand squeeze Katie gave her at the nail salon. It's nothing. A little kiss on the top of the head. A cute nickname. Most people would hardly notice it, but to Emma it's everything, everything she's never had.

She looks up at her father, hoping her eyes don't look watery. "Biscuits and gravy."

He rubs his hands together. "Sounds as good as it smells." He walks to the counter and pours himself a cup of coffee.

Emma tries to reconcile this sweet man being her father and that hard-faced angry woman in New Jersey being her mother. She can't imagine them together. What had they seen in each other? She clears her throat. "How'd you end up married to Isobel?"

Her father is silent for long enough that Emma turns from the stove to see if he's still there. He is. Staring off into space, his face sagging a little. "I guess it was a little like you kids say. It seemed like a good idea at the time."

Emma snorts a little as she returns to stirring the biscuit gravy, making sure to get rid of any lumps the flour might have formed.

"She was gorgeous. Like you. Those big eyes and all that hair tumbling around. There wasn't anybody around here quite like her. She was quite the firecracker, too. You could feel the electricity crackle every time she walked into a room. She was wild, but she was also funny and smart." He pauses and when he continues his voice is lower, sadder. "Too smart to be happy out here on a ranch, I guess."

"Or too dumb not to be," Emma says, trying to match that mental picture of a wild child with the angry woman behind the screen door in New Jersey. Emma looks out the window. The sun has risen just enough to touch the hills with golden light. The land stretches out and away and the sky is like a big blue bowl above them. She's been trying to capture that sense of space and light in her photos, but it's really something you have to experience to understand.

Mitch smiles. "You like it here, EmmaBear?"

She smiles back at him. "I do. I didn't know what to expect when I got off the plane. I wanted to know who you were and what had happened. I didn't expect to stay or feel like I kind of belonged here."

"No kind of about it." Mitch nods, wrapping his knobby hands around the coffee mug. "It's in your blood, like it's in mine and Katie's. Three Keys is more than a stretch of land."

The door bangs open and people tumble in. Sawyer and John and Katie and Mario and Linda and Otto and Addie, who stops to give Emma a hug around her hips on her way through to the dining room and makes Emma smile. They're all talking, three conversations going on at once. A cow who might give birth any day, a horse whose shoe seems a little loose, a calf pen that might need mending. She still only understands about a third of it, but that doesn't matter. It's the way it feels. The everydayness of it. The sense of being part of a team that works together.

Katie grabs the basket of biscuits and gestures toward the dining room with her head. "You coming or are you going to keep staring into space for a little longer?"

Emma jumps a little, but then sees the teasing smile on Katie's face. "I think I can probably stare into space later." She picks up the skillet of sausage gravy and pours it into a waiting bowl, sticks a ladle in and follows Katie into the dining room.

"Oh, Addie," Emma says as she walks into the room. "I almost forgot. I found some things in the attic you might want to play with while you're here."

Addie sits up very straight. "What? Where?"

Emma hands the gravy to Linda. "Some dolls and a tea set. They're in boxes under the kitchen table. You should take a look after breakfast."

"Tea set?" Katie asks, her voice cold.

Emma's hands falter as she passes the pitcher of water. "Yeah. Dad said I should check to see if there were any toys up in the attic Addie might like to play with. That's . . . that's why I was up there the other day." She opts not to bring up the whole wedding dress fiasco.

Katie's head swivels toward their father who is studiously applying himself to the biscuits and gravy. He must feel her gaze on him because he says. "Stuff was only gathering dust up there. Thought it would be better if it brought some little girl some joy. Some little girl who might miss her mama on occasion, too."

Katie slumps back into her chair. It doesn't take a lot for Emma to put two and two together. The tea set was Katie's and it was special to her. Now Emma has hauled it out and offered it to someone else without even asking.

Damn it.

She screwed up again and just when she and Katie had made so much progress. "I'm so sorry. I didn't know it was something special. I should have asked."

Katie stops her, placing a hand over hers. "There was no way for you to know that. You did what you were asked to do." She sighs. "Dad's right. It was gathering dust up there." She turns to Addie and smiles. "My dad and I spent a lot of fun afternoons having tea parties together with that set. I hope you and your dad do, too."

Hot tears prick at the back of Emma's eyes. Had Katie and Dad played tea party with this same set? Emma could totally see it. The big man and the little girl, sipping water and pretending to be fancy. The tenderness of it stabs at her. The picture of little heartbroken Katie and big heartbroken Mitch comforting each other over tiny cups of pretend tea vies with her relief that her sister has forgiven her so quickly.

Addie looks back and forth between Emma and Katie and Mitch, clearly understanding that something is happening, but not quite sure what. "Thank you, Miss Katie. I'll take real good care of it. I promise."

"I know you will," Katie says.

"Umm. I think that's my biscuit." Mario glares at Sawyer. The basket is almost empty. There's one left and both Mario and Sawyer reach for it at once.

"I beg to differ. You already ate at least four. I only had two. This one is definitely mine." Sawyer pulls it a little toward him.

"I don't think I had more than three." Mario pulls the biscuit toward himself.

Otto snatches the biscuit out of their hands, cuts it in half neatly with a knife, then tosses one half on each of their plates. "Children," he says shaking his head and passing the gravy bowl to them. In seconds, both their plates are wiped clean and everyone stands up to carry items into the kitchen.

"Can I stay with Emma today? Please?" Addie says, tugging on Otto's jeans.

Otto shakes his head. "No, baby girl. You're with me today. I've got about an hour of chores to do out in the barn and then it's just you and me."

Addie's eyes light up. "Really? Just us?"

He ruffles her hair. "Well, maybe we might let Mario and Sawyer hang around if they promise to behave."

Addie presses her lips together. "Mario never behaves."

"I resent that remark!" Mario says, tugging on one of Addie's pigtails.

"Oh, Mitch, I picked up the mail on my way in. Left a pile of it on your desk," Linda says. She stands, rubbing at her lower back.

"You okay there?" Mitch asks.

She blows out a breath. "Just my lumbago acting up. I'm not getting any younger, you know."

"None of us are," Mitch says, rising slowly and taking a moment to straighten out his knee with a creak. "You work too hard."

Linda smiles at him. "Show me someone around here who doesn't."

Sawyer makes a face, but his eyes stay bright. "Dear Lord, if this gets any sweeter I'm going to end up a diabetic."

Emma blows him a kiss. "That one's just for you, cuz."

He laughs and mimes catching the kiss in midair and planting it on his cheek.

Katie stays behind to help Emma clean up. When they are alone at the sink, her sister asks, "So do you have a plan?"

Emma hands her a plate she's just washed. "A plan for what?"

"A plan for the future. You told Addie yesterday that sometimes there's a plan and sometimes there's not. Is there one? Have you thought about what you want to do next?"

There had been a plan. There pretty much always had been. She's always been focused on the next goal. She finished high school at the top of her class and already had the goal of going to college. She'd finished college and already had the goal of getting a job. She'd gotten a job and already had the goal of getting a better one.

Then she'd come home to find the detective she'd hired on her doorstep with that envelope and she'd decided to come to Montana to meet her family. What's the goal past that one?

"I'm not sure." Right now, there's not much to go back to in New York. A tiny apartment. Friends who are all getting married and starting families of their own. No job, either. At least, not yet.

Could working out here be an option? Billings isn't that far. Surely they have an ad agency or two. Nothing compared to Tik Talk Media, though, that's for sure. Working for the large company had been her goal for so long and her benchmark for deciding whether or not she's a success. What would it be like to put that aside? Her heart sinks a little thinking about it.

Katie sets down the cast iron skillet, but before she can say anything else, her father stomps into the room.

"Katie, what the hell is this?" He throws a big white envelope down onto the table. Emma cranes her neck to see what it is. It's from Double Helix Testing. She frowns at it and looks up at Katie whose face is flushed bright pink. Uh oh.

To Katie's credit, she doesn't try to prevaricate. "I had Emma's DNA tested along with yours. To see if she's really your daughter."

If there ever is a moment to worry Mitch might have another heart attack, it's this one. His face turns a dark brick red and his teeth are clenched so hard a vein pulses in his jaw. "I believe I made it perfectly clear that I did not want you to do that."

Her sister takes a step backward, holding her hands up in front of her. "This isn't only about you. It's about all of us. It's about the ranch." Katie turns toward Emma. "I took your sample right when you first got here, before I got to know you, before I knew we could trust you. When I thought maybe you might be scamming us or looking for a handout." Katie holds up her hands as if to stop traffic. "I know better now. Still, I don't think it's a bad idea. Lord knows we can't trust Isobel farther than we can throw her and we only have her word that Dad is your . . . dad."

Emma bites her lower lip. Katie does have a point. The fact that she and Katie look like each other and both of them look like Isobel doesn't mean that Mitch is really her father. Finally, she nods. "She's right. I want to know for sure, too. How did you get the sample of my DNA, though?" She would have remembered spitting in a tube or swabbing her cheek.

Katie knots the dishtowel she's holding in her hands. "I stole your toothbrush." Her lower lip trembles.

Emma laughs. "So that's where it went! I thought Matilda or one of the dogs took it." She turns toward Mitch. "We'll be a lot better off if we're dealing with facts and not just feelings here. You've been amazing to me. You've shown me what it feels like to have a father. No matter what it says on the papers inside that envelope, I'll always have that."

Their father rubs his face. "Fine, then. Open it up."

Katie slits open the envelope and pulls out the report. Emma's insides are twisting and turning like they've turned into a pit of snakes. She's come to love it here. What if it turns out that Mitch is wrong and Three Keys isn't in her blood like Katie's and his? What if he's not Emma's biological father? Will he throw her out? Maybe she shouldn't have agreed so readily to have Katie read the results.

Katie looks through the first page, then the second, and third. She sets the whole thing down on the table.

Emma feels like she can't breathe, like there's no way to get air into her lungs.

Katie holds her arms out wide. "It's verified. You're a Locke. One hundred percent. Just like me. Welcome to the family."

Emma steps into her hug. For a second, she thinks she might be able to contain the tears, but it's too much. Way too much. She has a family. A sister and a father who want her. She belongs. Tears stream down her face and sobs wrack her body as she holds onto her sister for dear life. Then that familiar scent of soap and leather is there, too, as Mitch joins in the group hug.

"My girls. My girls," he repeats over and over again.

The three stay that way until Emma's sobs turn into hiccups and the hiccups turn into little gasps and the little gasps subside. When her father – *her father* – finally releases them, she says, "Sorry about that."

"I'm not," he says, sitting back down at the table to wipe away the tears that have run down his face after giving her one more pat on the back.

Katie sits down across from him and motions for Emma to sit down as well. "What now?"

Emma frowns. "What do you mean what now? You're my sister and he's my dad." She points at Mitch.

Katie and Mitch exchange a look. "Not exactly," Katie says. "There are some legal issues to take care of."

Shaking her head, Emma shoves her chair back. "No. No no no. That is not why I came here. I told you that from the beginning." She stands.

Katie grabs her hand and pulls her back down into the chair. "I know that. So does Dad. That doesn't change that we need to make some adjustments to our legal arrangements now that I have a sister."

The next two hours go by quickly and Katie and Mitch fill Emma in on the many legal issues that need to be decided. She understands a little more than she did when they all start talking about fences and calves, but not a whole lot more. She looks up at the clock and holds up her hands. "I need to start making lunch."

She pushes back from the table and sets up to make sandwiches for everyone at the counter. Her dad joins her and they turn out a substantial pile while Katie goes out to let people know that lunch will be ready.

About the time the sandwiches are finished, Mario, Sawyer, and John come trooping in. "Where are Otto and Addie?" Emma asks, immediately wishing she'd kept her mouth shut as Mario and Sawyer exchange a meaningful glance.

"He and Addie are back at the residents' building," Sawyer says, grabbing a turkey sandwich off the top of the pile and sitting down.

After making sure everyone has enough, Emma puts a few sandwiches on a tray along with a couple of apples and a few cookies and drapes a clean dishcloth over it. She shoulders the screen door out of the way and lets it bang shut behind her.

She stops at the bunkhouse door, not sure whether to knock or to walk right in. Balancing the tray on her hip, she reaches for the doorknob and turns it slowly, opening the door a crack to peek inside.

Otto sits cross-legged on the floor in front of the coffee table. Iris Twinklehoof, Addie's stuffed unicorn, sits to his right in all her pink and purple iridescent glory and the two dolls Emma found in the attic are to his left. Addie sits across from him, carefully pouring water from a tiny chipped tea pot into a cup. She sloshes a little into the saucer and frowns. "The water jumped." It's the tea set that Emma found in the attic, the one that used to belong to Katie.

"You just have to slow down a little." Otto puts his hand over Addie's and supports the tea pot with his other hand and helps her pour water into the tea cup for Iris without spilling.

She grins up at him, pleased with her accomplishment. She sets the teapot down and picks up her cup and takes a sip. "Do you like your tea, Daddy?"

Otto picks up his cup. It looks ridiculously small in his big hand, especially with his pinky finger sticking out like he's having tea with the queen. "It's delicious. You must share your recipe with me."

Addie giggles. "It's only water, Daddy. There's no recipe."

Emma clears her throat. "Would the lady and gentleman care for some refreshment with their tea?" she asks in a fake British accent.

Addie looks up and without skipping a beat says, "Yes please. That would be lovely." She takes a napkin and drapes it over Iris Twinklehoof's legs and then puts another one on her own lap. Otto very seriously does the same for the dolls.

Emma sets the tray down in the center of the coffee table and takes off the dishcloth with a flourish. "Luncheon is served, my lady." Then she curtsies.

Addie covers her mouth with both hands to try to stifle her giggles.

Otto looks up at her, those eyes drinking her in like he's parched for the sight of her. "Care to join us?"

Emma hesitates a moment, then shakes her head. She won't intrude on this moment. "Thank you, but no. I, uh, have work to do."

"You sure?" he says, sliding to one side. "There's room."

"Maybe some other day."

"Well, how about I take you out for that riding lesson tomorrow to say thank you," he looks up at her.

She smiles. "I'd like that." In truth, the idea terrifies her. The animals on this ranch have not exactly been cooperative with her and the horses are surprisingly huge when you get close to them. Beautiful, but also enormous and intimidating. It means time alone with Otto, though. She'd like a little more of that.

She slips back out of the bunkhouse. Addie will grow up always knowing she's loved. She'll never have a moment where she thinks no one wants her. Emma is beginning to get a sense of what that feels like. Mitch loves her. No questions. She's his daughter and that's that. Katie might not have made it quite to love yet, but she likes Emma now. That's clearer and clearer every day.

Emma's not sure how many more days she'll be able to stay. When she went upstairs after breakfast, there was an email from a Holly Doucette at Tik Talk Media reminding her about the interview in two days. She'd stared at the email for almost ten minutes before hitting reply.

Chapter 22

Otto

Otto finishes currying Bayberry, appreciating the bay stallion's tightly coiled muscles and his glossy coat. He's not a big horse, certainly one of the smaller ones on the ranch, but damn if he doesn't have drive. Otto would trade about anything to keep that trait in his mount.

"Am I riding him?" Emma fidgets as her glaze flicks over the horse, her voice a little higher and breathier than usual.

"No, ma'am. Bayberry is my ride. You'll be riding John's horse, Redwood. He's great for beginners. Or for physical therapy." Bayberry is a very forgiving horse, but he isn't a mount for a beginner.

When Emma's footsteps grow silent, he turns to look over his shoulder, the corner of his mouth lifting up at the confused expression on her face. "John had some injuries when he came back from overseas. Riding was one way he worked to recover."

"Oh, I didn't know that was a thing." She continues walking again until they come to a stop in front of Redwood's stall.

The tall, chestnut gelding picks up his head to greet them. Emma steps closer. There's a small smile on her face. She glances over at Otto and Otto could swear his heart stops momentarily. "I've never been this close to a horse before. Never even touched one."

Something inside Otto's chest swells, the same way it had when he first introduced Addie to a horse. There's something magical about the animals, and something even more gratifying to be the first person to get to introduce another to them. It's an honor. Redwood's soft eyes meet his and he runs a hand over the horse's muzzle while Emma pets the gelding's neck. Her touch is tentative at first, as though she doesn't know what to expect and doesn't want to startle the horse. But then she gets used to it, and her face beams as brightly as the sun.

"I'll be right back." Otto heads over to the tack room a few feet away and grabs the saddle, bridle, pad, and girth. He returns to find Emma still in the same place and still petting the horse. Otto slows for a moment, just so he can watch her. When she glances up he clears his throat. "Let's get this guy ready for you."

He opens the stall and the two of them step in. He reaches into his back pocket and hands a brush to Emma. "This is a curry brush. Run it over Redwood's back and sides."

Emma takes the brush, then tentatively begins running it over the gelding.

"You can press a little harder," he says.

"I don't want to hurt him. He's so pretty." She gazes up at the horse who seems to stand a little taller like he can understand her praise. Otto knows how he feels.

"You won't hurt him. Move in circular motions like this." Otto places his hand over hers to guide her. It feels small and cool and soft under his work-roughened hand and the contact sends a jolt of awareness up his arm. Her little gasp tells him that she's felt it, too. He leans in and gets a noseful of peach. Dear Lord, is he going to be able to get her on the horse or is he going to pick her up and carry her into the barn and make love to her right there?

Just the thought makes him cast a guilty look toward the office where Mitch is working.

Once Emma seems to be getting the hang of brushing Redwood, he steps back. Her brow furrows in concentration and the tip of her tongue peeks out of the side of her mouth. Just like Addie working hard to master some small task. Then the brush gets tangled in Redwood's mane and Emma makes a noise in the back of her throat. She looks back at him, those even white teeth sinking into that plump lower lip again. "Sorry."

"Leave it to the city girl," he teases, but walks over and helps remove the brush, then together they get the gelding ready.

"Grab the reins here under his neck like this." Otto demonstrates what he wants Emma to do. When she has a solid grasp, he walks out of the stall. "Walk him outside and wait for me. I gotta get Bayberry ready."

Emma's eyes go wide. "By myself? What if he tries to run away?"

"He won't. He's a solid horse. Nothing really spooks him." Otto watches as Emma takes in a deep breath and blows it out even and slow. "Just walk at his side."

She nods and leads the horse out of the stall and toward the door, her posture straightening with each step. He can tell she's nervous. Redwood probably can, too, but she adapts so fast, never letting her fear or inexperience stop her. It doesn't take much instruction before she can handle something on her own. Hell, did she watch YouTube videos before she came out this morning?

Otto makes quick work of getting Bayberry ready and heads out to meet Emma. Redwood has his head down and is eating the grass while Emma looks...perturbed, complete with a pouty lip. "Are all the animals stubborn? Or are they just like that with me?"

He laughs. "What do you mean?"

"I wasn't sure if he was allowed to eat the grass. I tried moving him but the darn thing wouldn't budge. Just like the cow. And the dogs who led me on the wild goose chase." Emma leans into the horse to try to move him. Her eyes narrow a little. "And the chickens."

Otto rubs the back of his neck. "That's not going to work. Don't tug the reins, but lead him. Click your tongue softly to get his attention."

She does as he instructs and the chestnut gelding lifts his head. She walks him a couple of paces away from the grass and stops. Then she turns and looks at him, a big smile on her face. "I'm ready. Or as ready as I'll ever be."

He gives Bayberry a command to stay put then walks over to Emma. "Come over here on his left side. Grab the reins and some of his mane in your left hand. You can place your right on the saddle. Make sure to relax. As easygoing as Redwood is, he can sense your tension. Now place your shin in my hands and propel your other leg over the horse."

Emma does as she's told and while she propels a bit too much, almost going over the other side, she quickly recovers. As expected, the ever-patient Redwood remains still. She shifts in the saddle and grabs onto the horn. "Whew."

"Don't rely on that. Let your body find its own balance. Relax and find the rhythm. Sit up straight and don't lean forward or back." He remains next to the horse and Emma for a few more seconds until she nods. God, she's strong, and she looks beautiful up on the tall horse, sun glinting around her like a halo. Like she belongs here.

Maybe she does. Maybe she just hasn't figured that out yet. Maybe this day will be one more step in that direction.

Otto swallows hard and makes his way over to Bayberry. Once he's mounted on the horse, he heads over to Emma. "It's an easy trail over to the pasture. Give a gentle squeeze with your legs and relax the reins. The horse already knows where to go, so you won't need to lead him much."

Emma complies. Redwood's first steps must've caught her off guard because she flinches, but she settles down a second later. They exit the gated area and head away toward the vast expanse of land that belongs to Three Keys Ranch. Emma looks over at him and the horse starts to drift to the left.

"Look ahead. It's like driving. Focus on where you want to go and the horse will follow. Remember, it can sense you. Plus it helps with the balance." Otto gives Bayberry a squeeze and trots until he's a little ahead of Emma. At least this way she can follow him. And he won't be distracted by her because it's getting harder by the second to remember that he's supposed to be teaching her to ride.

They ride in silence, taking in the surrounding hills, decorated by western yarrow and lupine. The breeze does little to cool his skin as the sun shines bright, the only clouds off in the distance. Even the cows rest in the shade of the trees.

They continue along the fence and Otto assesses the metal grids between the posts. Everything held up so far. Emma's body gently sways with each of Redwood's footfalls as she finds the rhythm of his stride.

"I didn't know anywhere in the world could be this quiet," she says, keeping her eyes trained on the horizon. "I don't think I even notice all the noise in New York City at night anymore. Cars and cabs and people and music and sirens all night. It kind of all melts into background noise after a while, like a steady beat underneath everything else. The quiet sort of got to me my first few nights here."

"Took me awhile to adjust, too. But it grows on ya." Mostly the silence is good for Otto. No cars backfiring or people shouting to startle him and set off all his fight or flight reflexes. Sometimes, though, when he's been out here in the quiet with only his thoughts and nothing to distract him, the silence allows his emotions to nearly drown him. Those are the times he's thankful for having John and Katie around. They know the look, the feeling, when the darkness turns threatening. They know how to guide him back into the light to the place where the silence is succor. "One of the most beautiful days I ever experienced was back in Afghanistan. It was different. Hot to the point where I was sweating through my socks. But the sky reminds me of this one." He gives Emma a wink. "The company is much better, though."

Emma smiles. "How long were you over there?"

"Deployed three times, enlisted for twelve years. Was my calling, until it wasn't. Things changed." His smile slips slightly from his face. "Lost too many friends, blood haunted my nightmares. Even times when I was at home with Addie, couldn't help but feel like I should be back at the base, avenging those who died." He blinks, looking back at Emma. "I've never actually told anyone that before."

Emma's cheeks flush, but she holds his gaze. There's something about it, something that makes him nervous and comfortable at the same time. Part of him wants to look away, but part of him can't. Otto turns back to frown at the horizon. He gestures to the sky. "What about you? I doubt Manhattan has days like these."

"Manhattan has its charms. You should go out there, check it out for yourself before you dismiss it."

They continue riding in a comfortable silence. But the wind from the north picks up and there's a scent of rain to it. Otto looks up to see the clouds racing above them. "Weather's coming."

Emma asks, "What does that mean? There's always weather. That's why they have the report every night on television."

He laughs, then turns serious as he points toward the dark clouds. "Real weather. A storm."

"Those are miles away."

"For now." He clucks to Bayberry and turns him back toward home. "Let's go."

It takes Emma a few minutes to get Redwood to accomplish the same maneuver. In the same amount of time, the temperature has dropped enough for Otto to notice. He glances over his shoulder. "We're going to have to move a little faster than we did coming out. Stay loose. It's all about finding the rhythm."

He gives Bayberry a nudge with his heels and they break into a canter. A moment later a little squeal from Emma reaches his ears. "You okay back there?"

"Working...on...finding...the...rhythm." The words come out syncopated.

He gives her another minute and then chances a glance behind him. She's found it and is moving smoothly with Redwood. Unfortunately, the clouds have gotten closer, too. Thunder rumbles in the distance.

He brings his focus back to the path in front of him. They're going to get wet. The storm front is moving faster than they are. The best thing he can do now is to get them in under shelter as quickly as he can. The first fat drop of rain hits the back of his neck, followed in rapid succession by a second and third. Within seconds, it's a steady sheet of rain, but he can see the barn. They don't have far to go.

"Hang in there," he calls back to Emma.

"I don't think I have much choice."

He smiles. Of course she's hanging with it. It's what she does.

In another fifteen minutes, they're back to the stables. And completely soaked. He gets off Bayberry and then helps Emma dismount from Redwood. She's shivering and her lips are slightly blue.

"H-h-how did it get so cold?"

"Welcome to Montana where you can get all four seasons in one day." He grabs a plaid jacket off a hook by the door and wraps it around her. "This should help."

He turns to the horses and unsaddles Redwood and then Bayberry and picks up the curry brush.

"I want to help," Emma says. She looks lost inside the big coat. Water drips off the end of her braid.

He gets a second brush and hands it to her and together they get the two horses back into their stalls. Emma brushes Redwood and he could swear he hears her whispering words of thanks into his mane for getting her back to the barn.

"You're still shaking." It's dry inside the barn, but not much warmer than outside. A cold wind blows through.

A bolt of lightning cracks with thunder hard on its heels and Emma jumps, eyes wide and peering outside. "Are we safe in here?"

"Safe as we'd be anywhere." He stacks up a couple of bales of hay, finds a few blankets to drape over them, and then sits. He holds his arms open. "Come here. We'll keep each other warm."

She hesitates for a moment and then joins him on the hay bale, taking off the jacket so they can drape it over both their shoulders. "You look like a contestant in a wet t-shirt contest."

He looks down at the white t-shirt he'd put on that morning. It doesn't leave much to the imagination. He chuckles. "Would I win?"

She nestles in closer and slowly stops shaking. "I think even the Russian judge would give you at least a 9.5."

"What about the American judge?"

She looks up at him, her lower lip caught between her teeth. A few seconds later she slips out from under the jacket and throws a leg over him so she's straddling him like she had just been straddling Redwood. She slides her hands up underneath his t-shirt and, even though they're cold, they leave a trail of heat behind them. "Oh, the American judge gives you a solid ten."

"You know," he says, untucking her shirt from her jeans. "We'd probably get warmer faster without these wet things on."

"I think I saw that on one of those survival shows. You're supposed to press your naked bodies together." She leans down and kisses him. She smells like rain and hay and horse and tastes like sunshine.

His fingers find the clasp of her bra and unhooks it, then he's lifting her bra and shirt off of her in one movement. Cupping her breasts in his hands, he takes a second to drink them in. They're every bit as beautiful as he'd thought they would be when he was trying to peek at them while she milked Clara. He touches his tongue to one pink nipple and she grinds herself against him. He swirls his tongue around her nipple and Emma arches into him.

Soon his own shirt follows hers onto the floor. The chill of the air contrasts with the warmth of their flesh as they press together and he pauses for a moment to savor the sensation. Her movements have picked up speed as she rocks back and forth against him.

He unbuttons her jeans and she stands so he can strip them down her legs and pull off her boots. Then she's standing before him, naked and rain-soaked, so beautiful that he can barely breathe.

He stands and she unbuckles his belt and pushes down his jeans until his cock springs free, then she pushes him back down and straddles him again. "Please tell me you have a condom," she whispers.

"Pocket," he growls.

She's fished it out and covered him in a matter of seconds and then she settles onto him, surrounding him with her wet heat. He groans as she sighs and she begins to move, up and down, forward and back, finding a rhythm that works for them both. He leans back so he can thrust upward as she crashes down on him, engulfing him.

She tightens around him. "Otto."

He grabs her ass, pulling her onto him and is rewarded by the sensation of her beginning to pulse around him. She cries out his name again and he watches as her climax crashes over her. Her head thrown back, hands clutching his shoulders for balance. A few more hard thrusts and his own orgasm shakes him to the core.

Emma slumps against him, her skin glowing golden in dim light of the barn.

"Sunflower," he whispers in her ear. It's like in the song. She's sunshine on a cloudy day. Slowly, he eases back onto the blanket-covered bales, pulling the jacket over both of them as she snuggles against his chest. He listens to the thrum of the rain on the roof and Emma's deep, even breathing as she slips into sleep and wonders what he'll do when she decides to leave.

All he knows is that it's going to hurt.

Chapter 23

EMMA

Emma checks her hair in the mirror one last time, fluffing it a little with her fingers. She put it up at first, but was afraid it made her look like she was trying too hard so she took it back down again. This interview is too important and she wants to look like the kind of effortlessly sophisticated and put-together woman who would work at one of the premier agencies in the country. She checks her teeth for lipstick and her mascara for smudges.

All good.

Emma hadn't brought a lot of work clothes with her, but Katie loaned her a black dress that will work. The dress is classic. Simple clean lines. It's a little too long on Emma, but Ms. Doucette won't know that. She'll only see Emma from the shoulders up.

She also won't know that Emma is going to be sitting on a pillow. Of all the advice everyone gave her when Otto took her out for her horseback riding lesson, none of them bothered to mention how sore her butt was going to be afterwards. Of course, riding Otto might have contributed to that state a little, too.

A warm smile spreads across her face. It was all worth it, though. She'd never connected with an animal the way she'd connected with Redwood on their crazy dash in from the storm and the connection with Otto seems to get stronger every day. Sure. He's handsome. The physical attraction has been there since the second he pulled his truck over to help her. He's also kind, though. And strong and smart.

She heads over to the laptop on the desk in her bedroom and clicks on the meeting link, then puts her Air Pods in her ears and sits down on the pillow with only the smallest of winces. The program launches and a window pops up with a message stating the host has not joined the meeting yet.

Emma checks the time. Ten minutes early.

Okay. Not a bad thing. It gives her time to be sure there aren't any technical problems. It also leaves room for her to worry, though. Does she really have what it takes to work at a firm that's this prestigious?

Is she getting ahead of herself?

Biting off more than she can chew?

She takes a deep breath and shakes herself. She won't self-sabotage. She can do this. She deserves this job. She's worked hard and proven herself over and over. She's got this.

Emma looks out the window. The only clue it had rained recently is the way the hills are now dotted with wildflowers. Closer to the house, Otto stacks hay bales.

There's something about him, about the way he moves, that always catches her attention. She can't take her eyes off of him, and she doesn't want to. He's strong – that much she knows – but there's a tenderness that pairs with that strength that's difficult for her to ignore. Her heart skips a beat as she watches him stop and wipe the sweat from his brow and massage the back of his neck. How a gesture so simple can be so masculine, Emma has no idea. If she's being honest, she's annoyed by it. She shouldn't be attracted to a man wiping sweat from his face, but here she is, practically drooling.

A ding cuts through the ear pods and Ms. Doucette joins the meeting. She's wearing a plain black dress that could be the twin of the one Emma is wearing, although she has a colorful scarf tied in a complicated knot around her shoulders. "Good morning, Ms. Wallace."

Emma smiles. "Good Morning, Ms. Doucette. Thank you for meeting with me today."

"I must say. Your resume and portfolio were quite impressive. I loved the diversity of the works you sent."

"I've been lucky," Emma says. And she also has hustled, always pushing herself on to the next thing, the next goal, the next skill she can acquire.

"Luck favors the prepared, doesn't it? You did some of the photography yourself? The landscape photos were magnificent."

"Yes. All the photos are mine." Emma tucks her hair behind an ear and hides a smile. "Montana is such a lovely place. The wild plants and open landscape are great for shooting amazing pictures."

"I liked the photos of the old buildings, too. Especially the shots where you transposed them with more modern architecture. You have a wonderful eye for contrast and a sense for how to use that contrast to make a big impact." Ms. Doucette pauses for a moment and takes a sip from her water bottle. "Tell me, Ms. Wallace, why do you want to work for Tik Talk?"

A question she's prepared for. "Your company has a reputation for only working with the very best. The best products and the best clients. The best materials and the best venues. You have a style that I really connect with. I can pick out a Tik Talk ad on a billboard or up on one of the Times Square displays without ever knowing you rep the product. There's a polish that I admire and want to be part of and that I think I can support with my own work."

"Yes. I can see that. Talk me through your campaign for Jazzby Salon. Tell me how that evolved."

It's one of Emma's best designs.

The next twenty minutes fly by as Emma and Ms. Doucette discuss the different design elements and how Emma made the decisions that led to the final product.

"Do you have any questions for me?" Ms. Doucette asks.

She did. Lots. "How many clients do your designers have at once? Do they get to focus on one at a time or are they working on several things at the same time?"

"Good question. Let me walk you through how a typical campaign gets developed here at Tik Talk."

Twenty minutes later, most of Emma's questions are answered, although she's sure she'll have more eventually. "Well, Ms. Wallace—"

"Please, call me Emma."

"Emma. It was lovely to speak with you. For the next stage of the process, we'd like to see how you would approach a project on your own. I'll email you an assignment today. We'll be using the results to make our final decision."

A project. Something they are testing her on. She pulls at the hem of her dress under the desk and swallows past the lump in her throat. Then she sits up straighter. This is good. She'll be able to show them what she can do. She just needs to believe in herself. "I'll be on the lookout for the email."

"You'll have a limited time to work on it. We work on deadline here a lot. We need to know that you're capable of working under pressure." Ms. Doucette smiles. "Are there any other questions you have?"

"Not at this time." Emma is too focused on her nerves and imagining what the project entails.

"If anything comes to mind, you have my email so reach out. I'm excited to see your submission. You're one of our top candidates."

And the pressure keeps on coming. Emma's palms sweat. "Thank you."

"I'll be sending the email shortly. Enjoy the rest of your day."

"You as well." And with that, Emma disconnects from the meeting. She slumps back in her chair and blows the bangs off her forehead. Okay, then. She's past one more hurdle on the path to her dream job. That's good.

Isn't it?

Emma pulls off Katie's dress and grabs a T-shirt and a pair of soft cotton shorts out of her dresser. Once she's changed, she stretches both arms over her head and does a yoga swan dive over to touch her toes. Everything feels tight and cramped. She needs to loosen up and chase away the self-doubt flowing through her mind.

Her computer dings and sure enough the email from Ms. Doucette is already there. She sits back and clicks open the attachment, chewing on her bottom lip as she reads through the assignment. She's to develop an entire package for an upscale new restaurant in New York City—logo, website, menus, catering brochure—and it's due in three days.

Emma's pulse rate spikes.

Three days. Talk about a short deadline. But the assignment gives her the freedom to let her imagination fly free.

So why is she just staring at the screen? Where's the bubbling fizz of excitement that she's had every time she's imagined herself working at Tik Talk? She shuts her eyes, seeing herself striding into the office on the 27th floor of a high rise in mid-town, nodding at the chic women and well-dressed men who share this space with her. Huge blow-ups of successful ad campaigns for everything from high end tequila to a non-profit that gets vaccines to underprivileged nations line the walls. She sits at her computer, loaded with all the best most up-to-date photo and graphics programs and an assistant brings her a cappuccino made just the way she likes it.

Oh, yeah. That feels good. Then, unbidden, she sees herself leaving the office late at night. It's dark, but she can't see any stars. There's too much light pollution. She's taking the train back to Brooklyn where the streets smell of garbage with a touch of raw sewage and she's climbing the three flights of stairs to the apartment that could probably fit into her bedroom here at Three Keys in its entirety.

And it's empty. It's just her. Alone. In the tiny studio. No stars. No scents of lupine and fireweed wafting through an open window. No Katie and Mitch. No Sawyer and Mario.

No Otto and Addie.

She shakes her head and pulls herself back upright, chasing away those dark thoughts. New York might not be where her family is, but that's her home. Where *her* life is. And sure she's part of the family, part of the ranch, but no one's asked her to move to Montana.

Or even hint at it.

She stares at the assignment. Time to get to work. This is not only an opportunity for her dream job, but one she needs to pay bills. Freelance work isn't consistent. Nor does it offer benefits.

She hates the feeling of instability. She grew up with it, never knowing how long she'd get to live in any one place, never being able to predict where she'd be shuffled to next. The opportunity with Tik Talk is the way to go.

Which means she needs to get to work on this assignment. Three days isn't a lot of time to come up with a concept and execute it in all these different formats.

Chapter 24

Otto

Otto looks down at his plate of bacon and eggs. It's the second day in a row that Mitch has cooked breakfast. Otto's gotten accustomed to biscuits and gravy and pancakes and fruit and hash and quiche and all the other dishes Emma seems to whip out effortlessly from the Three Keys kitchen. They've exchanged a couple of texts since they rode out the summer storm in the stables three days ago, but he hasn't laid eyes on her since. Yesterday, the Jetta wasn't parked by Katie's Prius and today she's not at the table, either. He looks over at Mario who's digging in without a problem and then at Sawyer who's eating with slightly less gusto, but still eating, hoping that one of them will ask where Emma is.

No such luck.

Mitch leans back in his chair. "Let me know if I need to order any supplies after y'all check fencing along the south pasture and make sure the irrigation isn't leaking to the west of it."

"We should be good with what we've got." Sawyer picks his fork back up and cleans his plate.

Otto does, too. It may not be what he wants, but it's still going to be a busy day. He needs the fuel. When he steps out onto the porch, Matilda is waiting with her posse. As he continues toward the residents' quarters, she falls into step beside him.

Mario chuckles. "Looks like one of your girlfriends is taking advantage of the other one being M.I.A."

Otto stops to give Matilda a scratch in the spot behind her comb that she particularly likes. "Speaking of which, where is Emma?"

"I would think you'd be more up on her whereabouts than the rest of us." Sawyer looks over his shoulder at Otto. "You could just reach out to her."

He could. He hasn't wanted to push. He doesn't know what to call what's going on between them. Well, he knows what to call some of it and he feels the heat rise to his face thinking about the moments they've shared. He's not sure what they mean, though. Not to him and not to Emma and not to Addie, who came home from the day in town with a lot of questions, including how would she go about getting a sister and could Emma be the one who gave her one. That had been a heck of a conversation and one he'd been completely unprepared for.

But not knowing, not seeing her, is eating at him. So he pulls his phone from his back pocket and texts her.

Everything okay? Missed you at breakfast.

He's already back to the residence when he feels his phone buzz with a response.

Working on a job that came in. Tight deadline.

Right. She freelances at whatever it is she actually does, which he still doesn't totally understand. He knew when he looked at how she'd helped Addie with her dolphin presentation that there was something about where everything was placed and how things worked in relationship to each other that made it easy to understand and nice to look at, but damned if he could explain it.

Apparently Emma could, though.

Need any help?

All good.

See you tomorrow night, then?

There's no answer for a minute or two. But then she responds. *Tomorrow night?*

That stops him in his tracks, literally. He's halfway to the truck and freezes. She forgot? Addie will be crushed if Emma isn't there. *Addie's recital.*

Right. Send me the address. I'll be cramming right up until the last minute.

He texts the address of the auditorium and the time. *I'll save you a seat.*

She sends back an emoji of a face blowing a kiss. He smiles, but still feels uneasy. Before he can put his phone back into his pocket, it buzzes again. He checks, expecting another message from Emma, but instead this one is from Veronica.

Who the hell is Emma?

Uh oh. Addie must have been chattering about her. How to answer? He decides to stick with the facts, but not offer anything else.

Mitch's daughter.

A new message comes through from his ex. *I thought that was Katie.*

His fingers tap the screen of his phone as he clenches his jaw. *It is. He has another daughter. Why?*

Addie is going out for mani/pedis with them instead of spending time with you?

He should have known that all had been too good to be true and would come back to bite him in the ass. *If you'll recall, I didn't have any warning I was going to have her that day and Emma and Katie offered to help by watching her while I worked.*

So you're getting babysitters to spend time with her instead of you.

Otto exhales. Of course she's going to come at him. Nothing he does is ever right in her eyes. But Veronica is not about to win this time. *I'm pretty sure she goes to daycare when you're working. How is this different?*

The three little dots appear and flash for a moment and then disappear. He blows out a breath. Maybe there won't be any trouble from this after all. Then the three dots come back. *We can talk about it when I get back from my business trip next week.*

Otto snorts. *Nothing to talk about.*

We'll see.

Of course Veronica is going to try to find a way to twist this into something to use against him. Damn it all to hell. He shoves his phone back in his pocket and follows Mario and Sawyer out the door.

Chapter 25

EMMA

Her father walks up behind her as Emma stands on one of the dining room chairs looking down at a mass of photos she's printed out and has arranged and rearranged what feels like a million times. She spent most of yesterday taking photos and looking for inspiration. Now she's trying to figure out what to do with it all.

"What's all this?"

"I'm working on a demonstration project as part of my interview for that company I told you about." She chews on her thumbnail and then leans down to move some photos and text blocks around. The final design will be done on the computer in a graphics and layout program, but Emma has always found having the physical pieces to move around helpful when she's starting a project.

"The tick one?" Mitch straightens one of the photos and it takes everything in Emma's being not to slap his hand away.

"Yep. Tik Talk," she says, getting down off the chair.

Mitch puts his arm around her shoulders. "Means a lot to you to impress them."

She leans into him, happy to have his solid bulk by her side. It makes her feel safe. "It does. It would mean a lot to work there. Everyone would know that I'd made it."

"You'd have to go back to New York to work there?"

She nods and feels a strange catch in her chest.

Mitch sighs. "I'll be real sad to see you go, EmmaBear. So will everyone else. You should have seen Otto's face when he came in for breakfast and saw bacon and eggs."

She burrows into him a bit, not wanting to meet his eyes. "This was never supposed to be forever." Hell, when she packed to come here, she wasn't sure if it would be more than a day.

"I know. Plans change, though. I sure didn't plan on having that heart attack. Or having you show up on our doorstep in time to be a big help to us."

Imagine if things had gone a different way, if Mitch had died when he had his heart attack. She would have arrived here and never gotten a chance to know him. She sincerely doubts that Katie would have invited her to stay. Those few short weeks ago when she'd gone skittering down those stairs on her ridiculous sandals. Katie would have sent her packing and they would never have had a chance to get to know each other and to start figuring out what it might be like to have a sister.

She definitely wouldn't have gotten to know Otto. Or Addie.

A little pang hits her. She'd nearly forgotten about promising to go to Addie's dance recital. All thoughts of the little girl had blown out of her head once she started working on this project. Thank God Otto reminded her. It would be tight, but she'd make it. She even set a reminder on her phone.

Mitch smooths his mustache with his free hand. "You know, EmmaBear, there are advertising companies in Billings. They might not be as big and fancy as this tick place, but you could end up being a big fish in a little pond instead of the other way around."

It isn't as if the thought hasn't occurred to her. She's gone as far as to look up what might be available for someone like her in some of the nearby towns. Tik Talk, though. It has been her goal for so long, to accomplish that would mean she's made it, that she's at the top of her game. She has to take a serious run at it.

Being here at Three Keys has been amazing. Finding her family and realizing there's a place for her is more than she thought she'd ever get even at her most wildly optimistic moments. She's happy here. There's no doubt about that.

Happy enough to stay indefinitely?

That's another question all together.

Something inside her still isn't quite satisfied yet and she's pretty sure it has to do with proving to herself and to the world she matters, that she's worth something, that she's enough. All those years of no one really wanting her, of no one really caring about her are about to be knocked down by the bulldozer of her professional success and she can relax and be happy.

At least, she hopes that's what happens.

"Nothing's for certain right now. The competition for this kind of job is fierce and being in their top three or five is no guarantee of anything. I really want to wow them and nothing I've come up with has felt quite special enough yet."

Mitch squeezes her to his side. "You will. It's impressive that you've come this far already. I'm real proud of you, honey." And with that he kisses the top of her head and ambles away, leaving Emma standing with her eyes full of tears and her heart full of love.

His strong arm. The smell of soap and leather. Her father's deep voice saying he's proud. Everything wells up inside her, threatening to burst out. She feels the energy like a physical force, a river of love and care rooted deeply in herself, bursting out and blossoming.

And that's when she gets it. She sees exactly how to lay out this menu and what the logo should look like to create that same kind of feeling in anyone who sees it. Oh, it won't be as strong and they won't know why they react the way they do – unless they're graphic designers, too – but it will work.

She gathers up the photos and blocks of placeholder text and scampers up the stairs to where her laptop waits.

Chapter 26

OTTO

"Daddy, are you sure she's coming?"

Otto has already heard the question three times today. He lets out a breath, smoothing out the wrinkles on her dress. He has no idea if he's doing this right. Nor why his ex left him in charge of such a pivotal moment. Not that he can't handle it.

He kneels down next to her and cocks his head to the side. Taking his index finger, he places it over his lips. His heart flutters, though it isn't because of messing up his daughter's appearance for this recital. It is for a very different reason.

Emma is going to be there tonight. She told him she would be. She's coming to Addie's dance recital. Not for him, but for Addie.

There's a reason he hasn't dated since he got to Absarokee. He has a child and she is his number one focus. Everything he does has to do with building a future for him with Addie. He has a steady job. He's earning money he can put away and save up for a chunk of land of his own where she could live with him as much as or more than she lives with Veronica. He didn't think he could add a woman into the mix. He didn't think someone new could understand his focus on creating that world for Addie and how important that is.

Until Emma.

Maybe it's because she didn't have a dad. Not really. Not until now. But Emma seems to understand what it means to be a father to a little girl and why that has to be the most important thing in his life. She's done what she could to be there for him as he works toward that goal in the short time they've known each other.

"Honey, I told you already," he says, looking up at his daughter. Her big eyes cut him to the core, filled with such cautious hope, he isn't sure what to say to that. "She's coming. Emma wouldn't let you down."

"I know." She twists her fingers, looking away. From his position, kneeling on the floor, he can see the manicure she received with Emma and Katie is barely chipped, which means Addie is doing everything in her power to ensure the paint stays on her fingers for as long as possible. "I just wish she was meeting us here and coming with us so I know for sure."

"She's going to meet us there," he says, standing. "Okay, I think I've adjusted your tights. How do you feel?"

Addie lifts one leg and bends it, then does the same thing with the other. She nods. "Good." She tries to curl her hair behind her ear. "But you have to redo my hair. I can't have one single strand out of place, Daddy. Not. One. Strand."

Otto tilts his head to the side. He wishes Emma was here. He's good at buying outfits, but doing hair? Makeup? He relies a lot on the moms who help their daughters with this sort of thing. Right now, though, it's just him, and he can tell that it means a lot to Addie for tonight to go perfectly.

But Emma isn't here. So, taking a move from her playbook he grabs his phone and launches the YouTube app. He hopes figuring out how to put his daughter's hair up isn't quite as ridiculous as learning to milk a cow from a video. He searches for "how to make a ballerina bun." Of course, there are at least a dozen how-to demonstrations.

"All right, honey," he says, giving his daughter a smile. "Let's do this."

Twenty minutes later, Addie's hair is as perfect as it's going to get. There is one damn bump he can't smooth down no matter what he does, but it will have to do. As long as he positions it in a way where Addie can't tell, it should be fine.

Apparently it is because she looks at herself in the mirror and jumps up and down, clapping her hands. "Spray it into place, Daddy! Then let's start on the makeup. Mademoiselle Chevelle says that we have to wear makeup so the people in the blood seats can see our faces."

Otto's eyebrows climb halfway up his forehead. "Blood seats?"

Addie shoves the makeup back at him. "Yes. Blood seats. You know, the ones that are really far away so it's hard to see."

Nosebleed seats.

He's also fairly certain the tiny auditorium where the recital is taking place doesn't have anything remotely close to a nosebleed seat, but far be it from him to argue with the wisdom of Mademoiselle Chevelle. "Okay, then. What do we have here?"

Addie pulls out a bag full of makeup from her backpack while Otto looks up more tutorials on his phone.

Another twenty minutes and several YouTube videos later, his daughter has on way more foundation, eyeshadow, mascara, blush, and lipstick than he thinks he'd let her out the door wearing when she's sixteen, but she's ready to go. Nervous and bouncing up and down on the balls of her feet, but ready. He reaches out and squeezes her shoulder. "Anything else I can do for you, baby doll?"

He doesn't want to admit it, but he's nervous too.

"Should we take a picture for Mom?" Addie asks, turning to her father.

"I would say yes." He holds up his phone and takes a quick snap of Addie, hoping the messed-up part of her hair isn't in the picture. Lord knows, Veronica is looking for anything Otto does wrong so she can call him out on it. Her lawyer already called his lawyer with questions about Emma and Katie and Addie's trip to the nail salon with them. He doesn't want to give her the opportunity to complain about one. Single. Strand.

"All right," he says when he finishes sending the picture. "Is there anything else?"

Addie shakes her head. "I think I'm set."

He pulls a shoebox out from under his bed and hands it to Addie. "Maybe one more thing. We don't want to get your slippers scuffed up walking to and from the truck."

She opens it and pulls out the pair of purple Chucks and clutches them to her chest. "For me?"

"Yep. Happened to see them in the store the other day and thought you might want them." That was a lie. He'd ordered them the day he'd listened to her and Emma talking about shoes and about how they were about more than covering your feet. He wasn't sure he understood what they meant, but he understood what he should do about it.

    Addie throws her arms around his neck and kisses his cheek. "Thank you, Daddy. These are perfect."

    "Just like you, pumpkin." He helps her get the shoes on her feet and laces them up. Then he stands and takes her hand. "Let's do this."

Chapter 27

EMMA

The seconds feel like hours, but Emma pushes on. She's so close to finishing up this project. She needs to have it done by six, and after unraveling a problem she hadn't expected a couple of hours ago, she can finally finish the design itself.

She blinks once, twice, before pinching the bridge of her nose and letting out a sigh. Every part of her body is filled with knots she can't unravel. A small, niggling thing in her brain tells her that she's forgetting something, but for the life of her, she has no idea what that is. She even stops mid-design in order to go over everything one more time, to make sure she hasn't missed anything.

It turns out she hasn't. That took forty-five minutes she doesn't have to spare, which means that ten-minute break she wanted to take to rest her eyes is subsequently erased.

She tilts her head to the right, stretching out her neck, before doing the same thing to the left. She's almost done. She has to keep going. No matter what, she has to keep going.

The alarm on her phone goes off, reminding her that it's time to get ready for Addie's dance recital. She will. She just needs five more minutes. Ten at the most. Okay. Maybe fifteen.

The second Emma submits her project, she starts to laugh. Running fingers through her hair, she stands up. Her back protests, groaning and grunting. She forces the stretch, blinking her eyes as she takes in the dim office.

She made it.

It took up until the last second, but she turned the project in on time.

Now, all she can do at this point is wait.

She glances at the time. There's no way she's going to make it to the recital to see it from the start, but she'll be there in time to see Addie dance. She rips off her yoga pants and pulls on a pair of capris and a short-sleeved cold shoulder top and rushes out the door. She can brush her hair and smear on some makeup as she drives.

She bounces into the Jetta, sticks the key into the ignition and turns it, and nothing happens. There's a clicking noise, but the engine doesn't start.

She tries again.

Still nothing.

She gets out of the Jetta and lets loose a string of swear words that turn the air around her blue. If she doesn't leave right this second, she'll miss seeing Addie dance.

"Whoa, there!" Katie says, coming out onto the porch. "Did a group of sailors land on Three Keys with the express purpose of having a swear-off?"

Emma whirls. "I'm late. It's Addie's recital. The stupid car won't start. I don't know if I can get there in time." She kicks the Jetta for good measure.

Katie's eyes go wide. "Addie's recital? Tonight? You're late for it?"

Emma nods, feeling tears start to well up in her eyes. She can't miss this. She can't let her down. Emma knows all too well what it feels like to be the little girl searching the crowd for a friendly face.

"Stay there. I'll get my keys."

Five minutes later, they're careening down the highway toward town in Katie's Prius.

"What time does the recital start?" Katie asks.

"Seven."

Katie frowns. "Even if the Jetta had started, you'd still be running late."

Emma flips open the vanity mirror on the underside of the sunshade on the passenger side. "I had this deadline. I thought I could get it done in time, but things kept going wrong." She fishes a lipstick out of her purse and applies it.

"You put the deadline before getting to Addie's recital on time?"

Emma opens her mouth to explain how important the job is to her but instead lets out a ragged sigh instead. Katie's right. She had put her job before Addie's feelings, which means she didn't consider Addie or, to a degree, Otto as important as her work.

Which was part of the problem with New York. If you don't operate on that level, you're going to get trampled. "Maybe I'm not cut out for this. Addie isn't even my kid."

"Is this about our mom?" Katie asks, speeding up to pass a slow-moving pickup truck.

Emma doesn't respond.

She never thought about having kids before. Not really. But maybe she isn't ready for the responsibility of taking care of someone, of having a person depend on her. It's intimidating.

Her own mother couldn't handle being a mom. If Emma isn't worth that love as a daughter, how can she give it to someone who doesn't belong to her in that same way? Look at all the different foster homes she lived in over the years. Not one of those families loved her the way they loved their own kids. Not one of them wanted to adopt her.

Katie clears her throat and says, "I don't want to overstep, but what happened with our mom hurt all of us. We've all got scars from it. It hurts like hell to break up scar tissue. You have to do it, though. Otherwise, it can paralyze you from the inside out."

Emma doesn't feel paralyzed.

She feels like she's spent her whole life running, moving forward as fast as she can to get to a place where she doesn't have to rely on anyone. Then she came here. It had only been a matter of wanting a few questions answered, but she's gotten so much more.

She's learned to value and appreciate the stillness of a Montana morning and to stop to literally smell the flowers. She's learned that making a meal for people is more than securing a place in a house or getting sustenance and that sharing that work with someone else, even in silence, can create communion between two people. She's learned that listening to someone can mean so much more than talking to—or worse at—them.

The time she's spent at Three Keys Ranch has shown her that there are other ways to live than the one she's ascribed to all these years. She's so close to realizing those goals, though. She just needs to run a bit more and she'll be there. Is this really the time to slow down?

Chapter 28

OTTO

Otto shuffles down the row to one of the few places that ill has two seats together. He didn't expect the auditorium to be full this early. Then again, all the other parents had to get their kid here early just like him. The difference being most came with a partner, one who could be backstage while the other secured a seat. He, however, is on his own. He checks the door. No sign of Emma yet. Maybe he should text her. Make sure she remembers. It had sounded like she'd forgotten when they'd texted on Thursday. She wouldn't forget again, would she?

He hates to admit it, but he's nearly as excited about her being here as Addie is. He won't have to be alone anymore. He'll have someone else to share in the joy of what an incredible kid Addie is. He'll be one of the people in a set of two.

No. That's not right.

He'll be part of a set of three.

Be making a family for himself and for Addie. And for Emma. Maybe it would be what would erase that last little bit of sadness from her eyes.

"Excuse me, is someone sitting there?"

Otto looks up. Oh, great. Gracie, the predatory redhead from the Girl Scouts meeting. "I'm saving it for someone."

Gracie's eyes narrow. "Seriously? You're so repulsed by me that you're going to pretend someone's coming so I don't sit next to you?" She shakes her head. "I just need a place to sit. I'm not trying to stalk you. Conceited much?"

His cheeks start to heat. "I didn't think you were stalking me. I'm saving this spot for someone."

Gracie checks her watch. "Well, your someone is late. The show's supposed to start in three minutes."

Otto glances behind himself at the door. Still no Emma.

He turns back to see Veronica coming up behind Gracie and tapping her on the shoulder. "Excuse me, Gracie. I'm trying to get to my seat."

Gracie's puffed up lips part and she looks back and forth between Otto and Veronica, a calculating expression on her face. "I'm sorry, Veronica. I didn't realize."

Veronica smiles, although it looks a little bit more like a baring of teeth to Otto. There's definitely no warmth in it. "Well, now you do. So if you would be so kind as to move and let me sit down before the show starts, I'd sure appreciate it."

Gracie shuffles away and Veronica sits down, chuckling and rolling her eyes. "I swear that woman would hit on a Billy goat. I've never seen anyone so man-crazy in all my days."

Otto stares at Veronica, speechless for a moment. "I thought you were in Los Angeles for work."

She shrugs, pushing back her blonde hair and smiling at him. "The meeting ended early and I was able to switch my flight. I wasn't sure I would make it here in time so I didn't say anything. I didn't want to disappoint Addie. It all worked out, though. It'll be a fun surprise to her that we're here together."

The lights began to dim and Otto doesn't get a chance to say anything about saving the seat for Emma before the first set of little girls wearing way too much makeup skip out onto the stage. He checks his phone one last time before shutting it off.

There's nothing from Emma.

She's not here. Maybe having her mom here will keep Addie from being too disappointed. It isn't doing anything for Otto, though.

Chapter 29

EMMA

Thank God the Absarokee Auditorium didn't operate by Broadway rules. The doors didn't lock once the performance began. Emma slips in, careful to let in as little light as possible. There's already a group of eight little girls prancing around on the stage.

None of them Addie.

Emma's only five minutes late. She glances at her phone. No. Ten minutes late. Katie drove like they were being chased by the hounds of hell. If she'd driven herself it would have been way worse. Most likely ending with the car being back in that ditch Otto pulled her out of when she first arrived.

She opens her program and squints in the dim light. She exhales, her shoulders drooping as the tension dissipates from her body. Addie's group is the one after this one.

The group on stage finishes and performs their curtsies and the lights come up a little so they can make their way off stage. She stands on her tiptoes and cranes her neck, trying to find Otto.

She spots the back of his head, about seven rows from the front and toward the middle. Her heart sinks. No way can she make her way there without causing a bit of a ruckus. Plus, there's no seat open next to him. Hadn't he said he'd save one for her?

Emma sighs and makes her way to an open seat by the aisle close to the wall about two rows back from Otto. The lights dim again just as she sits in the empty seat and the next group files out with Addie right in the center.

A smile spreads across her face as her eyes fall on Addie who stands straight and tall, and then begins to move with the same easy grace Otto uses as he goes about his chores. She's only six, but there's an awareness of herself and the space around her that already sets her apart from the other children.

Emma's heart swells with pride even if she doesn't have a right to it. She's only been in Addie's life for a short time, but she can't help it.

She glances over to Otto in time to see the blonde sitting next to him pick up Otto's hand and plant a kiss on the knuckles. The smile fades from Emma's face and is replaced by numbness. Otto extricates his hand and very deliberately puts the woman's hand back in her own lap. The blonde whispers something to him and his only response is a little headshake. Emma shrinks into her chair. Maybe she should go.

No.

She promised Addie she'd be here and Emma wants her to know she kept her promise. She'll stay, but she finds it hard to focus on Addie and not on Otto and the woman sitting next to him.

It's none of her business. Not really. He should be looking for someone else. She's going back to New York to where her real life is. Still somehow it hurts he's replacing her before she even leaves.

Chapter 30

OTTO

The lights come up and everyone starts gathering up their things. There is the usual slow rush as people move into the aisle single file. Otto turns on his phone, hoping to find a message from Emma.

Nothing.

"You did a great job on Addie's hair and on her costume," Veronica says as they wait their turn.

He eyes her suspiciously. She hasn't been one to give out compliments on his parenting. And what was with trying to hold his hand? "Watched some YouTube videos."

Veronica cocks her head. "Good thinking. Resourceful."

He frowns. What is going on here? They're finally moving into the aisle and out into the lobby area to meet Addie. It's a crush of bodies, but then the doors from the backstage area swing open and the girls stream out like rockets. He spots Addie instantly. Her eyes go wide and she's running toward them and right past Otto to wrap her arms around Veronica's legs. "Mama! You made it! I thought you said you couldn't."

Veronica crouches down to hug Addie back. "I figured out a way to get back early and came straight here."

Addie looks around behind her. "Where's Lars?"

Veronica's lips tighten. "He's not here. I don't think we'll be seeing too much more of him."

Ah.

Now it makes sense. Veronica and Lars must have broken up. Or at least hit a rough patch. Otto's not certain he wants to be some kind of consolation prize, even if it would mean putting his marriage back together and ending all the back and forth over Addie.

"Oh, hey, Emma!" Addie says, her tone surprisingly casual. Kind of the same tone Veronica used when she asked Gracie to get out of her way. Complete with the icy chill.

Otto turns around. Emm's hair is a little crazy and her lipstick is a little smeared, but she's here. His heart leaps at the sight of her. She didn't forget. She didn't blow them off. On the other hand, she also didn't get here in time to sit with him. He takes a tentative step toward her. "When'd you get here?"

"I was late," she says.

He wants to ask why, to find out what happened, hoping it's something entirely out of her control like maybe a giant sinkhole swallowing up the road into town, but Emma's already turning toward Veronica. "Hi. I'm Emma."

Veronica hesitates a second and then takes Emma's proffered hand. "Nice to meet you. I'm Veronica, Addie's mother. Nice of you to come to a recital for one of your employee's kids." It would be hard to miss the sarcasm dripping off Veronica's words and Emma's not one to miss much. She blanches a little.

Otto rubs the back of his neck as his ex-wife eyes him also clearly wanting some kind of explanation.

Addie grabs Veronica's hand as soon as she releases Emma and then grabs Otto's hand with her other hand so she's suspended between her parents like a little bridge. "Look, Emma. Both my mommy and daddy were here for my recital. They even sat together."

Is there a little dig there in his baby girl's words?

"They must be super proud. You were amazing up there. Definitely the best one." Emma smiles down at Addie, but her lower lip trembles a little. "I'm sorry I was late."

"That's okay," Addie says. "You did your best."

Ouch. Otto definitely recognizes that tone. Veronica's used it more than once on him when he's come up short on something. It says that while you might have done your best, it's still not quite good enough.

"Glad you made it," Otto says, trying to take the sting out of it.

"Of course," Emma avoids his gaze.

Addie tugs at his sleeve. "Can we get ice cream?"

Before Otto can say a word, Veronica says, "Absolutely. Want to go to the Pink Pony?"

Addie jumps up and down and claps her hands. "Yes! Please, Daddy? Please? Can I have unicorn bark?"

He laughs and rests a hand on his daughter's shoulder. "Yes. Pink Pony Ice Cream with unicorn bark."

Veronica turns to Emma. "Nice to meet you, Emma." Then she takes Addie's hand and sails toward the door.

Otto gives Emma an apologetic shrug, not sure what else to do. Once again, he's being pulled in two directions at once. His priority is Addie. If having him and Veronica eat Unicorn Bark on overpriced soft-serve makes his daughter happy, then he will do that.

But doesn't he deserve some happy?

Veronica is being nice to him now, but how long will that last? Will he ever be able to trust her again? Would he ever find the same joy he's found with Emma with Veronica? All those are questions for tomorrow. Addie has to come first right now. It's her night.

"I should go," he says to Emma.

"I'm really sorry about being late." She pauses for a moment, then looks him in the eye, brows furrowed. "I thought Veronica couldn't make it."

"She got an early flight back. I wasn't expecting her either."

"Daddy!" Addie's voice pierces through the crowd.

"Go." Emma offers him a weak smile. "I'll see you back at Three Keys."

He swallows past the lump in his throat and turns to head over to his daughter. His steps are sluggish, his chest tight. If only Emma had shown up on time. But what would've happened if she had when Veronica showed up?

Maybe it all worked out for the best.

Ten minutes later he is standing in the crowded ice cream parlor. Seems like everyone went to the Pink Pony to celebrate. The place is packed with little girls in leotards and proud moms and dads. They walk in and Addie runs off toward her friends.

"I'm pretty sure I know what she wants." He gets in line to order. "Why don't you find us a spot to sit?"

A few minutes later, he hands Addie her unicorn-bark covered ice cream and then finds Veronica and hands her a cup of ice cream. "Addie'll be over in a second. I told her it was okay to hang with her friends a bit."

"That's good. Gives us a moment to discuss us." Veronica swirls her spoon through the chocolate ice cream.

Otto's insides freeze up and not from the ice cream. He didn't think there was still an 'us' to discuss.

Veronica sets down her spoon and twirls a strand of hair around her index finger. "I think we need to give this one more try. You've made such improvements on your relationship with Addison that we owe it to ourselves to see if this could work."

He tenses.

His ex-wife reaches across the table to take his hands. "I think we should get back together."

Otto pulls his hands away and snorts. Is this some kind of joke? After so many years have gone by with him trying to do the right thing, to keep his family together, after so many years of her saying no, of her insisting it was impossible, she's finally changing her mind? She's finally saying yes? Now? When he's finally settling into this new life?

Veronica continues, seemingly oblivious to his distress. "I'm serious. I've seen how much you've grown. I see the effort you put into being part of Addie's life. You've changed so much. You're exactly the man I've always wanted you to be."

Otto furrows his brow. That might have sounded good to him a while ago. But now, it sounds like he's some sort of project that she's handling, like she's trying to turn him into what she wants rather than accepting—or appreciating—him for who he is. He tries to imagine it, to create a mental image of the three of them as a family again. Sharing a home with the two of them. Sharing a bed with Veronica. Just thinking about it makes his heart sink. It's not what he wants. Not anymore. "I'm not different. I'm who I've always been."

Veronica's lips tighten, a sure sign of trouble. She clearly expects him to be jumping with joy or immediately inviting her to move in with him.

He watches the emotions playing over her face. Frustration. Anger. Realization that she won't get what she wants that way. Finally, a forced equanimity. "I think we should at least talk about it."

"Sure, we can talk. But not now. Tonight is supposed to be about Addie." Not that what she has to say matters because he knows what he wants. He wants Emma.

And nothing Veronica can say will change that.

Chapter 31

EMMA

The alarm goes off and Emma drags herself out of bed. While she may want to pull the blankets up over her head, she knows her dad is counting on her. She already dumped food prep on him rather unceremoniously for the past couple of days and she has no excuse today.

Except for avoiding Otto.

Watching him, Addie, and his ex-wife walk out of the auditorium holding hands like a little family without so much as a backwards glance stung. Then she had no way home and had to call her sister to come back, spending another half an hour cooling her heels in front of Absarokee Auditorium as all the other families strolled out, reminding her how out of place she was. She's not a part of a family. She's on the outside looking in. Like always.

Just another sign she doesn't belong out here.

Emma drags herself down the stairs, holding her head so it doesn't move too much. Drinking with her sister when they'd gotten back to the ranch was a bad idea, but Katie had been adamant that tequila was the best way through this. She'd pulled a bottle out from a bottom cabinet and started pouring. It hadn't seemed like a bad idea at the time to Emma either, still smarting from the way Otto and Addie had turned their backs on her. Now, however, she's not sure how she's going to get through the day with a killer hangover.

With any luck, a big ass cup of caffeine will help.

She gets the coffee going and starts putting together what she needs for huevos rancheros. Beans, salsa, cheese, tortillas, salsa. She pulls it all from the refrigerator. The coffeepot dings and she pours herself a huge mug, dosing it up with plenty of milk and sugar. While she drinks it, she opens her email. Her heart does a stutter stop. At the very top is one from Ms. Doucette.

With a trembling finger, she taps the icon to open the email. The first line is "Congratulations."

She drops the phone and her hands go over her mouth. She did it. She got the job at Tik Talk. And she did it all on her own.

Everything she'd done her whole life led her to this point. All the hard work and drive. It's a sign. New York is exactly where she belongs, not Montana. She's thrilled she has a family now, but she made it this far without them. She has a plan and working at Tik Talk is the next step in it. She breathes it in. She's got a great job in a great city doing something she loves. She's incredibly grateful to have found her father and her sister, but this is a visit. Not a relocation. She's gotten way more than she dreamed was possible when she hired Ray to find her dad, but that box has been checked off on her to-do list and it's time to go home and get back to her real life, her real self.

She slams down the rest of the coffee and reads the rest of the email, scanning for important information. Start date is in a little over a weeks' time.

Well, looks like her time in Montana is coming to an end quickly.

The back door opens and Otto strolls inside with Addie. Emma's stomach flips, maybe from the alcohol or maybe from the image that flashes to the front of her mind from last night. Otto and Veronica walking away from her, each holding one of Addie's hands, a perfect little trio, a family. Maybe Addie will get that sister she wants, after all. Sure. It hurts. Otto is different than any man she's ever dated. Strong and dedicated with his priorities firmly in place. Regardless of how she feels, Emma won't get in the way if

Otto wants to reconcile with his ex-wife. Not when it would be in Addison's best interests.

"Hi, Emma," Addison says as she trudges past her and into the dining room, scratching her little bottom as she goes.

Emma shakes her head. "She looks more like she stayed up half the night doing tequila shots with Katie than I do." Then she turns back to the stove, ladling the beans into a bowl before handing them to Otto. "Would you take these to the table on your way?"

"Sure."

When he hesitates, she shoots him a perfunctory smile before turning back to the stove to flip some tortillas. This isn't the time for discussion, not that there's anything to say. She's leaving. He's staying. Possibly with his ex-wife.

Mario and Sawyer come in a moment later, and before long everyone is at the dining room table, the bowls of beans and eggs and cheese and salsa and sour cream making the rounds. When everyone's plates are full, Emma stands up and raises her glass of orange juice. No time like the present to fill everyone in. "I have an announcement to make."

Her father puts his fork down with an audible crack. Mario's head swivels between her and Otto as if he's watching a tennis match.

She takes a deep breath, almost hesitating. Should she tell her father first? In private? But she swallows and pushes the thought away, knowing if she did he'd only try to convince her to stay. "I've mentioned to several of you I had been working on a project for my dream job back in New York City. I found out this morning that I made it." Emma's face heats at the chorus of applause that fills the room.

Even Mario whistles and stands. She turns to her father and her chest squeezes. While he is smiling and clapping, his joy doesn't reach his eyes. Yeah, it's a bittersweet moment. She places a hand on his shoulder. "Just because I'm leaving, doesn't mean I won't be back to visit. That is, if you want me to."

Her father stands and wraps her in a big, giant hug. "I wouldn't have it any other way."

"When are you heading out?" Katie asks.

She pulls away from the hug and tucks a stray hair behind her ear. "A few days. They want me to start in a little over a week."

"Is that why you were late to my recital?" Addie asks.

Emma looks down at her plate. "I'm afraid it was. I needed to send off my project before I went into town and it took a little longer than I expected."

Sawyer takes a swig of juice and sets his glass down with a thunk. "Congrats. Last time someone in my family stood up to make an announcement, it was that they were expecting a baby."

Emma's eyes go wide and her father lets out a string of coughs as he punches the center of his chest. "Sawyer, what kinda drama you wishing on this family?"

Addie looks over to Otto. "How would Emma get pregnant? She's not married. You said people had to be married to be pregnant."

The room gets very quiet. Emma bites back a laugh. It must have been what Otto had told Addie when she asked him for a sister. What she wouldn't give to have been a fly on the wall during that conversation. She'd bet money he threw marriage into the mix to circumvent the conversation. Then again, how much information was appropriate to tell such a young child?

Though there were many ways for people to have children. Including adoption. Surely that would be okay for a kid to know.

"We'll talk about it later." Otto reaches across to Addie's plate and cuts up her food into small enough pieces.

"Do you think you and Mommy will give me a baby sister? So I can be like Katie and Emma." The little girl looks across the table to both Emma and Katie. "Mommy asked last night to be a family again."

If Emma thought her announcement was a big deal, Addison certainly topped her. Though, not in a good way it seems. Otto is ghost white, well, actually turning green. Mario looks like he might murder his friend. Sawyer throws down his utensils, cursing at the ceiling. And John stabs his food as if it's some evil entity.

Emma looks over to her sister, who offers a sympathetic smile. Well, guess the universe wants to make sure she gets the message about where she belongs.

Her father lifts his mug of coffee as she sits back down into her seat. "To Emma. We wish you the best of luck."

"To Emma," everyone but Otto echoes.

He just sits there staring at his plate. His face is blank. Neutral.

But it no longer matters. She's heading home to where she belongs.

Chapter 32

Otto

Otto fights not to run out in the middle of breakfast. Both Emma and his daughter seem determined to destroy him from the inside out. One announcing she is up and leaving, and the other throwing out false information. He grinds his molars. It isn't his daughter's fault. That's all on his ex-wife who shoulda kept her mouth shut in front of their daughter.

Then again, he didn't make the situation any better. Not when she kissed his hand, not when they ran into Emma after the recital, and not when Veronica broached the topic of them getting back together. No, he remained silent, saying he'd think about it.

More so because if he opened his mouth, a shitload of anger would have come flooding out. He didn't want nor need Addison to witness that.

But now here he is standing in the gravel driveway, watching as Veronica drives away with his daughter, knowing only a few meters away the woman he wants has also bailed on him. Only Emma isn't going to leave without him saying his piece first.

So, he turns on his heels and makes his way to the main house, entering the kitchen through the screen door.

Mitch and Linda are sitting at the table, a complicated chart between them. Linda leans back in her chair. "So that's why I think you're better off waiting to bring some new blood into the herd. Not long. Just be patient for a few months."

Both look over at him and Otto rotates his hat in his hand, feeling ridiculously like he's picking up his prom date and her father might have a shotgun in a nearby closet. "I was hoping to speak to Emma."

"Upstairs." Mitch points toward the hallway and then turns back to Linda. "I see your point, but I'm worried if we wait we're going to miss some opportunities."

Otto leaves them to their discussion and makes his way up the stairs to Emma's room only to find Katie and Nickel are with her. His gut twists at the sight of the open suitcase on the bed. He closes his eyes and takes a deep breath then knocks on the door jamb, praying she'll hear him out.

He opens his eyes just as Emma glances at him and then back at the pile of clothing she's folding and fitting into her suitcase. "Hi, Otto."

"Hi." He remains still, not quite sure what to do.

Katie stretches and stands from the bed. "Look at the time. John was expecting me back a half an hour ago." She gives Emma a hug and heads toward the door. "See you tomorrow, Emma."

Emma shakes her head. "You are not as slick as you think you are."

"I'm as slick as I need to be." Katie turns to Otto and lowers her voice. "Good luck."

Once she's gone, Otto walks into the room, looking for a place to sit. The bed seems ... presumptuous, but there are clothes stacked on the desk chair. So he leans against the wall, hat still turning clockwise in his hands. "Quite an announcement this morning."

She remains quiet, avoiding looking in his direction.

"Can't believe you took the job without talking to me about it." The hat in his hands stills, his finger wringing the brim.

"Was I supposed to ask for your permission?" Emma's tone is light, almost teasing, but when she looks up he can see the anger flashing in her eyes.

Fucking hell.

He hadn't meant it like that. He shakes his head. "I just thought . . . I thought that there was something between us . . . something more than . . ."

"More than sex?" She folds another t-shirt and shoves it into her suitcase. It's not nearly as neatly folded as the other ones.

"Well, yes. More than sex." Even that first time, in an abandoned parking lot, it had been about more than sex. He might not have realized it then, but he knows it now.

Emma rolls up a pair of jeans and jams them into the case. "Otto, it doesn't matter. Not after what Addie said."

Every muscle in his body goes rigid. Like hell would he let Emma leave believing that. "Addison is wrong. Yes, Veronica mentioned it. But it's not what I want." His blood is beginning to boil.

She throws down whatever clothing she has in her hands and crosses her arms. "Let me ask you then. Did you tell your ex-wife you weren't interested?"

His mouth opens, but no words come out. He sighs, shoulders slumping forward. "No."

He'd wanted to avoid a fight in the middle of the ice cream parlor, and in front of his daughter. Addison had witnessed enough.

Emma rolls her eyes. "Exactly."

Otto runs a hand over his face. This is not how he planned this. "Look, Emma—"

She holds up a hand. "Otto, please stop. What we had was casual. That was our deal from the start. You knew I was leaving. I never made promises to stay. You even knew I was applying for this job."

"Yet you got close to Addie." His fingers clench and unclench into fists at his side. "Did you not think leaving would hurt her?

Emma huffs as she shoves a pair of balled up yoga pants into the suitcase. "I have no intention of hurting Addie. Or you." Finally, she stops, blowing her bangs off her forehead in exasperation. "I came here for a visit and to meet my family. I never intended for what was going on between you and me to get serious. I made that clear from the start. Addie's a great kid and I was happy to help out with her and happy to get to know her, but I need to get back to my life, to where I belong. Addie will be fine. Trust me. Kids are resilient. They can bounce back from all kinds of stuff. Believe me. I know."

Like fucking hell.

He stalks over to the other side of the bed, the mattress between them. "You think where you belong is back in New York City, thousands of miles from your family? You're wrong. I've seen you out here. I've seen the way you look out over the land and up at the sky. I've seen you with your dad and Katie. Your life isn't back there. It's here."

When she opens her mouth to speak, he cuts her off. "And you're wrong about kids bouncing back. I can see that looking at you. Not having a family you could rely on growing up has skewed your whole way of looking at the world."

Tears gather at the corner of her eyes and Otto's throat closes. He hit below the belt on that one. So, he walks out the door, not trusting himself to say anything more. Not wanting to hurt her. Not wanting to put his heart out there. Because she's already made her choice.

And it is not him.

Chapter 33

EMMA

The strange thing about being back in New York is that it's like Emma hasn't even missed it while she was gone, and that scares her more than she's willing to admit. New York has been her home, a place she chose to make a life for herself. Returning here should be emotional. She should be relieved. Instead, she's drifting through life like a leaf in the wind.

Her alarm clock blares and she quickly shuts it off. She's already up, staring at the ceiling, listening to the cars honking and the people yelling. It used to sound like a symphony. Now it jangles her nerves. Was coming back the right choice?

It has to be.

This is her dream job with her dream company in her dream city. No recalcitrant dogs or stubborn cows or jealous chickens. Everything lines up here. Everything is better here. This is her happy place.

Except, it isn't.

She'd gone to Montana to find out who her father was and get a little information. She'd gotten so much more. Being with her family had filled a hole in her heart whose existence she had only guessed at. Not to mention those moments together when she felt as though she had been accepted and loved and welcomed, that she was part of something bigger than herself, something that meant more.

And then there's Otto. She tries not to think about Otto because missing him is the part that hurts the most. She wishes him the best. She truly does.

She just wishes the thought of him reconciling with Veronica and being a family with her and Addie didn't make her want to curl up in a little ball and cry. During their last conversation in Montana, she'd told him what they'd had was casual. Even as she'd said it, she'd known she was lying. She loves him. She loves his quiet strength, his gentle sweetness, his dedication.

It doesn't matter.

Not if he has a chance to put his family back together. She knows what finding family has meant to her. She's not going to do anything to take that away from anyone else.

Ever.

She thought work would be a good distraction, that it would bring in a new sense of purpose. She'd been excited to work with a team of people who were at the top of their profession. They're great. No doubt about that. Emma even is on top of her game with the contributions she's made to the team, too. She knows they're pushing her to do some of her best work ever.

But when she looks at everything, it doesn't give her anywhere the satisfaction she felt when she heard the milk hitting the pail the first time she milked Clara or when the whole table would fall silent when she put dinner out or when her father put his arm around her and told her he was proud of her.

She is part of a team at Tik Talk.

But back in Montana, she was part of a family.

Katie and her father aren't the only people she thinks of as family. She loves Otto. It wasn't a mere infatuation. It wasn't only a fling. It wasn't just sex.

One more reason for her stay away, though. Loving someone means wanting what's best for them. Otto has the opportunity to put his family back together and who is she to stand in the way of that?

She pads across the cold floor to her fridge, pulling out milk before turning to the small pantry and grabbing a box of cereal. The flakes tinkle as they hit the glass bowl, and she sighs. She shouldn't be this depressed. She shouldn't be sighing into a bowl of cereal. She should be brimming with happiness, with excitement, with joy to the point where she should be singing her thoughts.

But she can't even bring a smile to her face.

She pours the milk in her cereal, replaces the milk in the fridge, and eats in silence. She misses Katie's chattering, misses the snap of the newspaper her father reads, Linda's soft warm voice, and Sawyer's sarcasm. She even misses the way Mario clowns around all the time. She misses the sound of the rooster in the morning and the sound of silence at night.

After she finishes her breakfast, she stands up and takes the bowl to the sink. She doesn't mind doing her own dishes, but she misses talking to Mario and Sawyer while she works. She misses talking to her father and Linda.

She misses that big, blue sky.

"But, you made your choice," she says out loud, running the sponge over the bowl. "You came back here. You said your life was here. You said your happiness was here."

Emma will not indulge herself in any more tears. She's cried plenty already.

And of course the day doesn't get any better. Work should've pulled her out of this funk, distracted her enough. But no such luck. Instead of concentrating on the meeting she's in, she's daydreaming about being on horseback looking out over the Montana hills, breathing in the scents of lupine and Indian paintbrush.

So when her boss calls her name she snaps back to reality where she's sitting in a conference room and everyone is staring at her, especially her boss Marcy whose eyebrows are raised so high they're practically in her hairline.

She clears her throat, heat crawling up from her neck to her cheeks. "I'm sorry. Could you repeat the question?"

Marcy clicks the back of her teeth with her tongue. "Em, I know you're still settling in, but I need your focus or else we're going to fall behind. We already had to push the deadline back. We can't do that again. Now, can you give me estimates on a timeline based on the plan from a week and a half ago?"

Emma recites numbers like she recites her name. Marcy seems to approve. Emma had expected to be thrilled to work on the launch of a celebrity-fronted cosmetic line. The budget is huge. There are a dozen products to create labels and ads for. Somehow, it's left her cold. Hell, she'd been way more passionate helping Addie make her dolphin presentation.

Who is she kidding? Montana's to blame for all this. Damn its big blue skies. And damn her for missing the opportunity to be brave, to tell Otto what she feels. Why had she kept her mouth shut?

Oh, that's right. Because he threw her past into her face and then walked out. He'd made it clear he thought that growing up in the foster care system had made her damaged goods and then he'd left.

Last thing she wanted to do was chase after him, outing all their business to everyone, outing her heart to everyone. Not like most of them didn't already know she and Otto had a thing. But what if her father had found out? She didn't want to risk Otto losing his job, possibly losing Addie. So, she bottled up her feelings and left.

Now she has just about everything she's ever wanted, including a family. And a tiny box of an apartment within the boundaries of this concrete jungle, building walls around her. Along with a lease that doesn't allow pets. No time for a social life either based on her schedule these past two weeks. Late nights at the office followed by travel time meant the only extra time she had was for eating, bathing, and sleeping.

Deep down, her heart isn't in New York anymore. Or in this job. She'd thought it was what she needed to achieve to prove herself worthy, but worthy of what? Of love? Her family loves her and it has nothing to do with where she works or how much money she makes. They'd come to love her for her. They appreciate the way she works hard and doesn't let failure derail her or stop her. They know she can fall in chicken shit a dozen times and each time she'll get up, brush herself off, and try again.

Her whole life, she's been fighting for her place in the world. In Montana, she didn't have to fight. She just had to be herself and it all came together. She'd thought she'd gotten everything she needed from that place when she'd gotten on the plane to come back to New York, but it had changed her more than she had realized.

New York is supposed to be her happy place, but it isn't anymore. If she stays here, she'll be miserable. All the things she thought she needed to be happy feel unimportant and insignificant.

Things are different now.

She needs her family. She needs the peaceful silence of a Montana night and the glory of a Montana sunrise. She needs be part of something more. She needs to have a family. She needs to tell Otto how she feels. She won't try to take him away from Veronica and certainly never from Addie, but she has to be sure he has all the facts before he makes up his mind. He has to know that she loves him.

So, without warning, she stands up, pressing her fingers into the surface of the table, Marcy stops in the middle of her sentence and tilts her head to the side. "Emma? Is everything okay?"

Emma clears her throat. It has gone dry, especially since all of her colleagues now stare at her. "I have to go."

"You…what? What do you mean, you have to go? Are you ill?"

Emma grabs her folder and heads for the door, turning to look over her shoulder. "I'm sorry." They'll fill the position in a heartbeat. Anyone would be thrilled to work at Tik Talk. Well, anybody whose heart isn't back in Montana.

She has to face something else about her heart. It isn't just Montana that's her dream. It's Otto. Otto and Addie. That last little piece of emptiness she thought would be filled up by her job is still there and it's his. It may be too late. He may have moved on. But she at least has to tell him how she feels.

Emma steps out of the conference room and breaks into a run. She has to get to the airport. She has to get back to Montana. This isn't her dream job or her dream city. Not anymore.

The moment the elevator doors open to the main floor, she all but runs out of the building, thrusting her hand up into the sky and calling for a taxi. Time takes on a new meaning because it seems to be moving fast and slow at the same time.

"Where to?" the driver asks as she hops into the back.

"JFK."

As he pulls away from the curb, Emma rests her forehead on the cool glass window. She scans the scenery outside, the tall buildings, the people on the streets. No patches of green. Will she miss this place? When she's back in Montana, will she even spare a thought for the life she could have had in New York?

Probably not. Besides, she can always come back to visit. Actually, she'll have to come back and collect her things. Speaking of, looks like she'll need to borrow some clothes from Katie being her rash decision left her without a suitcase.

Hopefully, her sister will oblige.

Chapter 34

Otto

"Are you sure you don't want to talk this out more?" Veronica tilts her head so her hair falls to the side catching the light of the sun as it rakes onto the porch of the residence where she and Otto stand together. "I think it would be a good idea to at least give ourselves the chance to make things better. I think our family deserves that." She leans against the railing, back to the view, one foot propped against the porch posts.

"You didn't give us that opportunity when I wanted it." Otto tightens his grip around the railing, frustrated Veronica doesn't seem to understand the word no. "Now that you suddenly do, I'm supposed to drop everything and come running because you called?"

Veronica flips her hair back and visibly bristles. "I know I was the one who made the decision to walk away, but that doesn't mean I'm too stubborn to realize I made a mistake." There's a warning in her tone, something that hints at the fact that she's ready for a fight. He can see right where she's going. It won't be the first time she's complained about him being stubborn. It likely won't be the last.

"Veronica," He turns the words over in his head for a few moments, not wanting to say the wrong thing, but wanting to make himself clear. "I'm not being stubborn. You weren't wrong when you left me. I was in the wrong headspace. You didn't deserve what I was doing to you, to Addie. You leaving was the best thing that could have happened to me in that it forced me to take a hard look at myself and do something about my life." He pauses, sucking in a breath. "As much as I love you, and Veronica, I still do. I think we're better as friends than we are as romantic partners."

"We aren't friends, Otto," she says, looking down at the toes of her boots. "Let's not kid ourselves."

He isn't. Veronica will most likely make him pay in some subtle way for turning her down. He doesn't care. Now that he knows what love is really like, what it can be, he isn't going to settle for a substitute. It's Emma or nobody. "Here's the bottom line. As much as I loved you and Addie, I wasn't happy, and it's on me to make myself happy, nobody else."

"And you're happy now?" she asks, arching a brow.

"I'm working on it." He looks out across the rolling hills, smudged here and there with the green of pine. He'd never been to Montana before taking this job and now he can't imagine leaving it. "We should go talk to Addie."

Veronica pushes off from the railing, shaking her head. "Fine."

She throws open the door and strides inside. Otto follow more slowly, not really wanting to break his little girl's heart. He knows she'd like her mommy and daddy to be together. Addie sits at the kitchen table, a worksheet from school in front of her and Iris Twinklehoof in the chair next to her. She's up on her knees, leaning over the table, the tip of her tongue peeking out of the corner of her mouth as she concentrates.

She is magnificent. So smart and sassy. Maybe he should think about trying again with Veronica. Just the thought makes him feel all twisted up inside though. Someone else has his heart. Doesn't seem to matter that she doesn't want it, that she wadded it up and handed it back to him, then got on a plane and went back to New York City. It's hers and hers alone.

Otto slips into the chair opposite Addie and next to Veronica. "Hi, honey. Can you take a break from that for a minute? We wanted to talk to you about something."

Addie colors for another few seconds and then sets down her marker and folds her hands in front of her. "What did you want to tell me?" She looks like a bank manager.

Otto looks over at Veronica who motions for him to go ahead. He leans forward, placing his palms on the table. "We didn't want there to be any confusion about what's going on. We wanted to be sure you knew that Daddy and Mommy aren't getting back together."

"I already knew that," Addie says as though it's the most obvious thing in the world.

In that moment, Otto sees his ex. The attitude in his daughter's voice. The skepticism in her eyes. The twist of the lips. He glances over at Veronica who has to be seeing her mini me, but she is inspecting her nails.

"Your mother thought we should talk to you and communicate with you so we were all on the same page." Otto glances again at Veronica, hoping for a little back up, but instead gets a slight snort of derision.

"Are you guys going to fight again?" Addie asks, her voice flat.

Veronica finally looks up and shares a look with Otto. Even though they both could continue with their pettiness, they stop. Agreement flashes in their eyes. They're on the same page. For once. Relief washes over Otto.

"Good," Addie says, "because I want to know when Daddy is going to do something about Emma."

"Emma?" Emma had not been part of this conversation. At least not his external one.

Veronica's head comes up and she also says, "Emma?"

"Ever since Emma left, he's been grumpy," Addie comments, picking her marker back up. "Grumpier."

Veronica turns toward Otto. "Emma's the one who was at Addie's recital. The one who took her to get her nails done. Isn't she the owner's daughter? Were you seeing her?"

Otto feels color creep up his cheeks. "She's moved back to New York."

Because her life is there.

Wasn't that how she'd put it? Like whatever she'd been building here wasn't a life? Like what they'd had was insignificant? He sighs. Emma's job is as important to her as Otto's is to him. It's taken a little while, but he's come around to having a begrudging respect for Emma's commitment to getting ahead in her profession. It's part of all the other things that he admires about her. Her courage.

Her grit. If it's what she needs to make her happy, then he won't stand in her way. Above all else, he truly wants her to be happy and if living in a crowded noisy city is what that will take, then he wishes her Godspeed.

"Did she go because I was mad at her?" Addie asks, in a small voice. She's picking a little at the last of the nail polish that still remains on her tiny fingers.

"No! Of course not! Why would you think that?" Otto reaches across the table to take Addie's hands.

Addie shrugs and slips her hands away from him. "I was mad because she was late to my recital. Then we went for ice cream without her and the next morning she said she was leaving."

Otto knew Addie had been mad at Emma. He hadn't done much to change that, either. He figured it was just as well, maybe it would make her not miss Emma because he also knew how attached Addie had been becoming. And he knew how much it hurt to miss Emma, knew it all too well. "That was all a coincidence. One thing didn't cause the other."

At least, he's pretty sure of that. The whole reason Emma had been late for the recital was getting her interview package off to Tik Talk. She'd been charging hard toward that goal before she saw Veronica and him together with Addie at the recital. Although he doubted that had helped.

"Okay." Addie chews her lips a little. She doesn't totally accept his answer. He hopes in time she will. Her little shoulders don't need to carry that responsibility.

Veronica pushes back from the table. "We'd best be going then. Your stuff all ready to go, Addie?"

Addie nods and puts her schoolwork back into her backpack.

Otto stands and when Addie trots off to the bedroom to get her suitcase, Veronica sidles in closer to him, way too close. Her breasts brush against his chest. "You'll come around," she says.

He's sure he won't, but he keeps his mouth shut for now.

Then Addie is back with her suitcase. He crouches down to hug her good-bye. "See you on Thursday, Daddy?"

He nods. "I'll be there to pick you up from school."

He walks Addie and Veronica out to Veronica's SUV and helps get Addie settled in her booster seat. As he clicks her seat belt, she says, "If you and Mommy aren't going to be together, maybe you should ask Emma if she'll come back."

Then Veronica is revving the engine and he steps back so they can drive away, Addie waving from the back seat. He's still standing there when Matilda struts up. He reaches down to scratch her head. "You won't leave me, will you, girl?"

Matilda pecks his hand and struts away.

"Et tu, Matilda? Et tu?"

"You're speaking Latin to a chicken?" Katie walks up next to him. "You might at least want to try pig Latin."

He chuckles. "Matilda has apparently had enough of my charms. Kind of like everyone else."

Katie's gaze follows the cloud of dust that's Veronica's vehicle as it leaves the ranch. "Addie giving you a hard time?"

"Not really, but she thought that Emma left because Addie was mad at her and didn't invite her to get ice cream with us after the dance recital." He shakes his head.

"It's a good thing you talked to her about it." Katie sighs. "I spent a lot of years thinking that Isobel left because she was mad at me. Dad never talked about her and I made a lot of assumptions. Kids always think everything's about them. They don't understand grown-up relationships."

"I'm not sure adults do, either."

The problem is, he and Emma aren't in a relationship. They never got the chance to really see what they could have been because she left. He clenches his teeth together and looks away. Right now is not the appropriate time to be thinking about everything that could have been. He needs to focus on what is in front of him.

"Especially grown-ups who didn't grow up with good examples in front of them." Katie scuffs at the dirt with the toe of her boot. "Like someone who grew up without parents at all."

He looks over at her, sharply. "You mean, like Emma?"

Katie straightens up to look him in the eye. "Exactly like Emma. She's still trying to figure out what makes a family. She might have some ideas about moms and dads belonging together. She might not see where she could fit into someone else's life. She might leave so she doesn't get in someone else's way."

Otto's eyes narrow. "You been talking to her?"

Katie shrugs. "A little. Mostly texting."

"She doing okay?" No matter what passed between them, he'll always wish her well.

"You know what she's like. She'll always find a way to be okay. Is she happy? That I'm not so sure about." Katie stretches her arms over her head and looks out at the vista in front of them. "I think there was always a little bit of Montana in her. She didn't know what that meant until she got here and felt it, until she felt what having a home is really like."

Otto knows what all that feels like. He's okay, too. But happy? No. Not really. "She left, Katie. She made a choice."

"She can unmake it if somebody gave her a reason to." Katie turns to him, that piercing look that he sometimes dreads focusing on him. "You should go bring her home."

"Go to New York?" He stares at her.

"That's where she is." Katie turns back to the horizon, giving him time to think.

Go get Emma.

It's so simple. He reaches into his pocket, going for his keys before he realizes what he's doing. He stops. Is he crazy? Is this what he wants?

You know it is. And you have Addie's blessing. And Katie's.

Otto looks at Katie.

"It's okay," she says, nodding once. "I'll let Dad know where you're going. You know he wants her back, too."

That is all the encouragement he needs.

Chapter 35

EMMA

Emma deplanes in Montana. She has a rental car reserved, all she has to do is get off this plane and to the car rental counter. People in front of her get their luggage out of the overhead compartments so incredibly slowly that she gauges whether or not she could leap over the seatbacks to get out.

She takes a deep breath and blows it out. Did she just get a whiff of cow manure? She sure hopes so. She misses that smell.

Finally, she disembarks. She has no luggage to worry about so she speed walks in her heels to the rental car counter. There are only two people in front of her in line, but they take forever. She's about ten seconds from grabbing a key off the pegboard behind the counter and running when the man in front of her finally manages to sign and initial in all the appropriate places.

"Can I help you, miss?" the young man behind the counter asks her.

She shows him the reservation on her phone screen. "I need a car."

"Well, we've got those. Anything in particular you're interested in?"

She chews her bottom lip, an idea taking form in her mind. "I don't suppose you have a silver Jetta?"

"You're in luck," he says and gets the paperwork started.

There was a time she thought that Jetta was possessed or something, but it had brought her luck. It had brought her Otto. Maybe it will again.

She should call Katie to let her know she's on her way. No. She'll be there soon enough. It will be easier to explain why she's there and what she wants in person. Finally, she's got the keys and she's on her way to her rental car and out of the airport.

It doesn't take long to get out of the city. She rolls down all the windows and lets the air rush in. She's not sure she's ever smelled anything so good. It's like her entire chest is cracking open to let all that good air in.

There's almost no one else on the road. She's to that isolated stretch where she met Otto the first time, when she sees a red Ford 150 barreling toward her. It isn't. It couldn't be. But when she gets closer, she realizes it is. It's Otto's truck and Otto is at the wheel. He whizzes past her going in the opposite direction without giving her a second glance.

Where's he going in such an all-fired hurry? Into town? To see Addie?

To see Veronica?

Emma bites her lip and pulls over to the side of the road and dials Katie's number.

"Hey, Emma. What's up?"

She smiles hearing how happy her sister is to hear from her. "I don't have a lot of time. I have a quick question. Is Otto around?"

There's a moment of hesitation. "I don't want to ruin the surprise, but he's on his way to the airport. He's heading to New York to convince you to come back home."

Otto? Going to New York? Willingly? And he's doing it for her? Tears prick at her eyelids. "Seriously?"

"Very seriously. He booked a seat on the first plane out."

"Unbelievable." Here she is in Montana, without so much as a spare pair of panties with her so she can speak her truth to him, and he's halfway to the airport to fly to New York City to find her.

"Why?" Katie asks.

"Because I'm halfway between the airport and Three Keys Ranch and I think he just went past me going in the opposite direction." Emma rests her head on the steering wheel.

"You're where? Why?"

"I... I want to come home." The tears that threatened now spill over. "I want to be with you and Dad. I want to be with Otto."

"Then you better skedaddle, little sister. Or you're going to have to chase him all the way back to New York."

Emma looks back down the road toward the airport. Otto's truck is already a tiny dot in the distance. She needs to stop him before he gets to the airport. "Right. Gotta go, Katie! Talk to you soon!"

Quickly, she dials Otto's phone, but it goes directly to voicemail. That's right. He turns it off in the car so he won't be tempted to text and drive.

"Shit!" She pulls a U-turn and pushes the gas pedal to the floor, determined to catch up to Otto before he gets on a plane to go to the city she no longer wants to live in to convince her to come back to where she already is and where her heart will always be.

Chapter 36

OTTO

Otto must have lost his mind. What the hell is he doing? After talking to Katie, he went back to the residence and packed a bag. There was one last flight into New York City for the day. With leaving the truck in long-term parking, he'll barely enough time to make it.

But seriously, what is he doing? He's had no communication with Emma since she left. Not even a text.

Katie has, though.

And she wouldn't steer him wrong. Plus, he's not sure when anything has ever felt so right. Not since following his daughter out to Montana.

Behind him, a silver Jetta pulls up practically right on his bumper. What the fuck? "It's a big old open road. No damn reason to tailgate."

He slows a little. The Jetta stays with him, flashing its lights. Whatever. He pulls over on the side and it zooms past. As he watches, the car suddenly swerves, then spins out and goes directly into the ditch.

Holy shit!

He puts the truck in park, gets out, and jogs toward the car, swearing under his breath. He has to get to the airport, but he can't leave whoever this incredibly bad driver is out on this isolated stretch of road. One more time, he wants to be in two places at once. Will it ever stop? As he gets closer, the passenger door opens and a shapely leg emerges, wearing the highest heeled shoe he's ever seen.

He slows to a walk.

Emma sticks her head out of the car and smiles up at him, her face open and pretty as a sunflower. "Hi, there. Can I maybe use your phone to call for help?"

"Are you okay?" He extends his hand down to her to help her up out of the ditch, his heart beating hard against his chest, eyes glancing over her for any sign of injury.

She takes his hand and scrambles up. She's even less appropriately dressed than the first time he saw her out there. The tight black skirt with a silky white top complete with high-heels are definitely not made for Montana.

High-heels for fuck's sake.

Worse than those platform sandals.

He tenses, heart skipping a beat. Why is she here? He takes a deep breath, calming himself down enough to speak. "Why are you here?"

She meets his gaze and takes a deep, audible breath. "I wanted to see you. I had to see you."

Her words are as shaky as her legs are. Otto pulls her closer against him so she has some stability. His pulse thunders in his ears, chest swelling from her words. She had to see him. She put a rental into a ditch – again –to stop him so she could.

"Oh, yeah?" He cocks his head to the side, a teasing smile on his face.

She nods once, her cheeks turning a soft shade of pink. "I don't want to leave things the way they are between us. I would never want to step in and ruin your family or your happiness, but I had to see you. If you're with Veronica, I won't stand in your way, but I had to tell you that I loved you and that I'm moving to Montana for good."

Otto is silent for a moment. "Loved? Like, past tense?"

"Wha—?" She shakes her head, hair blowing in the breeze. "I love you, Otto. I love you more than I can comprehend, and I want... I don't even know what I want. I just want to love you."

His lips curve into a wide grin. His heart is so full it may burst. He's missed her and doesn't want to wait another second apart, so he ducks his head and gives her a long, lingering kiss. "I'm in love with you, too. You are the only person I ever want, Emma."

"Really?"

He nods. "Really. Now let's get this rental car out of the ditch and go home."

Epilogue

OTTO

"Hurry, hurry, hurry!" Emma flips pancakes onto plates as quickly as she can. "Eat up!"

"Can I have two?" Addie looks up at Emma, lifting her plate up.

Emma kisses Addie on top of her head and puts another pancake on top of the one on Addie's plate. "Of course, you can. But go eat it. I need to get in the shower!"

Otto comes up behind her, slips his arms around her waist, and takes the spatula from her hand. He takes a good deep sniff of her peach-scented hair. "How about I take over so you can get dressed? I know you want to look nice for your first day at your new job and I've been known to flip the occasional flapjack." She's been back for barely a month and already scored a job with an advertising firm in Billings. His girl. Smart and pretty, too. He is one lucky son-of-a-bitch.

She turns in his arms and gives him a kiss on the lips. "My hero. Once again. Thank you!" She ducks under his arm and makes her way out of the kitchen and up the stairs to their bedroom. Otto still can't believe he's living in the main house. Mitch insisted, though. Once Otto had joint custody of Addie, Mitch said the residence was no place for a little girl. It felt strange at first, but the strangeness is already wearing off. Now it feels right. Like he's in just the right place. There's no other place he wants to be than with his girls on this ranch.

He finishes off the pancakes and takes the rest out to the table in the dining room.

"Otto!" Mitch says, motioning for him to take the seat next to him. "Linda and I were just discussing whether to lease out some of the south pasture. We've got more than we need and there's been some flooding nearby. Folks could maybe use a hand. What do you think?"

"I think it's good to lend a hand when we can. We may need a return favor someday." It's nice to be consulted. Mitch has been giving him more responsibility around the ranch and Otto is determined to learn everything he can from the older man. Addie is carefully cutting her pancakes into little squares and then dipping each square into the puddle of syrup on her plate. At this rate, it'll be lunch time before she's done eating. He looks down at his watch. "As much as I hate to say you need to eat and run—"

"What do you think I'm doing?" Addie asks around a large bite of pancake.

"No need for attitude," he says, putting his hands up. "Just trying to keep you on a time check."

"I'm sure it's not helping to have you stare at her as she's trying to eat," Emma says from behind him.

For a moment, Otto can do nothing but stare at her when he turns to face his girlfriend. Her long hair is still slightly damp, though thoroughly brushed, pulled into a high ponytail on her head. She wears a sleeveless blouse tucked into a steel pencil skirt that fits her curves in all the right places. Her heels clack on the wood floor, emphasizing her long, shapely legs.

How he managed to win her over, he doesn't have a clue. But he's determined to show how much he loves her every day.

"I can't be late again. Principal Tanner said I'll have to stay after school if it happens again," Addie says.

"Which is why I'm driving you to school today." The past week he's asked Mario to drop off his daughter since his friend has been heading into town anyway, claiming to have some errands to run.

Otto suspects those errands are of the female variety. Mario's been uncharacteristically serious lately.

Emma sits down on Addie's other side and plops a pancake on her own plate. She takes a bite, but then pushes it away.

"You nervous?" he asks.

"Of course, it *is* my first day. Weren't you nervous when you started working for my father?" she asks.

Otto chuckles. "I still get nervous around him. For different reasons." He glances over at Mitch who shakes his head.

Emma's lips curl up in the corners, her face turning a dark shade of pink. Otto grins. He loves being able to make her blush. He hopes it will never go away. She stands up to take her plate back in the kitchen and stops to give him a kiss.

"Ew! I'm eating!" Addie covers her eyes with her hands.

Later, as he's dropping Emma off in front of her new office in Billings, he grabs her wrist before she gets out of the truck. "Do you know how much I love you?"

She closes her eyes, resting her forehead on his. "Do you know how much I love you?"

"Do you know how much I want to barf?" Addie asks from the back seat.

He and Emma laugh. There is no better way to start the morning, and he wishes that for the rest of their lives their days will be filled with laughter.

Acknowledgments

First and foremost, thank you to my Heavenly Father for blessing me beyond all measure.

Thank you to my family for your support and encouragement. For picking up the slack and adjusting your lives so that I could get this manuscript done. Thank you for the laughs we shared about how I was writing a romance book, yet how you pushed me to finish it. Thank you to my dogs, who are pure psychopaths with never-ending energy and never-ending love. Thank you for showing me what "drive" really is, for demonstrating what pushing past your limits means. Would I have a nicer house without chewed moldings, broken doors, and tumbleweeds of fur? Of course, but I wouldn't have the abundant laughs and stories to share about you two.

Thank you Jes at Black Bird Book Covers for the amazing cover. Your work is incredible.

And lastly, THANK YOU with all my heart to those men and women, their families and friends, and to those four-legged soldiers who voluntarily sacrifice their lives, well-being, and time to defend this great country we live in. Your sacrifices and memories will never be forgotten.

About Author

Paris Wynters is a multi-racial romance author whose stories that celebrate our diverse world. When she's not dreaming up stories, she can be found assisting with disasters and helping to find missing people as a Search and Rescue K-9 handler. Paris resides in New York along with her family. For fun, she enjoys video games, and watching hockey. Paris is a graduate of Loyola University Chicago.

Connect with Paris Wynters online:
Website: www.pariswynters.com
Facebook & Instagram: @ParisWynters
Tiktok: @ParisWyntersBooks